Dear Mystery Lover:

In the vein of Janet Evanovich's Stephanie Plum mysteries (*One For The Money, Two For The Dough*) comes Bruce Most's Ruby Dark.

Last December, DEAD LETTER enthusiastically brought the Ruby Dark mysteries into our line of paperback originals. Now, after a highly successful debut in *Bonded for Murder*, Bruce's feisty bail bondswoman is back for another mysterious adventure in the Mile High City.

If you haven't checked Ruby out yet, *Missing Bonds* is a great opportunity. A little brazen—and a lot of fun—she's a tough fifty-year-old woman with a past as shady as her clients. In this go-around, Ruby takes a chance and puts her money on what the law calls a "repeat offender" named Bullet Joe. None too happy after Joe skips bail, Ruby tracks him down but winds up running head on with murder.

So strap yourself in for a rough-and-tumble ride through Denver's wealthiest and seamiest sides with the irrepressible Ruby Dark.

Yours in crime,

Joe Veltre
St. Martin's DEAD LETTER Paperback Mysteries

Other titles from St. Martin's Dead Letter Mysteries

WINTER GAMES by John Feinstein
THE MAN WHO INVENTED FLORIDA by Randy Wayne White
WHISKERS AND SMOKE by Marian Babson
FLY FISHING CAN BE FATAL by David Leitz
BLACK WATER by Doug Allyn
REVENGE OF THE BARBEQUE QUEENS by Lou Jane Temple
A MURDER ON THE APPIAN WAY by Steven Saylor
MURDER MOST BRITISH ed. by Janet Hutchings
LIE DOWN WITH DOGS by Jan Gleiter
THE CLEVELAND CONNECTION by Les Roberts
LONG SHADOWS IN VICTORY by Gregory Bean
BIGGIE AND THE POISONED POLITICIAN by Nancy Bell
THE TRAIL TO BUDDHA'S MIRROR by Don Winslow
A VOW OF FIDELITY by Veronica Black
THE SENSATIONAL MUSIC CLUB MYSTERY
by Graham Landrum
THE GOURMET DETECTIVE by Peter King
MANDARIN PLAID by S. J. Rozan

Also by Bruce W. Most

BONDED FOR MURDER

Missing Bonds

Bruce W. Most

St. Martin's Paperbacks

NOTE: If you purchased this book without a cover you should be aware that this book is stolen property. It was reported as "unsold and destroyed" to the publisher, and neither the author nor the publisher has received any payment for this "stripped book."

MISSING BONDS

ISBN: 0-312-96273-8

Printed in the United States of America

St. Martin's Paperbacks edition/August 1997

10 9 8 7 6 5 4 3 2 1

1

The motorcycle banked sharply into the parking lot behind the office of Ruby's Bail Bonds and roared down on David Piszek. David was walking toward his car, his mind on the evening's law class, which he was not looking forward to. By the time his attention had fully shifted to the presence of the onrushing motorcycle it was already too late for him to dodge its path. The cyclist, dressed head to toe in black leather, wore a black helmet with an impenetrable dark visor and was staring dead into a low evening sun. Suddenly the bike braked and skidded to a stop just a few feet from him, its rear wheel fishtailing out slightly.

The cyclist pulled off the helmet and flounced short, coal-black hair. David, his heart still getting acquainted with his Adam's apple, blinked. It was Cyndee Valone, his aunt's personal attorney.

He yelled above the rumble of the engine, "Jesus, Cyndee, you could have killed me!"

A big, loopy grin crossed her face. "Did you piss your pants?" She playfully snapped one of the black suspenders he wore over a blue-striped shirt. Valone was a large woman, around six feet, just slightly taller than his aunt. Her black outfit made her look big enough to go one-on-one with an NBA power forward.

"I hope you don't take clients out for joyrides on that thing," he said.

"Half my clients would *steal* a bike like this." She patted the maroon gas tank with a black-gloved hand. "So would I, for that matter. Brand new wheels. How do you like it?"

He shrugged, his nose wrinkling at the acrid smell of oil and gas. "Okay, I guess. I've never been into bikes."

"Just *okay*? This is a Triumph, David. Direct from England. A Thunderbird. They haven't built new Triumphs since the eighties when the Japanese drove them out of business. Brando rode a Triumph in *The Wild One*."

"I'll stick to my old green Duster. By the way, how can you afford this thing, Cyndee?" Contrary to popular opinion, not all lawyers are rich, especially small-practice independent attorneys whose cases are mainly penny-ante civil suits and small-time felons.

Valone hung her head in mock shame. "I can't afford it. I've had to put my daughter on bread and water so I could make the payments." She looked up brightly. "But it's for a good cause."

"What's that?"

"My sanity."

David smiled. He knew she worked as hard in private practice, and with as much passion and idealism, as she had worked in the public defender's office. He glanced at his watch. "I've got to run, Cyndee."

"You headed for class?"

"Yeah. Contracts."

"How are your studies going?"

David shrugged. "Tough trying to juggle bail bonding and night school. Neither my aunt nor criminals seem to keep civil hours."

Valone nodded her head at a distant memory. "First year law's a bitch. Speaking of your aunt, she in?"

"Yes, she's up there."

"I've got some news on her license."

"Is she going to keep it?"

"Looks that way—oh, there's the Angel herself!"

Ruby Dark came down the metal stairs from her second-floor office, down the backside of the Planned Pethood Spay-Neuter Clinic, which occupied the first floor of the Victorian home that sat across the street from Denver Police Headquarters. Ruby wore a loose print dress, the low evening sun catching her piles of shoulder-length red hair. As she walked toward them, she dipped in and out of black fingers of shadows creeping across the parking lot.

"So it's *your* bike making all the racket," Ruby chided lightheartedly in her trademark truck-driver voice.

"My new Triumph," Valone said proudly, patting the gas tank again.

"She damn near killed me!" David said to his aunt.

"That's okay. The world won't miss one less lawyer."

"Ha, ha."

"Speaking of lawyers, did you two hear the joke about the brass rat?"

Valone and David frowned. They had heard more than their fair share of lawyer jokes from Ruby Dark.

She ignored their unenthusiastic response. "A man finds an interesting-looking large brass rat in a junk shop in New York City, but the dealer refuses to sell it. 'I'll pay you whatever you want for it,' says the man. The dealer says ten thousand dollars. The man thinks that's outrageous but decides to buy it anyway. He pays for the brass rat and heads out the store and down the street. Pretty soon he notices several rats following him. He walks a little faster. More rats join in. They're coming out of the sewers, old buildings, alleys, everywhere. The street is filled with rats, waves of them. The man starts to run. More rats join in. He's freaked. So he runs all the way to the East River and hurls the brass rat as far as he can into the water, and all the rats jump in after it and drown. So the next day the man hurries back to the junk shop and asks the dealer, 'Do you have any brass lawyers?' "

David and Valone laughed courteously. Then the lawyer said, "Now that you've trashed my profession, Ruby, maybe I won't tell you the good news I stopped by with."

"What good news?"

Valone lifted her chin and was silent.

"Do I have to apologize first?" said Ruby.

"Feet kissing would be sufficient."

Ruby made an exaggerated bow and sweep of her arm.

"That'll do," said Valone. "I talked to the State Insurance Commission this morning. Cooler heads prevailed. They're not going to suspend your license."

A smile of relief crossed Ruby's face. "Thanks, Cyndee."

"*And* . . . ," continued Valone, "I think we've got a good shot at making the criminal charges go away, now that the Cherry Hills Village DA understands exactly what happened. I don't think he relishes the idea of letting a bondsman off the hook, but solving the Kray murder earned you Brownie points around town and puts him in a tough spot. Charging you wouldn't be good PR. He knows you've got newspaper buddies who would rush to your defense."

David still broke into cold sweats when remembering that night. He and his aunt and three bounty hunters had stormed a wealthy Cherry Hills Village home hunting for a millionaire who had skipped on a million-dollar bond for murder. It had turned out they had raided the wrong house, just as later the skip turned out to be the wrong suspect. The tip given to Ruby had been phony—an elaborate setup, in fact, most likely concocted by her arch rival and industry slimeball, Cadillac Johnson. But the damage had been done. The woman and her two daughters who lived in the home and who had no connection to the skip, had been terrorized by the goons Ruby, against her better judgment, had brought along. The initial headlines had been ugly and the Cherry Hills Village DA had promptly filed a raft of criminal charges, though David had not been among those charged. His aunt had managed to keep his name out of it, and for that he would be eternally grateful.

"What about the lawsuit?" Ruby asked.

"That's proving a little stickier," conceded Valone. "Your offer to pay for property damages and therapy fees was well received by the woman, and I think she realizes you personally didn't act maliciously, even if Curly and Moe did. But she's got Sydney Ellsworth for counsel. He smells a fat contingency fee."

"Bloodsuckers."

"Hey, we have to make a living, too, Ruby," Valone said in mock apology.

Ruby laughed. "Thanks for all your work, hon. If we have to have lawyers, I wish more of them were like you."

"My bill's in the mail. Oh, by the way, I also stopped by to tell you I think Bullet Joe's jumped."

"What makes you think that?" Ruby's eyes, as dark green as some of the chile peppers she was so addicted to, were wild and restless.

"He didn't show up for sentencing this morning and I can't find him. The judge issued a bench warrant."

Ruby stepped into one of the shadows, darkening her face. "He's never skipped on me before, and I bet I've bailed him out at least a dozen times."

"He's never faced the Big Bitch before."

"Who are you two talking about?" interjected David, "And what is the Big Bitch?" He slung off his backpack of law books draped heavily on one strap over his shoulder and set it at his feet. He knew he'd be late to class if he lingered any longer, and Professor Gideon Rothschild was not a man who trifled with tardiness. Yet of late, David had found himself less attentive to his law studies and more caught up in his aunt's world of criminals and cops and skips and bounty hunters and, yes, even murder.

"Earl Brown, a.k.a. half a dozen other names," said Ruby, answering his question. "Most people call him Bullet Joe."

"*Bullet Joe*? What kind of name is that? Sounds like a bad nickname for a hit man."

"Actually, it's an old baseball player's nickname. At least that's what Bullet Joe told me once. He's one of those walking baseball encyclopedias. You're a baseball fan, David. You haven't heard of a Bullet Joe?"

"I've heard of Shoeless Joe, but not a Bullet Joe."

"You know how much I hate baseball. It's our National Snooze Time. But I have to admit it's got a great tradition of nicknames. There's not another pro sport except maybe pool with names like Oilcan and Catfish and the Yankee Clipper and Hammering Hank. Course, none of the players these days have nicknames like they used to. Too much money. Got bench warmers making a million bucks a year and they all want to be called Mister."

"Okay, so this Bullet Joe loves baseball like everybody else but you, Aunt Ruby. I can safely assume he wasn't being sentenced for spitting in the new ballpark."

"Armed robbery."

David turned to Valone. "What's the Big Bitch he's facing?"

"Mandatory life as an habitual criminal."

"What's he done?"

"Pick any page in the penal code. I think he's got it covered, except for assault, rape, and murder. Burglary, receipt of stolen goods, shoplifting, parole violation, pissing in public, auto theft, drug possession, criminal mischief, felony menacing. He's been arrested sixty-three times and served time for a dozen offenses."

David looked at the two women. "Jesus, no wonder the man jumped. Why are you two so surprised?"

"I'm surprised because he's a prison homey," said Ruby. "He's more comfortable in jail than out. It's where he's spent most of his life since he came back from Vietnam. Hard time wouldn't scare him. He might almost be happy about it. There's a lot of certainty in mandatory life."

That was his aunt, mused David. Always going with her gut instincts instead of common sense. What idiot would willingly face mandatory life in prison?

"I don't see how guys like that can walk the streets," said David.

"There's no doubt Bullet Joe couldn't go straight if he had a cop on each arm," said Valone. "But in some ways he's really a good-hearted man. When he has money, he always shares it with his friends.''

Ruby laughed. ''Yep, that's Bullet Joe. He'll steal for friends.''

David rolled his eyes at the women's romantic view of a stone-cold sociopath. ''How much was bond?'' he asked Ruby.

''Forty-five grand.''

''What did he pay for it with, his charm?''

''Third-party collateral. A friend.''

Every bondsman has skips, of course, but his aunt had fewer than most in the business. She had a sixth sense as to who was a good risk and who wasn't. She turned down several requests a day because they didn't ''feel'' right. And she had a fierce reputation for tracking down those who unwisely chose to jump bail. She didn't lightly write off a skip as a ''cost of doing business.'' Now she had thirty days or sixty days or ninety days—whatever time limit the judge chose to give her—to come up with Earl ''Bullet Joe'' Brown . . . or forty-five grand.

''Where have you looked for him, Cyndee?'' Ruby asked.

''I made a few calls, but I haven't had time to really hunt for him. That's your job.''

''When did you last talk to him?''

''Two days ago.''

''What was his mood?''

''He sounded okay, considering he was facing life in jail. He was more interested in talking about the Rockies.''

Ruby shook her head. ''Something changed his mind between then and today. Well, thanks for letting me know right away, Cyndee. At least we can get a quick jump on him. I suspect he's still around town. His folks and friends are here. I don't think the man's been farther from home in his life than Grand Junction.''

''Got to run,'' said Valone. She slipped on her black helmet and the Triumph roared out of the parking lot.

David glanced at his watch again. He would be late for

certain. "I've got to run, too, Aunt Ruby. Are you going looking for this Bullet Joe guy?"

"Not tonight. We'll start tomorrow."

"*We*?"

"Sure. I want you along to learn a few things."

"Learning a few things" about the bail bonding business was not high on David's agenda. As much as he loved his aunt—his half aunt, technically—he considered his work for her as temporary, a necessity for paying his way through law school. The bail bonding business was not his life's aspiration. He wanted to be on the other side, a prosecutor sticking criminals *in* jail, not bailing them *out*.

"So where do *we* start tomorrow?" he asked.

"Looking for Judas."

2

In the world of skip tracing, there is always a Judas. There is always someone, sometimes several people, Ruby told David, willing to betray the skip for thirty pieces of silver.

To find a Judas, his aunt used what she called her "ripple" method. You dropped a pebble into a quiet pool of water and watched the waves ripple outward. You started with the inner circle, the known associates closest to the jumper: spouse, lover, parents, siblings, relatives. They were the ones most likely to know where the skip may have gone or where he hangs out. Sometimes they actively hid the skip. Sometimes they betrayed him.

If that inner circle proved fruitless, you moved to the next circle rippling outward: friends, drinking buddies, former spouses, and former lovers. Ex-spouses or ex-lovers were often the best sources, especially if they still harbored anger at the skip. Most often, it was within these two circles that one would find Judas.

But sometimes it required going farther out among the spreading rings: the sibling of a lover, the parents of a spouse, co-workers and employers, landlords, neighbors. These sources could provide valuable clues about who among the inner circles might know the whereabouts of the skip, and in some cases, though more rarely, they themselves knew where the skip could be found.

Still another circle included people with a nodding acquaintance of the skip: bartenders, pizza shop employees, video-rental clerks, even paperboys who might spot the skip's car parked in the driveway at a particular address Ruby would give them.

All the while Ruby was canvasing these sources, she tapped into more bureaucratic sources for information: police records, phone records, marriage records, motor vehicle records, city directories, military records, financial records, property records—anything that might provide a clue.

In the case of Earl "Bullet Joe" Brown, the inner circle consisted of his parents, with whom he lived off and on; Sean Powell, the third-party cosigner who was financially responsible for Bullet Joe's bond if he failed to turn up; and an ex-con named Mickey "The Mayor" Squires, a close friend of Bullet Joe's. A phone call to the cosigner got an answering machine. Bullet Joe's parents were next on Ruby's list.

"Why don't you just call them?" David asked as they drove up to a semi-rural area on the northwest side of the city. "It would save a lot of time." They were in her big dark Buick, her skip-hauling car with the special locks on the rear doors and the iron rings bolted to the floor, where she could chain a skip. Her two-seater 1982 red Lamborghini with the personalized license plates reading "BONDED" was too cramped for the job.

"They don't have a phone," said Ruby. "And if they did, I still wouldn't call. He might be there."

"He'd be stupid enough to stay at his parents' place?"

"Nobody said Bullet Joe was bright. Besides, David, I keep telling you, skips are creatures of habit. If they weren't, we'd all go broke in this business."

Bullet Joe's parents lived in the Silver Spur Mobile Home Park among thirty or so other metal cartons crammed together at the end of a dirt road. Their trailer occupied space No. 17 in the back southwest corner of the trailer park, a three-point shot away from a weedy, cracked concrete pad with a netless bent basketball hoop mounted on a rusty metal pole. Heat rippled in waves off the empty concrete. A few scattered cottonwoods provided dribbles of shade from the late-morning sun. Thirty yards behind the row of trailers several kids played in a sluggish irrigation ditch.

"Helluva place to live," commented David.

"Beats sleeping in your car."

Ruby parked in front of a trailer two spaces away from the Browns. "Now I want you to cut between these trailers and go 'round to the back of their trailer," she instructed.

"You really think Bullet Joe might be in there?" David felt the familiar tightness in his gut that he always experienced whenever he knew they might be closing in on a potentially dangerous skip.

"Doubtful. But just in case, I don't want him climbing out the back while I'm jawing at the front door."

"What am I supposed to do if I see him? Hit him over the head with my law dictionary?

"Sure, why not? It's heavy enough to bring down an elephant."

"Did you bring your gun?" She rarely did, and he hadn't seen her put it in her purse. "What if he gets nasty?"

"No. He's not a dangerous man, David. He's basically a burglar."

But you've never known him to skip, either, David said to himself, and the man's never faced the "Big Bitch" before.

He wouldn't have worried with Big Jim Brodie, Ruby's bounty hunter who'd been murdered while tracking a skip in the Kray case. Big Jim would have grabbed Bullet Joe by the scruff of the neck with one hand and cuffed him with the other. But David didn't stand six-feet-four and weigh 265 pounds, and rough stuff wasn't his thing.

He started to get out of the car, then stopped. "By the way, what's this guy look like?"

"I don't think there'll be too many guys besides Bullet Joe crawling out a window," said Ruby, "but if you really want to be sure . . ." She held up a mug shot. The man was in his forties, balding, with thinning hair on the sides and back. He had the unfocused, sightless stare so prevalent in mug shots, but he looked harmless enough. "He's six-two, a hundred and ninety pounds, brown hair, brown eyes, no distinguishing marks or scars," she added.

Not someone David wanted to tackle.

He stepped out of the air-conditioned Buick into the breathless heat. A fourth consecutive scorcher. It felt like a hundred degrees. Denver rarely was this hot, the natives and semi-natives reassured him. Besides, it was a "dry" heat, they always added, as if a dry heat was better than the sticky, sopping summer heat of Missouri, where, as he'd known from experience, one hundred degrees made it feel like a rain forest. "Dry" heat was still heat. And it was so dry, his skin felt brittle, as if it would curl up and blow away in the faintest of breezes.

As instructed, he cut between the two trailers and headed for the rear of the Brown trailer. It was a single-wide Lamplighter, a mustard yellow with chocolate brown imitation shutters. The backside had no door, and the windows would have been a squeeze for a man of Bullet Joe's size. The lawn was more dirt than grass, and what grass there was looked in its last days. Weeds cozied up to the trailer's metal skirt. Four metal wires sagging between two metal clothesline poles stood empty. He could smell the irrigation ditch. It was not a smell he would want to go to sleep to. Beyond the far end of the trailer, two men worked on a rusty orange Maverick, one man under the car, only his legs showing, and the other leaning over the engine under the open hood. A boom box the size of a file cabinet blared country music. Neither man noticed David as he stood guard by the trailer.

He heard Ruby knock at the front door, then voices, then the squeak of a door opening and closing. He braced himself. If Bullet Joe was in there and he chose to run, it would be now. But nobody tried crawling out, and soon Ruby called David through one of the windows. He walked around the front of the trailer and up concrete steps. A porch railing of wrought iron was painted a brown that didn't match the trailer trim. Ruby pushed open a screen door and he stepped into a tiny combination living room, kitchen, and dining room where a television was blaring.

Immediately, his lungs recoiled. The trailer reeked of cigarette smoke. There was no air-conditioning, no fans. The stale air was smothering. The windows were open, propped up with sticks, but with no breeze they might as well have been nailed shut. A small bird sat silently in a cage just inside the door next to a plastic crucifix. He looked droopy. Maybe he was their mine-shaft canary. When he keeled over dead from the heat, the elderly couple would know it was time to get out.

Ruby introduced David to Bullet Joe's parents. They were matching bookends—large bookends. Each must have outweighed their son by forty pounds. Both looked in their late sixties, though David couldn't be sure because he knew smoking aged one quickly. The woman, who sat on a ragged couch, was dressed in flip-flops, black shorts, and a faded pink top. Curly grayish-brown hair framed a heavy face, damp with sweat. The man, sprawled in a sagging recliner, wore black pants and a white T-shirt. He had big sandpapery hands with liver spots, and pure white hair. Unlike his wife, his large, rumpled bulldog face looked as dry as a mummy's.

"How you doin', Mamma Brown?" asked Ruby.

"Oh, we're gettin' 'long," said the woman in a voice loud enough to be overheard at a tractor pull. "Social Security and Eddie's pension, tiny thing that it is. 'Course, Earl brings us money when he gits work, which ain't real often. Works now and then over in them greenhouses."

"Yeah, when them motherfuckin' wetbacks ain't took the jobs," muttered Eddie Brown.

David and Ruby had passed several greenhouses and mushroom farms shortly before reaching the trailer park. But David doubted their son was losing out to migrant workers. More likely it was because he had a criminal record thicker than a small-town phone book.

Ruby waved her hand in front of her face. "Don't you

guys have an air conditioner or fan you can run? Or a neighbor you can visit who has air-conditioning? This heat isn't good for you two.''

''We're doin' fine, Angel,'' Eddie Brown said stiffly. ''Don't need no help. We been living in this trailer fourteen years. We been through heat before.''

Angel. What many of his aunt's clients and informants and other lowlife called her. Angel of the Outlaws. The lady who gets people out of jail.

''You were a lot younger fourteen years ago, Eddie.''

''We're fine.''

The couple's attention drifted almost simultaneously from Ruby to a large color television a few feet away. Loot from one of their son's burglaries? speculated David. A chipped plate with a blotch of ketchup and a half-eaten corn dog sat atop the TV next to a VCR. Next to it stood a nearly empty fifth of Captain Morgan spiced rum. Bullet Joe's or theirs? At the moment, Mamma Brown was drinking from a red-handled Thirst Buster mug from Circle K. Eddie Brown wasn't drinking anything.

''Earl check in on you now and then?'' asked Ruby.

''Now and then,'' echoed the woman.

Ruby reached over and turned the volume on the TV way down. David caught the flickering electronic images of a talk show. A row of desultory-looking guests sat in a row of chairs while a female host waved a black microphone around in her hand like a baton. He couldn't catch the topic, but he assumed it was another cultural high-water mark of American television like ''Wives Who Made It With Their Husband's Father'' or ''Families Who Sold Crack Together.''

''When was the last time you saw Bullet Joe?''

''Don't call him that!'' The old woman's voice rose and hardened. David was struck by the ferocity of it. ''I hate that name.''

Ruby spoke more softly. ''When was the last time you saw Earl? Or talked to him?''

The agitated woman quieted and thought about it for a few moments. "I don't remember."

Ruby sat down in a chair. David lingered by the door in the faint hope of snatching a passing breath of fresh air. He ran his hand along the back of his neck to wipe off perspiration. He glanced at the bird. It was still alive.

"Was it recently? Talk to him yesterday or today?"

"It was *several* days ago," chimed in the old man.

"You're sure?"

"Yeah, I'm sure. He come by last week. That's the last time we talked to him."

"How would you remember, you forgetful old goat," said Mamma Brown good-naturedly. "You never remember anything. Like the other day. You put your Saint Christopher medal someplace and you still can't find it." She looked at Ruby. "How do you lose something you hang around your neck?"

"Earl ain't been home in several days," said the old man not so good-naturedly. Suddenly he bounded out of the recliner, as if shot from it, moving with more swiftness and strength than David would have guessed for a man of his size and age. He retrieved a cold beer from the refrigerator, popped the top with the same big hand holding the can, and slumped into the chair in almost the same position as when he'd left it. He stared at the TV again without offering Ruby or David anything. This didn't disappoint David.

"Why do you want to know, Angel?" asked Mamma Brown. "Is my boy in trouble again? You don't come around unless he's in trouble."

"Nothing serious, hon. Just his lawyer needs him to sign some important papers before his sentencing, and we can't find him."

David assumed his aunt was worried that if she told them her son had failed to show for a sentencing and the judge had issued a bench warrant—and that she wanted his ass for a forty-five-grand skip—they might become more uncooperative than they already were. Judas didn't always give up knowingly.

"Yeah, he told us he might be going away again—maybe for a long time." The old woman's hazel eyes welled up. "You know, Angel, I can't see him when he's in prison. I can't get all the way down there. I don't drive none these days and Eddie won't take me. Earl writes us letters, though. He's always been a good boy about writing us letters."

He's had a lot of practice, thought David.

"He don't belong in no prison," flared Eddie Brown, turning red in the face.

"Yes, he does, Eddie," said his wife, bowing her head. David could see through the thin gray hair to her skull. "You know that's where he belongs. When he does wrong, that's where he belongs."

"Ain't his fault," said Eddie. "It was the damn war that done that to him." He looked at Ruby with mournful eyes. "He got sprayed with that shit they used to kill all that jungle stuff. What'd they call it?"

"Agent Orange?"

"Yeah, that's it. Earl told us he was sprayed with it in the Mekong Delta. Sprayed a lot of them fellas over there. That's why people don't give him no jobs, 'cause they think he's poisoned."

"That's foolish, Eddie," said Mamma Brown in her loud voice.

"It was Vietnam," said her husband, enunciating each syllable as if it were a burning ember. "It's the damn war that done it to him. He was a fine boy until he come back from the war. The last time he slept here I could hear him screaming in the middle of the night. He'd curl up in a ball whenever it rained, like he did in Vietnam. He come back from them jungles all fucked up, Angel."

"That's why he was goin' to one of them Vietnam vet groups," said Mamma Brown.

"A lot of damn good it done him," said Eddie Brown. "He's still got them dreams and he's still goin' to prison. Stupid idea, you ask me, sitting around talking about the war over 'n over. How you gonna forget 'bout it if you keep refightin' it? They say the war was terrible. Hell, I was in Korea. I saw a lot of shit there I just as soon forget. But you don't hear me talking 'bout it with everybody. I don't even talk 'bout it to her. If you don't keep jawing 'bout it, it goes away. We didn't have that post-whatever."

"Post-traumatic stress disorder?" said Ruby.

"Yeah. We never had that. Wanna know why? 'Cause we didn't keep goin' on about it. We come home from the war and went about our business."

"This veteran's group Earl went to, you know where they meet?" Ruby asked.

"Someplace over on Ashbury," offered Mamma Brown. "I think it's called the Veterans' Center."

"Where does Earl go when he doesn't stay here?"

"I don't know . . . around."

"Around where?"

Mamma Brown shrugged her thick shoulders.

"Who does he hang out with?"

"Friends. But they don't come around here. He never brings 'em around here. I don't know who they are. He don't talk about 'em."

"He ever mention a guy named Sean Powell?"

"Yeah. He's the one who bailed Earl out last time, wasn't he?"

"Yes," said Ruby.

"We used to bail Earl out," Mamma Brown said wistfully.

"I know, honey."

His aunt must have taken a flyer on this trailer for collateral, thought David.

"We could afford it when Eddie was still working at the machine shop and the bonds were smaller. But the bonds kept gettin' bigger and Eddie wasn't working no more and—"

"I know, Mamma Brown. So did you see or talk to Sean Powell lately?"

"No," said the old man. "We never talk to him."

"But you might find him at that Veterans' Center where Earl goes," added Mamma Brown.

"He went there too?"

"I think so. I think Earl told me that once."

"What about his ex-wives? He seeing any of them?"

"Not if he knows what's good for him," said the old woman.

"What about Sandra? He talk to her?"

"That slut's in Albany or Tucson or someplace like that," Eddie Brown said savagely.

"Vicki moved to Salida last year," said Mamma Brown. "And we ain't heard about his first one in years, which ain't no loss to the world."

"Is Earl drinking again?" Ruby asked.

Mamma Brown nodded sadly.

"Where? Does he have drinking buddies or favorite bars?"

"I don't know. He don't tell us everything about his life."

Ruby stood up and leaned over the old woman, forcing her to look up into her face. "Sure he does. I know your son. He tells people everything. He talks too much for his line of work. People take advantage of him."

"He don't tell us 'bout his drinking. He knows we don't approve."

"You two aren't hiding Earl, are you? You're straight with me when you say you don't know where he is?"

"We got nothing to hide, Angel," snapped Eddie Brown.

"He's your son, Eddie. I'd hide my son."

"But he done a lot of wrong things," said Mamma Brown. "We won't hide him."

Ruby straightened up. "That's good, honey. That's the attitude to take. I know you don't want to see him on the run. That's how people get hurt, when they're on the run. If you see Earl—if he stops by or gets word to you—I want you to call me. Borrow a neighbor's phone and call me right away. My phone number's right here. Day or night, got that?'' Ruby put a business card in Mamma Brown's big hand.

Eddie Brown said nothing. Mamma Brown nodded her head. ''Is he gonna be okay, Angel?''

''He'll be fine as long as he doesn't keep running. He's probably just a little dazed and forgetful with the booze. That's why I don't want you to tell him we were here.''

3

Free of the hot, oppressive trailer, David made a beeline for the cool interior of the Buick. But Ruby snagged his arm and steered him around the end of Brown's trailer. She yanked off the lid of a banged-up metal trash can and peered inside. A swarm of flies roared up and took off for more hospitable accommodations.

''You think their son is hiding in there?'' needled David.

Ruby ignored him and began rifling through the garbage like a bag lady, though careful not to soil her silk blouse. Muskmelon rinds, a crumpled potato chip sack, coffee grounds, crushed beer cans, and an empty box of corn dogs formed the top layer. David recalled reading about a professor in Arizona who dug through landfills as a form of modern archeological and sociological inquiry. He wondered what profound things the professor could say about this family.

''What *are* you doing?'' he asked.

Ruby dug a little deeper. ''I located a skip once by going through his ex-wife's trash. She swore to me she hadn't spoken to him in a year, but I found a copy of a money order she'd sent him—with his address on it.''

''Hey, whattya doin'?'' yelled a male voice behind them. David turned to see the man who'd been leaning over the engine of the orange Maverick. He was standing up now, facing them.

"We're looking for a fugitive," said Ruby, still pawing through the trash.

"In the fuckin' garbage can?"

Ruby replaced the lid and walked toward the man while she wiped off her hands with a tissue from her purse. He was a burly, clean-shaven Hispanic in a blue basketball jersey and a tattoo on his right bicep that David couldn't quite make out.

"Hot day to be working on a car," Ruby said in her most sociable voice as she briskly approached him.

"Whattya lookin' through their garbage for?" he repeated. The other man remained on his back under the car, only legs in black pants sticking out, knees pointing up.

"You know Bullet Joe Brown?" Ruby asked, stopping within three feet of the man. She had to talk above the boom box that was still blaring country music. A male singer, but David didn't know who and didn't care. He hated country music.

The man's eyes narrowed. David could make out the tattoo now: hands clasped in prayer, wrists handcuffed.

"Maybe you know him as Earl Brown." Ruby nodded toward the Browns' trailer. "Their son."

"Who wants to know?"

"The name's Ruby Dark." She whipped a business card out of her black purse and handed it to him. "He jumped bail. On my dime."

The man glanced at the card, then flicked it to the ground, leaving black fingerprints on the starch-white card. It wasn't his dime.

"So have you seen Earl in the last coupla days?" Ruby asked. David thought maybe they should go back to digging through the garbage can for all the help they were getting here.

"No, I ain't seen him lately," said the man.

Suddenly the man under the car scooted out and sat up, squinting in the sun. Only it wasn't a guy. It was a woman, pecan-colored skin, double-pierced earrings, long black hair bound up in the back with a purple elastic band. She was attractive, except for the oil stains on her face and all over her white sleeveless T-shirt plastered in racing decals. She picked up the business card lying next to her and read it.

"I seen him," she said.

Everyone faced her.

"When?" asked Ruby.

"Two days ago."

"Sunday?"

"Yes."

"*No hables con esa puta!*" said the man.

"*¿Porqué no?*" the woman snapped back.

"*Son policia.*"

The woman stared at Ruby but seemed to be talking to the man. "*No lo son. Mira la ropa. Nunca ves una mujer policia vestida en ropa asì. Es ropa buena.*"

"*La policia puede parecerse como quieren estosdì as. Son mutantes.*"

"*No somos policia,*" Ruby suddenly interrupted. "*Y gracias por el cumplido de la ropa.*"

The man and woman stopped talking and stared at her. So did David. He didn't know his aunt spoke Spanish.

"Where did you see him?" Ruby asked in English.

"Here."

"Don't talk to her," said the man, glaring hard at the woman. "I still say they're cops."

"Earl's a criminal, Rene," said his companion. "He belongs in jail, not running around."

"Why are you so sure you saw him Sunday?" said Ruby.

"Because I remember we were working on his dad's car that day. Eddie's car. This one." She nodded toward the orange Maverick behind her. "Earl wanted to use it, but it wouldn't start. Eddie had driven it earlier in the day, but the car's got a lot of problems. We're always working on it for them. For an old machinist, Eddie doesn't know cars very well. Earl was hopping mad it wouldn't run. We said we'd look at it, but he was in a hurry. He wouldn't wait.

Took off on foot out of the park. Turned out to be a pretty simple problem. Just a coupla loose wires.''

''Know where Earl went when he left here?''

She shook her head. ''But I saw him come back later, in the evening. He pulled up in a real nice car. A Lexus LS 400. White. He wasn't driving. Some other guy was. Earl couldn't afford a car like that.''

''What did he do?''

''Went into his folks' trailer.''

''Were they home?''

''I suppose. The Maverick was here.''

''Did he stay?''

''No. He came back out in a few minutes in new clothes. Seemed in a real hurry.''

''New clothes?''

''Well, they weren't *new*. Different clothes. And he was carrying a plastic grocery sack when he came out.''

''Did the driver go in with him?''

''No, he stayed in the car.''

''Did you get a look at him?''

''No. The windows were tinted real dark.''

''You catch the plate number?''

''Didn't pay any attention. No reason to.''

''Anything special you noticed about the car besides that it was a real nice car?''

She thought for a moment. ''I remember seeing a bumper sticker on it. On the right rear. I noticed it when they drove away.''

''Sticker? What kind of sticker?''

''It was a black and white silhouette of a man's head. And it had some words on it, but I couldn't make them out.''

''Have you seen Bullet Joe or the car since?''

''No.''

Ruby looked at the man, but he added nothing.

''You've been a lotta help,'' she said to the woman. She pointed to the business card still in the woman's hand. ''Call me if you see Bullet Joe or the Lexus again.''

Ruby turned to leave, then stopped and turned back to the woman. "I'd like to ask you a favor." She dug into her purse, pulled out three twenties, and handed them to the woman. "Go buy the Browns a fan. It's hotter than a bagel bakery in there. A good fan. A big window fan. Not one of those wimpy oscillating jobs. Put it in a window and make sure they run the damn thing. And don't tell 'em I bought it for 'em. Get a new one, scratch it up, and tell 'em you found it dumped on the side of the road."

The woman took the money tentatively, as though she expected Ruby to snatch it back at any moment.

"Are you crazy, Aunt Ruby?" David said the moment they were inside the cool comfort of the Buick. "They'll never buy a fan for the Browns. That money'll go for booze or new spark plugs."

"She will."

Ruby punched a tape into the cassette player and the car filled with the sound of a jazz piano and vibes. David shook his head. Sometimes he just couldn't figure out his aunt.

As they drove out of the trailer park he asked her why she wasn't going back to talk to the Browns. Assuming the woman was telling the truth, it was obvious Bullet Joe's parents had lied about not seeing their son recently.

"They're old. Maybe they forgot. And assuming they did lie, they probably wouldn't tell us anything new. Besides, I don't want to tip my hand about the Lexus. It might get back to Bullet Joe and our mystery driver. Let's see if we can't track it down another way."

4

A call from Ruby's car phone still got the answering machine at Sean Powell's home. A call to the cosigner's employer, a retail computer store where Powell worked as a technician, turned up that he hadn't been to work in two days. The owner was concerned. Powell was his best technician and the store was already shorthanded. He missed work occasionally because of health problems, which the owner attributed to Powell's stint in Vietnam, but it wasn't like Powell to miss work without calling in. He'd worked at the store for three years, and even sick, he had a better work record than most of the young studs today who wanted a job but only showed up when they felt like it. In fact, Powell's work record had been so exemplary, the store had moved him up to technician supervisor four months ago. No, the owner had never heard Powell mention a man named Earl "Bullet Joe" Brown.

"Can I safely assume from this guy's job description that he doesn't drive a white Lexus?" David asked after Ruby hung up.

"A 1987 Chevy pickup."

They drove into lower downtown and stopped at Tattered Cover's LoDo bookstore where Ruby bought five science fiction paperbacks.

"I didn't know you read science fiction," said David.

"I don't. It's for the mayor. He reads a lot. Mostly science fiction, but he'll read anything as long as it's free."

"The *mayor*? The mayor of Denver?"

"No, the mayor of The Bottoms."

"The Bottoms? Where or what is The Bottoms?"

"You'll see."

Ruby drove a short distance to the west side of the big brick and steel edifice of Coors Field, past railroad tracks and down toward the river, to an area where, according to Ruby, early Italian and Chinese immigrants worked truck gardens.

The only thing they could truck out of here now are weeds and concrete, mused David as they passed abandoned graffiti-stained buildings, vacant fields, warehouses, and a few industrial businesses. Two makeshift tents poked up through a yard of weeds in the shadow of an empty seven-story flour mill, but David didn't see any people. He couldn't believe he was in the center of a large metropolitan area. The place had the isolated feel of a prairie ghost town.

They stopped at The Bottoms Café & Saloon, a shot-and-beer dive where a handful of shabby cars and pickups sat in its gravel lot. A favorite hangout of the mayor, said Ruby. She was in and out in a minute.

"The mayor's in his office."

"They know him?"

"Everybody knows everybody in The Bottoms."

The Bottoms turned out to be a shanty town along the east bank of the South Platte river. David always laughed when he heard people call the South Platte a river. After growing up by the wide Missouri, this tiny strip of water was an insult to the nomenclature. A man could pole vault across the South Platte, or wade across and never get his knees wet. However, David had to admit that for a small river it had a helluva big smell.

The mayor's office was in a shack crudely assembled out of lumber, old tires, bricks, metal sheeting, and whatever other scrap material the builders had scavenged. Bits of clothes, a hat, and a blanket hung on the building. A flower pot with wilted pansies rested on the center of a huge wooden cable spool tipped on its side to make a table. An empty bottle of MD 20/20 wine lay nearby. Above the entrance—a canvas flap served as the door—a board with black letters painted on it said MAYOR OF BOTTOMS. Half a dozen similar shacks were scattered along the riverbank. Not a place to winter, thought David, yet he knew they did.

"Hey, Mayor!" Ruby yelled as they walked toward the shack from her car. Two men standing three shacks away—one of them stark naked—watched suspiciously but said nothing.

A moment later a huge, shirtless, fierce-looking black man with a shaved head appeared, a silver earring in his left ear, and stylish blue-tinted sunglasses.

"Angel, how ya doin'?"

"Okay, hon. I heard you just got back in town."

"Rode the rails down from Missoula. I was taking a summer vacation. I heard the place was going to pot down here so I thought I oughta return. I shoulda stayed in Missoula. Helluva lot cooler up there. Besides, it's gettin' too damn crowded down here, what with the ballpark and all. Too many developers got their greedy little eyes on this spot. You know this is the last major chunk of undeveloped land downtown? Word is, somebody wants to turn the old flour mill into condos. If that's true, this place is gonna go to hell in a handbasket fast."

And none too soon, mused David.

"Mickey, this is my nephew, David Piszek," Ruby said, sweeping an arm in David's direction. "He works with me. David, this is Mickey Squires, mayor of The Bottoms."

"Howdy," said Squires. Despite his fierce appearance, he had a surprisingly gentle voice and a soft handshake.

"Hizzoner runs a tight ship," said Ruby.

"Not as tight as the rescue missions. They got too many rules for us. We got only five rules here, son: no drugs, no guns, no hard liquor, no stealing, and no violence. I'll beat the shit out of anyone who breaks those rules. Women are always welcome. Especially women as pretty as Angel. You bring any beer?"

Ruby held up the bag of books. "Something better."

A big grin with yellow teeth broke open on Squires's face. He took the bag and sat down on a yellow sofa in front of his shack. The first book he pulled out was Dan Simmons's *Hyperion*. "All right!" he said. He patted the couch and invited Ruby to sit down.

"That's okay," she said, obviously not wanting to place her white slacks anywhere near the vicinity of the filthy cushions.

"Damn hot to stand."

"We won't be long. You seen Bullet Joe lately?"

"Yeah, he was here a coupla nights ago."

Ruby stepped closer to Squires. "When did he arrive, exactly?"

"Hell, I don't know, Angel. I don't keep no watch. In the evening, sometime. A little bit before dark, I guess."

"He come in a white Lexus?"

Squires laughed, a full belly laugh. "A Lexus? Bullet Joe? He can barely afford bus fare."

"Somebody else was driving the car."

"No, I didn't see any Lexus. Yours is the nicest car we've seen in a year down here, Angel. How about a ride around the block in it?"

"Bullet Joe say how he got here, Mickey? Bus service is pretty rare out here."

Squires cracked his knuckles. "Yeah, I've been meaning to talk to RTD 'bout that. Maybe I can bring it up the next time we have a regional mayors' conference."

"Bullet Joe," she reminded him.

"He said he hitched a ride, but he didn't say who with. Walked the last stretch. Maybe the driver didn't like the neighborhood. He jump bail, Ruby?"

"Yeah."

"He said he was in some deep shit. I asked him what it was, but he wouldn't tell me."

"He was going down for the count."

Squires wrinkled his face and shook his head. "He wasn't a guy afraid of doing hard time. He was afraid of something else. That's why he wanted to stay. I don't know what was bothering him, but it wasn't hard time."

"He stayed here?"

"Sure. You never turn away an old pen pal unless he was a baby raper or a snitch."

Ruby looked around.

"Naw, he ain't here now, Angel. He slept on the couch but he was gone by morning. Don't know where. He didn't leave a note. Didn't see him leave. Ain't seen him since."

"When he was here, did he mention a guy named Sean Powell? He bailed him out the last time."

Squires shook his head. "But he talked about a guy named Todd Jennings."

"Who's Todd Jennings?"

"You don't know who Todd Jennings is?" Squires's voice was playful. "I thought you knew everybody in town, Angel."

"Most people, but apparently not Todd Jennings. So who the hell is he?"

"He runs a big construction company here in town. Earthmovers and all that kind of shit. Rich S.O.B."

Rich enough to drive a Lexus, thought David.

"I'm not into earthmoving, Mickey. Don't have any clients into earthmoving . . . except for a gravedigger I once bailed out. In what context did Bullet Joe mention this Jennings guy?"

"There wasn't any context. At least none I could understand. BJ was incoherent most of the time he was here."

"Drinking?"

"That, and the nightmares again. 'Nam shit, you know. Pulls you back like . . ." Squires clenched his fist but couldn't seem to find the right analogy, so he let it go. "Wouldna thought much about the name 'cept I knew he worked once for Jennings. In a legit job, if you can imagine Earl in one. Worked on heavy equipment for him, I think."

"When was this?"

"I don't know . . . three, four years ago, maybe."

"He said he was in deep shit. You think Jennings was connected to whatever that was?"

Squires shrugged. "Got me. He didn't make much sense while he was here. I tried to get him settled down for some rest, but he was real freaked out."

"If you were looking for him, hon, where would you look?"

"He liked to stay at the Taylor Hotel if he had any money and he didn't want to put up with his old man."

"Down on Welton by Seventeenth?"

"That's it. And the bars around Coors Field, of course."

"Any bars in particular?"

"Anything within distance of an Andres Galarraga homer."

5

The Taylor Hotel was one of the last downtown hotels, the kind of place that once had charm—maybe even elegance—when downtown was king. Now it was merely old and dingy and stuffy, a place where people on Social Security or small pensions went to die. The dimly lit lobby was full, mostly with people watching a fuzzy color television or staring blankly out the dirty windows at the passing world. An old woman with arthritic hands smoked a thin brown cigarette and watched intently as Ruby and David walked across the yellowed linoleum floor to the hotel desk.

The desk clerk, a heavyset black man with a three-day growth of white beard and who looked as weary as the residents sitting in the lobby, said Bullet Joe had stayed last night but had checked out early this morning. No, he hadn't said where he was going. He looked pretty whacked-out.

"Did he arrive or leave in a white Lexus?" Ruby asked.

The desk clerk laughed.

They scoured a handful of bars around the Taylor Hotel, but nobody had seen Bullet Joe—at least no one admitted to it. By then, Ruby's pager had beeped several times. She returned two calls from her car phone but decided to return the rest from her loft.

Ruby's fifth-floor loft was only a few blocks from the Taylor Hotel, but it might well have been a world away.

Granted, her loft overlooked an alley and the building was probably as old as the hotel, if not older—built at the end of the last century for the manufacture of mining equipment. But there the resemblance ended. The loft sported a high, timbered ceiling, refurbished red brick walls, and a hardwood floor pieced out of wood from a high school gymnasium over on the Western Slope. The interior was well-lit and airy; the furnishings were contemporary—a kitchen, lots of bookcases, plants, and original abstract art. A white baby grand stood against one wall.

David sat on a green leather couch and drank an iced tea while Ruby made her calls. The loft was cool, a refreshing break from the smothering heat outside.

"I gotta go over to the jail to see about a coupla possible clients," said Ruby, setting her cordless phone down on the coffee table in front of him. "Attempted second-degree murder and a possession charge. It shouldn't take long. You want to come along?"

"I'd prefer to stay here and study."

"Suit yourself. When I get back, we'll grab something to eat before we hit more bars."

He tried to study. He genuinely tried. He opened the book and stared at the words, but the print kept blurring. He listened to the faint whir of central air-conditioning. He was tired—tired from the heat, tired from looking for a lowlife like Bullet Joe, tired from trying to juggle his law studies with the time and stress of the bail-bonding business. He thought about taking a nap on his aunt's bed—the one that lay beyond the door built from the walk-in safe once used by the manufacturing company—but he let the cool green leather couch wrap its arms around him and pull him down into sleep.

He was dreaming of standing before Professor Rothschild, who was peering imperiously down on him from an impossibly high bench, dressed in his black judicial robes. David was standing as a defendant and not as a prosecuting attorney. Mercifully, the noise of his aunt's return from the city jail woke him. Hastily he retrieved his book, which had fallen to the floor, and opened it.

"Any luck?" he said, trying to push the grogginess from his voice.

"One out of two. I didn't trust the possession charge. He smelled like a skip."

Too bad Bullet Joe hadn't smelled like one, he thought.

They went to an upscale Italian restaurant three blocks from her loft. They were seated on the top floor of the narrow structure, having climbed three flights of stairs to get there. "You must be in incredible shape," David joked with the young hostess who'd led the way.

"It saves on health club fees," she admitted with a friendly smile.

He would have liked her phone number but was too embarrassed to ask for it in front of his aunt. He'd come back another time.

Ruby ordered fettucine Alfredo while David ordered a Caesar salad.

"You're in one of the finest Italian restaurants in town and all you're going to eat is rabbit food?" said Ruby.

"I'm not hungry. It's too hot to eat. Besides, it's a helluva lot better for me than that heart-attack-on-a-plate you ordered."

Ruby poured olive oil onto her bread plate and dipped a breadstick into it. "My eating habits may get me to heaven a lot sooner than you, David, but trust me, St. Peter's gonna reject you for the sin of *dullness*."

"Don't you want to live a longer life, Aunt Ruby?" he asked.

"Eating fettucine Alfredo doesn't guarantee that I won't. I bet I still outlive you. But to answer your question, no, not if I have to give up my favorite foods and exercise in my free time. So I'll come up short a few years. Big deal. I'm not obsessed with longevity."

"I prefer that option," said David.

"We all end up in the same place, you know, it's just a

matter of who gets to the door first. Unfortunately, our culture is obsessed with longevity. It's become a virtue, like not lying, or being faithful to your spouse, or reading the classics. To me, the virtue is living life, not just living a *long* life.''

''But don't you think it's a senseless waste of life if you end it earlier than necessary because of things you didn't do to prevent it?''

Ruby rolled her eyes. ''I kept hearing that phrase after Jerry Garcia died. 'He was only fifty-three. It was the drugs and the drinking and all that hard living that killed him. What a waste.' We should all wish we wasted our lives like he did. Here's all these people living timid, boring lives, afraid to take risks because they're afraid of death and afraid of dying *early*, whatever the hell that means. They'll outlive Garcia, all right, but in the end they'll die anyway and nobody will care. But Jerry Garcia will live *forever*.''

''I think his Grateful Dead fans would have wished he'd lived longer—though at least some of them will have to get *real* jobs now.''

''It wouldn't have been the same music if he'd been more cautious. You know what Jackie Onassis said to one of her friends when she was dying of cancer at the age of sixty-four?''

''I didn't know you followed the tabloids.''

Ruby ignored his sarcasm. ''She said, 'Why in the world did I do all those push-ups?' Promise me that if I ever end up in a hospital with a bunch of tubes sticking out of me and ICU nurses hovering over me like angels of death, you'll pull the plug.''

David visibly recoiled. ''I couldn't do that, Aunt Ruby. I couldn't pull the plug on you or anyone.''

She pointed her breadstick at him. ''You better, hon, or I'll come back from the dead and haunt your ass.''

The length of an Andres Galarraga home run from Coors Field encompassed a lot of bars in LoDo. Ruby and David worked Market and Blake streets first, since these bars had become center of the action. The majority were new, large, and overlit, with lots of still-shiny wood, and most of the bars played off a baseball or sports theme. They were packed. It was a 7:05 home game against the Braves, and fans were warming up with a few cold brewskis and watching huge multiscreen television displays simultaneously showing ESPN baseball games, dirt-bike races, in-line skating, windsurfing, and sky diving with jumpers wearing snowboards strapped to their feet and hair flying behind them—hair that hadn't seen shampoo in three months. One bar had made it easy for patrons who were too drunk to hold up their heads: TVs built into the floor. Two bars had put in computer terminals so patrons could surf the Net and settle baseball trivia bets.

In each bar, David hung back by the door and scoured the crowd for Bullet Joe, while Ruby bulled her way to the bartenders and flashed his mug shot. None of them were any help. "Kids," Ruby called them. "They've got one eye on the TV and the other on the cash register. They don't know their customers. They don't know the cops. They don't know the street."

Finally, after two hours of fruitless searching, Ruby and David dipped into a coffeehouse that sat below street level. The place was half empty. They found a small table in the back. No folk singers, no poetry readers, which David found refreshing. But original, local art—most of it modern—covered the walls, which explained the place's name, Java Gallery. Ruby ordered some blend from Tanzania, while David ordered bottled fruit juice.

"We're looking for Bullet Joe in the wrong places," muttered Ruby. "He wouldn't hang out in bars where Yuppies stand three-deep and the baseball memorabilia looks like it was made last week in Korea."

"So where is he?"

"Somewhere he can hide in the dark corners."

They finished their drinks and headed north along Blake Street. They passed the ballpark, its clock tower and bright, lacy light towers looming over them. They could hear the crowd inside. David guessed that the game was still in early innings, unless it was a pitcher's duel, a rarity at Coors Field.

Past Twenty-first, up around Park Avenue West, the bars grew dingier, with fewer patrons, where men in dirty caps with car-parts logos drank from long-necked bottles . . . bars where the help knew their customers.

"Yeah, I seen him in here," said the bartender in a Denver Nuggets T-shirt, after Ruby flashed Bullet Joe's mug shot. "But it ain't been in a while. Baseball nut, right?"

"Who isn't?" she said ruefully.

"You know where ya oughta go, lady?"

She waited for him to tell her where to go.

"Home Plate."

"That's over on Larimer, right?"

"Yeah. On Twenty-first. Owner's a former ballplayer. Eight years in the minors and maybe a coupla years, total, in the majors. White Sox and Mets. Played in the Polo Grounds, he told me once. Guy's gotta be well into his fifties. Name's Jimmy Moon. A true baseball fan would hang out at Jimmy Moon's."

Home Plate was flanked by a Mexican café ("Great chile rellenos," said Ruby) and a pawnshop. Two doors away, old men sat outside a corner liquor store, their shopping carts parked nearby. Home Plate had iron grills over its windows, neon beer signs, and the tired look of a team that was twenty games out of first place in mid-September. David squinted in the dim interior light. Half a dozen people sat scattered among the booths and at the bar.

"Hey there, folks," yelled the bartender. Thinning hair and a growing paunch. "If you're looking for a crowd, come back when the game's over. If you just wanna drink in peace, you came at the right time."

They went up to the bar and sat down. David noticed the pictures first. At least two dozen black-and-white photos mounted above the well bottles. "To Jimmy," autographed, often in easy, large strokes. He recognized most of the faces, though all of them had played before he was born. Anybody who followed baseball would know them. Don Drysdale. Minnie Minoso. Eddie Mathews. Willie Mays. *Willie Mays*! Enos Slaughter. Don Larsen. Joe Adcock. Then he spotted the bat. It stood upright among the bottles, ready to swing for the fence. At first, David assumed it was part of the decor—or to let customers know there'd be no nonsense at Home Plate. Then he realized that the bat was mounted and cracked, and that something had been written on its thick end. It was a special bat.

"You Jimmy Moon?" Ruby asked.

"The one and only." The bartender slid white drink napkins in front of them. "What'llya have?"

"Information," said Ruby.

He frowned. "Not a brand we carry, ma'am. Leads to trouble and I can't make any money off it."

"Sure you can." Ruby reached into her purse and pulled out a twenty-dollar bill. She laid the bill and Bullet Joe's mug shot on the bar.

The bartender looked at it, then pushed it back to her. "Like I said, it leads to trouble. I like my customers to keep coming back."

"This one's not coming back. He skipped on his bond. I'm left holding the ticket."

Jimmy Moon looked unsympathetic. "Musta had better things to do with his time."

Ruby started to dig into her purse, but the bartender put his hand forward and said, "It ain't the money, ma'am."

David cut in, pointing to the photos. "You collected all those pictures when you were a player?"

The bartender turned to him and beamed. "Yep, son. Crossed paths with all of them at one time or another, usually on the other teams. Played in both leagues, you know. I knew I wouldn't be up for the big one very long, so I thought I oughta at least collect a few souvenirs while I was there. Always knew I'd open a bar someday and the pictures might come in handy."

"And the bat. Is that your bat?"

The bartender looked back at it for a moment. "Wish it was. It belonged to Ted Kluszewski. Hit one of his three home runs in the fifty-nine World Series with that bat. Cracked it the next time up, so he gave it to me."

"You played in the World Series?"

"I kept the bench warm. They called me up late in the season, but I never took a swing. We lost, you know."

"To the Dodgers, right?"

"That's pretty good, kid. You weren't even in diapers."

"Dodgers had gone to L.A. by then, hadn't they?"

"Yep. That's why I hated losing to them so much. I never forgave 'em for leaving Ebbets Field."

"You two through reminiscing?" said Ruby.

"No ma'am, we're just getting warmed up."

Ruby pushed the money and the picture back toward him. "You sure you don't know this guy?"

"I didn't say I didn't know him. I just said I wasn't passing out information."

"Look, she's right," David said. "He's not coming back. He's set to do life. It would be a big favor if you could help us out."

The bartender shook his head slowly. "I'm sorry to hear that. Bullet Joe was a nice guy. Sure knew his baseball." He fell silent.

"That reminds me," said David. "I understand he took his nickname from a ballplayer. But I've never heard of a ballplayer named Bullet Joe."

"Well before your time, son. Well before *my* time. The guy was named Joe Bush. Bullet Joe Bush. He was a pitcher back in the teens and twenties. Played for a bunch of teams—Yankees, A's, Browns, Senators."

"I never heard of him."

"Fans back then did. A pretty good pitcher. ERA around three-five. Pitched in several World Series. Pretty decent hitter, too, for a pitcher."

"Thanks. I'll have to read up on him."

The bartender leaned on the bar and picked up Bullet Joe's photo. He ran his tongue on the inside of his lip. After a few moments he handed the photo to David, and said softly, ''He was in here tonight.''

''When?''

The man glanced at a small digital clock behind him. ''I'd say he left three or four hours ago.''

David tried to act calm. ''You wouldn't know—''

''Said he was going to the game if he could get a ticket. They're tough to get at the last minute, these days.''

''Was he with anyone?'' asked David.

''No. Sat right there alone for two hours and drank.'' He pointed two stools over from Ruby.

''Did he leave with anyone?''

''No.''

''Did you see him get in a car?''

''Didn't see a thing after that door swung shut.''

''Did he happen to say where he was going after the game?''

''Nope. Just said he was going to the game. He talked baseball. Though he did seem kinda preoccupied. He kept watching the door. But he didn't say why. He musta been watching for you two.''

David slid off the bar stool. ''Thanks. We really appreciate it.''

Ruby thanked him too and headed for the door.

The bartender held up the twenty-dollar bill. ''I told you, I don't take money for information, ma'am.''

''Then open two bottles of beer and pour 'em down the sink if it'll make you feel better, hon.''

As they went out the door and headed the two blocks to the ballpark, Ruby patted David on the back and said, ''I guess baseball's worth something, after all.''

6

The game against the Atlanta Braves was sold out. Every last ticket.

"Now what?" asked David as they turned away from the ticket window. "We can't sit out here and wait for him—*if* he's in there. Fifty thousand people will pour out of this place at the end of the game."

"We improvise."

Ruby took off toward a man selling tickets across the street. He was one of several hawkers within a fastball pitch of each other. David hurried after her.

"How much for two?" said Ruby as she and David approached the man.

"Hundred twenty bucks."

"That's robbery."

"You wanna see the Rockies play, you gotta pay."

"Still high."

"Okay, lady, I'll take a hundred. Cash."

"Scalping's illegal," David reminded him as authoritatively as he could. "We could have you arrested." He'd heard that some of the scalpers working sports facilities these days were gang members muscling in on the lucrative trade.

The man, in his early twenties with thin blond hair and a diamond earring, seemed unimpressed with David's threat of arrest. "You want the tickets or not? I'll make it eighty bucks."

"That's ridiculous," said David. "The game's already in the sixth inning."

"It's okay," said Ruby. "I have a short attention span for baseball." She dug into her purse.

"They're great seats," the scalper assured them. "Right behind third base."

"I don't care if they're in the basement, honey, just so they get us in."

As he handed her the green-and-cream-colored tickets, Ruby handed him one of her business cards.

"What's this?" he said.

"Just in case you get caught. Bail for scalping is a thousand bucks."

They went in the first-base entrance, under a huge purple Coors Field sign, and onto a concrete concourse full of beer stands and concessions and milling fans. They couldn't see the field well at first, just bright glimpses through the silhouettes of people standing or walking by. They snaked through the crowd and stopped directly behind the last row of seats looking directly at the first-base line. The sun was down but the sky hadn't turned black. The mountains beyond the left center field fence were silhouetted in a deep purple. The outfield grass glowed an odd green under the powerful lights.

"It's a beautiful ballpark, isn't it?" said David.

"I wouldn't know," responded Ruby. "I've never been inside one before."

David turned to her. "*Never*? That's unbelievable, Aunt Ruby. That's . . . unAmerican."

"I told you, I hate baseball."

He looked back out on the field. "Take my word for it, this is one beautiful ballpark. I've been in a few. Dad and I used to watch the Kansas City Royals at Royals Stadium. Had artificial turf. I hated that. This beats the places I've been in. It doesn't have the mystique yet of Fenway or

Yankee Stadium. It'll need a decade or two of seasoning for that. A ballpark's not worth much until it has some lore behind it. But it's already got a great old-time baseball feel to it."

"You folks'll have to step back of the yellow line," said an usher in purple vest and straw hat.

David looked down at a yellow line that ran two feet behind the seats. They were standing inside it by a foot.

"So much for that old-time feel," cracked Ruby.

They walked along the concourse toward home plate. David glanced at the huge electronic scoreboard behind left field. The Braves were up three-to-one in the top of the sixth, at bat with a man on second, two out. The Rockies would never beat these guys. Ruby bought two long red licorice ropes from a vendor and stopped behind another row of seats. She looked down at the yellow line and stepped over it.

"Got any ideas how we're going to find Bullet Joe in here?" she asked as she scanned the inside of the stadium. All three decks were packed. "What did you say, fifty thousand?"

David looked at her sharply. "I figured you had a plan."

"I said we'd improvise. You've been here before. I haven't. I was hoping you'd have an idea."

"*I* was hoping we could catch a few minutes of the game in those seats you bought. I've never gotten to sit that close to third base."

"Business calls."

David sighed. "What a waste. But I do have an idea how we might narrow things down."

Ruby looked at him, alert. "What?"

"We know Bullet Joe didn't have a ticket when he left the bar. He could have bought a seat from a scalper, but I doubt he could afford it. My bet is he bought a Rockpile ticket. They're cheap seats and they don't go on sale until two or three hours before the game."

"Where's the Rockpile?"

"There, just above that big green wall that looks like the

Green Monster at Fenway.'' David pointed across the way, toward dead-center field, at a cantilevered deck of seats detached from the rest of the seating. ''I've bought a few Rockpile tickets myself. It's just the kind of place a guy like him would sit in.''

''Then let's try it.''

They walked down the third-base side, past a children's playground and along the concourse behind left field, until they stood directly under the Rockpile. Miraculously, David had noticed on the way, the Rockies had retired the Braves in the inning without a run and were up to bat. They'd even put a man on base.

''What's the access?'' Ruby asked, looking up.

''Two stairways on either side that come out maybe two-thirds the way up the deck.'' David pointed to stairways at each end as if he was a flight attendant pointing out the emergency exits on a 747. ''He could be sitting behind us when we come up, but that's better than the middle entrance.'' He pointed to a sloped concrete tunnel. ''That comes out right at the bottom of the deck. It's where they roll in people in wheelchairs. He'd spot us for sure if we went in that way.''

''Then you take that stairway and I'll take the other one,'' Ruby said, turning away.

''Wait a minute!'' David called after her. When he got close to her, he half-whispered, ''Shouldn't we get security? There are cops around.''

''They're not going to help us unless we know he's definitely there. Let's find him first.''

''What if he's armed or something? They check for bottles and cans here, but not for guns.''

''He won't be armed. I've got handcuffs and pepper spray if I need it.''

''All right,'' said David, far less sure.

He climbed the zigzag set of stairs, pacing himself to his aunt's progress across the way. Partway up, he heard the crowd cheer. Another Rockie must have gotten on base. David surfaced on the left side of the Rockpile. First he looked out toward the field, then nonchalantly looked left, right, and back toward the top of the Rockpile. The faces belonged to families, young men with no shirts and baseball caps on backward, and dull-eyed old men who had probably drunk too much. But none of the faces belonged to Bullet Joe.

A rustle went through the crowd. The stadium announcer blared over the PA system, with great emphasis, that Dante Bichette was up to bat. Two Rockies were on base and the RBI leader in the National League was in the box, twirling his bat in his peculiar warm-up swing.

David glanced across the center of the Rockpile and saw his aunt scanning the crowd. Suddenly something riveted her attention, and it wasn't Bichette. She had focused on a man seated toward the lower middle of the deck. He wore a tan shirt and no hat. He had thinning brown hair and sat with a slight hunch. David couldn't see the man's face, but from the back he resembled the man in the mug shot.

Ruby glanced at David and gave him a subtle, confirming nod.

The man turned his head in David's direction, as if he sensed being watched. David tried to appear caught up in the game—just one of the fans. Bullet Joe wouldn't recognize him, but out of the corner of his eye, David saw the skip slowly look the other way, in Ruby's direction. Ruby started toward him. Bullet Joe looked back at David, who was moving casually down through the stands. Bullet Joe glanced back at Ruby and then to the exit at the bottom of the Rockpile. He was five rows away, in the middle of a row. He couldn't get to an aisle to run. Not a smart place to sit, thought David. The man would have to clamber over seats and through fans if he was going to reach it.

It was at that precise moment, while Bullet Joe watched Ruby and David descend toward him, that David heard the unmistakable crack of the bat. A hard hit. The crowd's roar began to swell, then plateaued for a moment as everyone in the ballpark followed the high, slow arch of the ball in the bright lights. Mesmerized, they held their breath, hurrying off a prayer to the baseball gods that the ball would clear the fence. A moment later it did, in deep center field, just to the left of the Green Monster wall. The crowd rose to its feet in unison and exploded in a deafening cheer.

David instantly lost sight of Bullet Joe. He stopped, suddenly realizing they might not reach the skip before he reached the lower center exit. David whirled and ran back up the stands, then down the exit stairway to the concourse under the Rockpile.

He reached the bottom just as Bullet Joe raced past him faster than a man in his forties had a right to run. Ruby was two-stepping her way down the other stairway faster than a woman of fifty had a right to hustle. He pointed her toward the fleeing Bullet Joe and took off in the skip's wake.

Ahead, Bullet Joe plowed into a hawker carrying a steel rack of lemonade. Liquid flew everywhere as the hawker let out a loud "Goddammit!" and sprawled backward onto the concrete. Bullet Joe stumbled but managed to stay on his feet.

"Stop that man!" David yelled at two uniformed cops twenty feet away. They had looked up at the sound of the hawker's scream, and David frantically pointed to Bullet Joe who, spotting the cops at nearly the same instant, veered toward a row of spectators who were hanging over a railing and cheering Bichette's victory trot around the bases.

Suddenly Bullet Joe was gone.

"Jesus!" said David. The damn fool had pushed his way through the spectators and leaped over the railing.

David arrived at the railing at the same time as the cops, pushing people aside. He looked down into the visitors' bullpen a good eighteen feet below. Bullet Joe should have broken his ankles, but he'd landed in the sand around the two home plates where an Atlanta catcher was warming up a reliever. The catcher had jumped back, staring in amazement at the sudden appearance of a man in the middle of his sandbox. Bullet Joe was scrambling to his feet.

"Who the fuck is that nut?" one of the cops asked David.

"A bail jumper."

"He armed?"

"We don't know."

"Shit!"

Ruby arrived at just that moment, out of breath. "Where is—"

"There!" David pointed at Bullet Joe as he headed for the bullpen door that opened onto the playing field. A purple-vested usher guarding the door was approaching him, both hands outward in a stop sign. "Sir, you can't come—" he managed before Bullet Joe barreled over him. The skip yanked open the door and stumbled out onto the playing field. He hesitated, then began running down the warning track toward the right-field corner.

One of the cops barked into a radio clipped to his shirt, and the two of them dashed off along the concourse in the same direction as Bullet Joe.

"Shit!" said David. He took a deep breath, climbed the railing, and leaped into the bullpen just as his aunt yelled for him not to. He landed in the same pile of sand as Bullet Joe had, beside the same bewildered catcher, rolled once, and was on his feet again, headed for the bullpen door. The usher had struggled to his feet and was blocking David's way, a single hand raised to stop him, while bracing himself for another hit. David, still moving fast, reached into his back pocket then swung his hand from his hip, his palm open. "I'm a cop!" he yelled. The usher hesitated, distracted by David's open palm. He expected to see a badge. By the time he realized nothing was there, David was past him and out the door.

Bullet Joe was well down the warning track when David ran onto the red cinder. Ahead, the usher sitting along the right-field line near the foul pole was racing toward Bullet Joe. The Atlanta right-fielder had turned his attention from Bichette's dugout welcome and was warily watching Bullet Joe. He was closer than the approaching usher but made no attempt to intervene. If anything, he backed away a few steps.

David could sense the rest of the ballpark's attention turning away from Bichette and focusing on the bizarre scene in right field. The cheers had turned to an uneasy murmur. Two purple vests were running from the left-field line and another from the direction of home plate, but no cops. David glanced over his shoulder toward the bullpen door to see if any cops or Ruby had followed him. They hadn't. He didn't expect to see his aunt. She was a tough lady, but she wouldn't jump the railing.

At that moment, as he looked back toward the bullpen, he caught sight of the huge electronic scoreboard above left field. David—and everyone else in the ballpark—witnessed Bullet Joe as he dashed along the warning track in two-story-high JumboTron video-vision. It was at that precise moment that David suddenly wondered what the hell he was doing out here, chasing a three-time loser in front of 50,000 people and God knows how many more watching the game on cable TV.

A voice in his head told him to stop running, to find the nearest exit and escape this insanity as fast as possible. But he kept going, gaining ground on Bullet Joe, who had veered off the cinder track and onto the grass of right field, where he made a beeline toward the low retaining wall that ran along the right-field foul line.

The usher had closed the gap on Bullet Joe. Like the bullpen usher, he put up his hands in a signal to stop—and, like the other usher, he found himself barreled over by the skip, who sent him sprawling backwards onto the grass. A gasp rippled through the crowd, along with a few cheers and uneasy laughs.

David ran by the prone usher and was only a few yards behind Bullet Joe when the skip reached the low retaining wall and hurled himself over the top into the lap of Dinger, the Rockies' oversized purple dinosaur-mascot who'd been hamming it up with the younger fans in the front row. It was like jumping onto a giant fur ball. Dinger sprawled backward into a seat, cushioning Bullet Joe's fall.

Another gasp rose from the crowd, this time with no laughter or cheers.

David was nearly at the wall—almost within grasp of Bullet Joe, who was scrambling to his feet—when suddenly he felt himself being tackled from behind. He went sprawling to the ground.

"No! No! Get *him*!" he yelled, pushing against the purple-vested usher who'd pinned him down. "He's an escaped convict, you idiot!"

The usher didn't hear—or didn't care, or didn't like being called an idiot, or had figured David for another crazed fan. David tried to push him away, but before he could make any headway, another usher arrived to help keep him down. From the corner of his eye he saw Bullet Joe winding his way through the crowd, stopping periodically to turn and point in David's direction, as if telling the crowd that David was the bad guy.

It took another hour for David and Ruby to sort it out with the police and ballpark security. Fortunately, no one was hurt—not even Dinger—but no one had found Bullet Joe, either. Somehow he'd eluded the police and vanished into the crowd.

David and Ruby stood outside the first-base entrance. The ballpark lights were shining brighter now against the coal-black sky. David was exhausted. He ached all over, his body scraped and cut from his wrestling match with the ushers. But worse was the pain of his humiliation, his anger. His name would be in the papers and on the damn television tomorrow. His law professors and fellow students would get a good laugh out of it; they'd needle him unmercifully about his line of work. A law student schlepping for a bail bondsman! Could one go any lower?

And his parents! Would they—especially his father—hear about it back in St. Joseph, Missouri? Would it be in the papers or on the local sports news—or replayed ad nauseum on ESPN—that their son was working for the black sheep of the Piszek clan?

Fans began to spill out. The game was over.

Ruby stared up at the massive brick structure of the ballpark. "God, I hate baseball."

7

It was mid-morning the next day when Ruby's Lamborghini pulled up in front of Sean Powell's home.

"This is the collateral for a forty-five-grand bond?" said David, staring at the house.

It was a tiny ranch-style home, tan siding and light blue trim, at least forty years old and not much bigger than a good-sized apartment. A swamp cooler squatted on the roof, an ugly appendage. Like many of the other homes on the block, the garage had been converted into a spare room in an attempt to squeeze out a little more living space. There was a small, curtained window just above where the garage door handle had been attached. Two thin strips of empty concrete ran up to the spare room and abruptly stopped—no Chevy pickup in sight. "Tacky" was the word that jumped into David's mind.

"He's lived here four years," said Ruby. "He's built up equity. He's held a steady job. Along with the pickup and a few mutual funds, he has enough assets to cover the bond."

"You don't need me to work for you, Aunt Ruby. You need a professional appraiser or an accountant. Let me guess. This one just 'felt right.' "

"He seems pretty stable, yes. And like I told you earlier, Bullet Joe doesn't have a history of jumping bail."

"Let's hope the guy's home with just a bad case of the

flu." They had called both Powell's house and his employer earlier in the morning, with the same negative results as the day before.

A concrete walk led them to the front door. A milk box with "Royal Crest" on a blue label sat to one side of the concrete stoop, which was partially shaded by a small, tan aluminum awning. The shrubbery along the front of the house was thick and well tended. A blue spruce cast a sharp shadow over the house. In fact, most of the neighborhood trees were mature and towered over the tiny homes. Neat beds of bright flowers were everywhere. But neither the flowers nor the trees could mask the low-rent feel of the neighborhood.

"Is the guy married?" David asked.

"Yes. They have one kid."

"The wife work someplace?"

"I don't know."

Ruby rang the doorbell again. A simple two-note chord chimed inside. She banged on the storm door, then flipped open the lid of a small brass mailbox. It was stuffed full. Ruby took the mail out and riffled through it. David started to object about the impropriety of reading someone else's mail, then figured that with his aunt, it wasn't worth the effort. Besides, the mail appeared to be mostly junk.

Ruby put the mail back and lifted the lid to the milk box, which contained a single-gallon plastic bottle. Ruby touched it. She didn't say anything, but David surmised it was warm. If the milk had been delivered cold that morning, it would be sweating in the heat.

"Maybe they've just taken a brief trip," he said, not believing his own words. "Family emergency or something." *Or maybe a vacation with Bullet Joe.*

Ruby opened the storm door and tried the knob to the main door. It was locked. A large dead bolt sat just above the knob. She stepped back off the stoop and surveyed the front of the house. All the windows were closed and either shuttered or covered with curtains.

"Stay here," she said, and walked back to the car. She

returned a moment later carrying her Peerless handcuffs and a Prowler-Fouler stun gun, a black tube of high-impact plastic that shot a beanbag of buckshot hard enough to knock a middle linebacker on his butt. Her bounty hunter had owned it before his death.

"You think Bullet Joe's hiding in there?" David asked his aunt, eyeing the cuffs and stun gun.

"No. But I'm not taking the chance. Besides, they'll make a good excuse."

"Excuse for what?"

"Come on."

They went around the end of the house, past the converted garage. David looked furtively up and down the street as they walked back. He didn't see anyone outside. Who would want to be outside in this heat? But he was sure they were being watched. Someone was probably calling 911 already to report two prowlers—although two people driving a red Lamborghini weren't your ordinary prowlers. Why did his aunt always do things that made him feel so uneasy?

They passed through the gate of a high wooden fence and into the backyard. Like the front, it was well tended. A garden bloomed in one corner, and flowers were planted along stretches of the fence. Two white metal yard chairs sat in the shade of a Russian olive tree. A crabapple tree shaded another corner of the yard next to an alley. The grass was thick and green and mowed. It was the kind of place where David would love to stretch out with a law book and a cold beer.

Ruby walked along the back of the house. Here, too, the windows were closed and curtained, except for the window on the rear door. They stepped onto a concrete patio covered by an extension of the roof. A redwood picnic table occupied much of the small patio. A lone blue plastic plate and an opaque glass sat on the table, next to plastic salt and pepper shakers and a napkin holder. Several ants were busy carting off treasures from the surface of the plate. David peered into the glass. A dead fly floated in pale liquid. Two unused napkins lay on the table. David put them back into the napkin holder. A third napkin had blown off the table and caught in the spokes of a man's eighteen-speed mountain bike leaning against the house. Odd, thought David, that someone who obviously took such great pride in his yard would go off and leave milk on the front porch and food on the picnic table.

Ruby knocked on the back door. She rattled the door knob. It was locked. She pressed her face against the plate-glass window. Suddenly she drew back and smashed it with the barrel of the stun gun.

"Jesus, Aunt Ruby, what the hell are you doing?"

"Breaking in."

"No shit!"

She gingerly reached in through the broken glass to unlock the door.

"What are you going to tell the cops when they show up?" He was sure that what neighbors *hadn't* called 911 when he and his aunt first pulled up were hastily doing so at this very moment.

"We'll tell them we had reason to believe the man of this house was harboring a fugitive."

"We've been through this one before, Aunt Ruby, and it didn't turn out well." Dark images of the home they'd mistakenly broken into in Cherry Hills Village flashed before his eyes.

Ruby opened the door. The stuffiness and heat of the house spilled out onto the patio. It brought something with it. A smell. David had encountered the same smell twice before in his life and did not want to encounter it again.

The smell of death.

8

"Don't go in there, Aunt Ruby."

She went anyway, of course: through the door and into the kitchen. Glass crunched under her feet.

"Mr. Powell!" she yelled.

The smell held David back, like a giant hand pushing on his chest. He couldn't breathe. He didn't want to enter, knowing what he would find there.

His eyes followed a shaft of light through the open door into the shadowy kitchen. It highlighted the edge of a refrigerator, the end of a countertop, and part of a round wooden table, which lay on its side.

"We have to call the police, Aunt Ruby."

"Powell!" she yelled louder. She held her Prowler-Fouler at the ready.

"We can use the car phone," he said loudly. "They can be here in minutes, Aunt Ruby. Let's just wait until they get here."

As if the police weren't already on their way after the noise she'd made breaking in. David cocked his ear but heard nothing but birds. It must be the quietest damn neighborhood in the city.

"Sean, it's Ruby Dark!" Her voice was farther away. She moved deeper into the house.

David inched to the open door and yelled in, "Aunt Ruby, I think you're compromising a crime scene."

"*Mrs.* Powell?" Her voice was still farther away.

"Not a good idea," he muttered uselessly, knowing his pleas were futile with his hardheaded aunt.

"Is anyone here? I'm a bail bondsman. I'm here on a legal search for a fugitive."

David peered inside, careful not to touch the doorjamb. His body cast a shadow into the kitchen.

His eyes tried to adjust to the muffled light. There had been a fight here. Shards of glass lay everywhere. A shiny metallic toaster had been knocked to the linoleum floor. Flour had spilled from a canister and across the counter onto the floor, where footprints in every direction had smeared the fine white powder. A kitchen drawer had been yanked open, its contents strewn onto the floor. Part of a newspaper was scrunched next to the overturned table. A closed prescription bottle lay nearby.

And the dark smears. As David's eyes adjusted to the shadows, dark smears emerged. Everywhere. The countertop. A cabinet door. The tabletop. The doorjamb leading out of the kitchen and into a tiny living room. Three large smears on the floor appeared glossy black and cracked, almost like pieces of black tile.

"Oh, shit!" he said to no one.

And no one replied. The house was silent. He didn't even hear his aunt.

"Aunt Ruby!" He heard the edginess in his own voice.

Dammit, why does she always do this! Why can't she stay out of things where she should stay out of things!

He tiptoed into the kitchen. His foot recoiled at the crunch of broken glass. He stepped in again, ignoring the sound this time.

The smell was stronger now. He swallowed hard—a gag reflex. He'd thrown up the last time he'd smelled death, retched like he'd never retched before. This smell wasn't as overpowering as the last time—*that* body had rotted in salt water for an entire week before they found it. But the smell here still made his stomach do a song-and-dance number. He remembered what his aunt's detective friend,

Morgan Reed, had told him about finding rotting bodies. A little secret among the pros. Don't keep sticking your head outside for fresh air. That's what does you in. Buck up to the smell for the first few minutes and your nose numbs up. Then, you're home free.

David went farther into the kitchen, avoiding a large, coagulated dark stain. He felt his foot step into something sticky. He froze but didn't look down. This was a crime scene. He was compromising a damn crime scene.

"Aunt Ruby, where the hell are you?"

"Down the hallway, David."

He moved into the living room. Furniture was knocked over here, too. Pictures—the kind one bought at so-called Starving Artists sales—had been knocked from the wall. A lamp had fallen off an end table. Books were scattered. David nearly stepped on the broken glass from a gold photo frame. The picture was missing.

Blood was everywhere here, too. The couch. The walls. The carpet. A lampshade.

God, it must have been a titanic struggle. From the looks of it, it should have awakened the whole damn neighborhood. Why hadn't anyone called the police? Even to an amateur's eye, it was clear that this fight had happened at least a day or two ago, maybe longer. Yet apparently the police had not been here.

Still, he had hope. Maybe the fighters had miraculously walked away. Maybe that was why the place was as it was—the neighbors had called the cops, who'd arrested the combatants and carted them off to jail—more likely the hospital—and left the mess behind.

Then he saw Ruby standing in the hallway, staring motionless into a room. His hope faded.

"We shouldn't be here, Aunt Ruby," he said softly.

She kept staring. "You can call the police now, David." Her sandpaper voice was subdued but steady.

"Who is it? Powell?"

"Yes."

He started down the hallway toward her.

"I wouldn't," she said.

He came anyway, not knowing why. Ghoulish curiosity, he supposed. Or maybe because, if he was going to be a prosecuting attorney someday, he should have more than a passing acquaintance with death. He looked over his aunt's shoulder into the bathroom.

The fight had ended here. Like the kitchen and the living room, bloodstains were everywhere. A large pool of glossy black blood, streaked with footprints, covered the linoleum floor. The corpse was in the tub, its head slumped against the tiled wall, legs dangling over the front edge. The features were bloated, the skin waxy in places, greenish in others. Flies and maggots had already taken up residence around the eyes and nose. The body was still clothed, but David couldn't determine the original colors of the clothes. The man had been stabbed. It would take the medical examiner and a calculator to figure out exactly how many times.

David closed his eyes and turned his head away. He went back down the hallway and outside, then called 911 from Ruby's car phone.

He hadn't thrown up this time. He could look at a man butchered to death and not throw up. That must be a sign of toughness. Morgan Reed would be proud. David had worked for his aunt for less than a year and he'd already seen three dead men. It was getting to be old hat.

Damn!

9

"Now we know why Bullet Joe ran last night," said David as they walked away from the murder scene. Detectives had questioned them for over an hour. In the morning, David and his aunt would write formal statements at police headquarters. For now, as the lead detective had put it, they were "free to go," though not before he castigated them for breaking and entering and for disturbing evidence at a murder scene.

"Why?" said Ruby.

David looked at his aunt. Surely she could see the obvious reason. Yet she gave him a skeptical gaze that said, "Don't assume the obvious. Prove it."

"He killed Powell."

"Why's that?"

"I don't know *why*. I don't know the man, I don't know the situation that occurred in there. Motive is not a factor in determining whether he did it or not. A lot of people may have had a good motive to kill Powell, but only one of them did the act. And Bullet Joe may have had no motive—at least no rational or apparent one. People kill for the bizarrest of reasons. All you have to do is prove that the person committed the act."

"You have proof he committed it?"

"Of course I don't. But it would explain why he jumped bail and why he ran at the ballpark," David said, exasperation in his voice. "And it would explain his hurried trip to his parents' trailer in that Lexus. He was changing out of bloody clothes. That's what he was carrying in the plastic grocery bag—his bloody clothes. Probably dumped them in the river."

"That suggests whoever was driving the Lexus was involved." Like a law professor—a comparison his aunt would abhor—Ruby posed this as a complicating factor, not as a statement of fact.

They ducked under the yellow crime-scene tape strung across the driveway. David said, "A guy like Bullet Joe is more—"

"My God, what happened?" A woman stood on the sidewalk at the end of the driveway. In her thirties, plain-faced and hennaed hair, she was dressed in shorts and held a heavy-looking plastic Safeway bag in each hand.

They stopped. "There's been a murder," Ruby said.

"Oh, my God! My God!" The woman set down the bags. Her wide blue eyes took in the surrounding police cars, the uniforms, the yellow ribbon strung around Powell's house, and the knot of neighbors grouped together across the street. She waved meekly at them.

Her eyes finally focused on Ruby and David. "Who? Was it Mrs. Powell?"

"No," said Ruby. "Sean Powell."

"Oh. Murdered! My God, how awful! How was he murdered?"

"Why did you think it was *Mrs.* Powell?" asked Ruby.

"I—" The woman looked too shaken to speak. Finally, she said, "They fought a lot. I thought maybe . . ."

"Lots of couples fight."

"But really loud, you know what I mean? I live right here"—she pointed to the house directly to the right of Powell's—"I could hear 'em fight late at night. Louder than most couples fight."

Probably because you keep your ear glued to the window, thought David.

"Do you know what they fought about?"

"No." The woman looked offended at the question.

"Were they physical fights or just shouting?" Ruby asked.

"I don't know. I thought I heard things thrown now and then. Things breaking, stuff like that."

"Any signs that he beat her?"

"I never saw any. But we didn't see much of them—my husband and me. They kept to themselves pretty much. I was surprised by the fights, really. I thought Vietnamese women always obeyed their husbands." She looked at them uncertainly. "Don't all those Asian cultures require that . . . you know, the man's in charge and all that?"

"I didn't know she was Vietnamese," said Ruby. "What was her name?"

"Susan. She went by Susan. I don't know her Vietnamese name, but she came from Vietnam, I know that. She told me once. Probably one of them boat people, you think? So she musta changed her name when she got here. To be more American, you know. Kinda silly, you ask me. She doesn't *look* American. Nobody would mistake her for a *real* Susan. She speaks English okay, though. Got that accent, but understandable. Not that I talked to her much, like I said. When I did, she was friendly but kinda reserved. I saw their boy more than any of them, at least when he was younger. Riding his bike or carrying a basketball. Like American boys, you know. A nice kid. Always said hi. Nicer than most kids these days. Allen's his name. He must be nineteen or twenty now. He's going to the community college, I think. He wasn't all Vietnamese. He was one of them mixed kids. What do they call them—you know, American and Vietnamese kids?"

"Amerasian."

"Yeah, that's it. Of course, that makes sense, don't it, her husband being American and her being Vietnamese."

"Have you seen Mrs. Powell or her son in the last day or two?"

The woman thought about it for a moment. "No, not

that I remember. But sometimes I don't see any of them for days.''

''Were you aware of any fighting in the house recently, say in the last coupla days?''

''Is that when it happened—his murder?''

''I can't say. Did you hear anything?''

''Maybe a coupla days ago. Sunday, I think. Maybe in the afternoon. I heard some crashing and yelling, but I didn't think nothing of it. My husband and I were watching a Rockies game on TV.''

''Did you see anyone leave their house around then? His wife or son or someone else?''

The woman shook her head. ''No.''

''Do you know if Mrs. Powell or her son were home at the time you heard the noise?''

''No.''

''Was there a car parked here or in the alley that wasn't their pickup? An unfamiliar car?''

''I don't watch the street that closely.''

Sure you do, thought David.

''Ever see a white Lexus parked here?''

''I don't know what a Lexus looks like.''

''A sedan. A very expensive car.''

''I don't remember seeing any fancy car around. Except that one.'' She pointed to Ruby's Lamborghini.

''Ever see this man?'' Ruby shoved Bullet Joe's mug shot under her face.

She studied it for a moment and shook her head. She looked up wide-eyed. ''Did he do it?''

''Why don't you put your groceries away, honey, and go over there to talk to the detectives—though I'm sure they'll find you if you don't find them. Ask for Detective Reynolds.''

The woman looked puzzled. ''Aren't you with the police?''

''We're just good friends of theirs,'' said Ruby, an impish grin on her face.

10

"This is getting to be a bad habit, Ruby," said Morgan Reed, closing the office blinds and shutting off the night view of Denver Police Headquarters. Fraternizing with bail bondsmen was a no-no for a cop, but it was especially a no-no for Morgan Reed. His superiors, angered at his stubborn refusal to help bury an internal police investigation, had already cut short his illustrious career in homicide by banishing him to auto-theft. But for Morgan Reed, fraternizing with Ruby Dark was worth the risk.

"What's a bad habit?" asked Ruby.

"Finding bodies."

Tell me about it, thought David.

Reed tossed a copy of *The Rocky Mountain News* on Ruby's desk and settled his large, ungainly body into a high-backed leather chair.

She left the newspaper lying between them and went to flip through her collection of jazz albums. She knew what was inside the paper. So did David. The police reporter had seen her name in the police report and had written an article, under the tabloid headline "Angel of Death," about the Angel's propensity for finding murder victims—including the body of her own husband, shot to death three years before in the parking lot behind the office.

"I don't sell Tupperware for a living, Morgan," she said,

putting an album on the turntable and gently setting the needle down.

He tapped his forefinger on the newspaper. "I just hate seeing these kinds of stories about you, Ruby."

She shrugged. "View it as great PR."

Billie Holiday began singing "That Ole Devil Called Love."

"I don't think *I'd* want someone bailing me out whose clients, or connections to those clients, keep turning up dead."

She looked at him playfully. "You'd love it if I bailed you out."

A love-struck schoolboy grin broke on Reed's face. "Maybe it would be worth it," he chuckled. But the concerned tone of his voice quickly returned. "But I worry about you attracting violence, Ruby. This business with the skip the other day at the ballpark, that was damn foolish and damn dangerous. The man coulda been armed, and you coulda been hurt. Somebody else coulda been hurt."

Why the hell was he worried about Ruby? David muttered to himself. *I* was the idiot chasing the sonofabitch across the damn park. *I'm* the one who could have been hurt.

"I had David with me," said Ruby.

Reed glanced at David as if having him along provided about as much protection as an old lady on crutches.

He turned his attention back to Ruby and pointed to a bulletin board with half a dozen photos pinned to it, including a photo of Bullet Joe. It was Ruby's picture gallery of current skips. "You need *professional* help looking for these guys," said Reed. "Quit doing your own bounty hunting."

"You know I've been reluctant to use bail enforcers since Big Jim's murder. I don't want somebody else to get killed tracking down my skips. That, or I can't trust 'em."

"You're risking David's life."

David almost fell out of his chair at Reed's sudden and unsolicited expression of concern. He had always felt tension between the detective and himself, as though Reed saw him as the little brother always hampering his efforts to put the move on the big sister—which, David admitted to himself in moments of cold self-honesty, was sometimes true. He was less sure why he was protective of his aunt. He liked Reed well enough. He was a good cop. Apparently he was a good father, too, raising two daughters by himself after his wife's death from Lupus. He liked dogs and baseball, always favorable attributes in David's eyes. Besides, his aunt was damn capable of taking care of herself. In fact, she kept Reed at arm's length well enough on her own. She seemed to keep everyone at arm's length.

"I was with David," Ruby defended herself. "I'm not sending him off alone to bring in skips. Besides, I can trust David."

"Don't you two get yourselves hurt or killed because of what happened to Jim. Bounty hunters get paid to take risks."

"If I'm really worried about bringing somebody in, I'll get a pro."

Reed looked unconvinced.

"You want to volunteer?" she said.

"I would if I could, Ruby, but you know I can't."

"You'd be damn good, hon. You'd make more money than you're making now."

"I like being a cop."

"But it doesn't seem to like you."

Defensiveness flared in Reed's face. "It'll change someday. Management changes. New elections, a new police chief. I'll wait it out. I'll get back to Homicide. Besides, what would you do without me as your pipeline?"

"I'd find another sucker," said Ruby as she shelled red chile pistachios from a bowl and popped them in her mouth. "Speaking of which, anything new on Powell's murder?"

"Homicide's real eager to talk to your skip—what's his name?"

"Bullet Joe. Earl 'Bullet Joe' Brown. Why are they suddenly so eager to talk to him? I already told 'em he'd skipped and that Powell had put up the collateral for his bail.''

''They got real eager after they found his prints at the crime scene.''

David whistled.

Reed ran a large hand through his silver-blue hair. ''For a career criminal, the man was pretty damn stupid, if you ask me. Left a bloody handprint the size of a catcher's mitt on the wall. He might as well have left his name and address while he was at it. This one's a ground ball for Homicide.''

''Guess that puts him away for life—again!'' David tried to restrain the note of triumph in his voice.

''They haven't convicted him yet, David,'' Ruby said. ''It only proves he was there, not that he committed the murder. I've known Bullet Joe for years. He may be a sociopath, but he's not a killer.''

David mulled that one over. ''Well, it would be a bit strange that he'd go to a *ballgame* after killing a man . . . or at least after finding the body of a friend.''

''Hell,'' interjected Reed, ''I've arrested guys sitting in bars and having a beer two blocks from where they whacked somebody.'' He popped shelled pistachios into his mouth, then dropped his hand down to the level of Collateral, who lay at his feet. The dog nibbled the rest of the nuts out of his hand. ''Except for getting caught, they didn't care, and I'm not even sure they cared about gettin' caught.''

''I don't have an answer,'' said Ruby. ''Maybe it's the Vietnam stuff.''

''Your skip fought in 'Nam?'' asked Reed.

''Yeah. He and Powell both did, according to Bullet Joe's parents. They went to the same vet rap group.''

Reed nodded. ''That would help his defense.''

''Why do you say that?'' asked David.

Reed twirled his finger round and round his temple. ''A crazy vet. PTSD. Refighting Vietnam. Mistaking Powell for a Vietcong. Homicide thinks the weapon was a knife from

Powell's own kitchen. A good lawyer would argue no premeditation and plead temporary insanity.'' Reed tipped a hand toward David. ''Even a first-year law student could bargain it down to manslaughter.''

David smiled. ''Personally, I think it's a crock, but in Bullet Joe's case it doesn't make any difference, anyway. He's already facing life.''

''It could keep him out of the gas chamber,'' said Reed.

''The taxpayers will be thrilled.'' David looked at his aunt. ''If Bullet Joe didn't kill Powell, what the hell was he doing at the crime scene?''

''When I find his ass, I'll ask him.''

Reed looked over at David, a big grin on his face. ''Finding him shouldn't be too difficult. Fifty thousand eyewitnesses and a national television audience watched him beat his feet across the park. I saw the video. Homicide keeps playing it over and over.''

''Looking for clues, no doubt,'' Ruby chimed in.

''You looked great out there, David,'' Reed went on. ''Really. You woulda got him if that usher hadn't made such a great open-field tackle.''

David tried to crawl inside his chair. At least his father hadn't called—not yet, anyway. He wasn't a big sports fan. Maybe he hadn't seen it, even though every damn sports show in the country had played a clip of the chase. Surely the stations in St. Jo were no exception. He'd seen the clip himself. His only hope was that he might not be that recognizable.

''Homicide got any other evidence against him?'' Ruby asked as Billie Holiday began singing her rendition of ''Ain't Nobody's Business If I Do.''

''Nope. Just his prints and the information you gave them.''

Reed looked at Ruby as if he suspected she hadn't given Homicide everything. She hadn't. She hadn't mentioned the Hispanic woman who'd spotted the mysterious white Lexus, or the Mayor of the Bottoms, who'd seen Bullet Joe the night of the murder, or Home Plate's owner, who'd served him drinks. Ruby wasn't about to give up her informants.

"What about Powell's wife and son?" asked Ruby. "They been located yet? Or their pickup?"

"No. They seem to have disappeared off the face of the earth. Could be they're just away visiting relatives and don't know about it. Maybe your skip took them away and killed them. Maybe they were involved and they're in hiding. If they are, it'll be tough finding them. The Vietnamese community here is pretty tight."

David watched Collateral suddenly get up from beside Reed's chair and go into the back room. He could hear the dog furiously lapping water out of his dish. Neither man nor beast should eat his aunt's red chile pistachios, or any of the other hot snacks she kept around.

"Does Homicide think the wife's involved?" asked David. "A neighbor told us they fought."

"I don't think so. Not unless it turns out she weighs two-fifty and is a professional wrestler. Her husband fought his attacker. The M.E. found defensive wounds on his hands and arms. His killer probably was pretty strong."

"Bullet Joe would fit that," said David. "And the wife's apparently Vietnamese. I've never seen a two-hundred-fifty-pound Vietnamese woman."

"Homicide's money is on the skip," said Reed. "But you know, I wouldn't automatically rule out the guy's kid, or even his wife. I've seen some pretty small ladies do some mighty big damage when they get their dander up."

"I don't see how she could have done what we saw," said David. He shivered at the memory.

Reed said, "Catch someone by surprise, you can do almost anything. The M.E.'s report indicated that the aorta had been severed by a deep stab wound. If it was the first stab, he woulda been pretty helpless after that. He coulda fought, but not hard. For all practical purposes, he would've already been dead. They couldn't have saved him if he'd been lying in the emergency room at the time."

Ruby shook her head. "The house was ransacked, like

someone was looking for something. I wouldn't think the wife or the son would need to do that.''

''Make it look like robbery.''

Ruby was unconvinced. ''People who commit crimes of passion aren't that together. Homicide say anything about the empty picture frame?''

''What picture frame?''

''In the living room. I noticed a small gold picture frame with the glass broken. The picture was gone.''

''I noticed that, too,'' piped in David.

Reed put out his hands as if to say, ''So?''

''Let's assume the photo was of the family, or maybe the wife,'' said Ruby. ''If she killed him, she might have taken it to make it more difficult for Homicide to know who they were looking for.''

''Makes sense,'' conceded Reed.

''Or . . .'' Ruby paused for maximum emphasis. ''. . . or the killer took it so *he* knew what she looked like.''

11

Before Reed had slipped off into the night, Ruby asked him if he knew anything about Todd Jennings, owner of a local construction company, or if any of Reed's buddies in Homicide had linked the name to the case.

Reed didn't recognize the name, nor had he heard anyone mention it in any capacity with the case. "Why?" he'd asked.

"Nothing," Ruby had said.

"If it was nothing, why are you asking?"

"Goodnight, Morgan."

Todd Jennings did not own a white Lexus. A quick computer check with the Department of Motor Vehicles turned up a Chrysler New Yorker Landau, an Audi Cabriolet convertible, and a Dodge Viper registered to Todd Jennings. A well-heeled collection of cars, but no Lexus.

A deeper computer search put Jennings in a three-story, 5,000-square-foot stone and wood house in the foothills west of the city, in the kind of neighborhood where valets parked your car in your garage and lawyers took ten percent of gross. As David and Ruby pulled into the Jennings driveway in her Lamborghini—at least they *looked* as if they belonged here—David glimpsed a large sunken Jacuzzi and one end of a lap-pool behind the house where you could lounge in the water with a glass of white wine while watching the moon and the city lights come up at night.

Surprisingly, the hired help did not answer the door. The door was opened by an elegant woman in pearls and a long red silk ankle-length sheath—the style worn by Asian women, though she was no Asian. She appeared to be in her mid-thirties, with perfect white teeth, short blond hair, and a satisfied air about her.

"Mr. Jennings, please," said Ruby.

The switchboard at Jennings's construction company had said he wasn't in the office today. He wasn't out of town, but the switchboard didn't know where he was. A "wrong number" call to Jennings's home got a woman's voice. At least someone was there. Ruby decided to take a flyer without knowing if Jennings himself was around. She could have asked for him, but it was easier to hang up on people than to get rid of them in person.

"He's not available at the moment," said the woman, glancing at Ruby's bright red car in the driveway.

Ruby handed her a business card. "My name is Ruby Dark. It's urgent we speak with Mr. Jennings. Are you Mrs. Jennings?"

The woman stared at the card she held in long thin fingers with polished red nails. Her eyes widened a little as she read it. "Yes, I am," she said almost absently, her voice soft and wispy.

"I'm looking for someone your husband may know. We just need a few minutes of his time."

"Uhh . . . please wait here." The woman closed the heavy door, her eyes still on the card.

David didn't think the door would open again, but it did a few minutes later.

"He can see you briefly," said Mrs. Jennings with a brittle smile. She ushered them through the foyer and toward the back of the house. Now David understood why the women was so well-dressed. This was the kind of house where casual dress was out of place, where the hired help probably wore formal attire while dusting shelves and cleaning toilets. David self-consciously pulled at his open-collared shirt.

They arrived in a huge living room whose floor-to-ceiling windows and muted red draperies framed the pool David had glimpsed earlier. Beyond the pool, horses grazed on a slope that fell away from the edge of the yard. Beyond the horses, the buildings of downtown Denver rose darkly in a layer of smog so murky, it made David gasp to think that he breathed the stuff every day.

The room was thick with the Oriental art David had noticed in rooms they'd passed on their way through the house. Small Oriental-looking sculpture and pots of blooming orchids cluttered tea tables and antique chests and bookshelves. Delicate monochrome ink drawings on silk hung on walls, and a large gilded bronze statue of a seated Buddha contemplated the world from a pedestal of its own. Sprawled across the floor was a red, intricately patterned Persian carpet large enough to raise as a circus big top. In the center of the room, his back to the windows, stood a tall, slim man in a short-sleeved shirt and slacks under a painter's smock with streaks of color on it. He held a palette in one hand and a brush in the other. His brown hair was silver-streaked at the temples—so neat that the silver might have been painted on—and he looked twenty years older than his wife. Directly in front of him stood a heavy wooden easel holding an eight-by-six-foot canvas whose surface David couldn't see. A canvas sheet lay rumpled under the easel to protect the carpet. Jennings paid no attention to his visitors' approach; his eyes were fixed in the direction of a tall, threefold Chinese screen. David couldn't see its front. Jennings dabbed his brush on the palette and lifted the brush toward the canvas with the grace and assurance of someone who had painted for a long time.

"Todd, these are the people who wanted to speak with you," said Mrs. Jennings as she led David and Ruby into the center of the room.

The painter never looked up, nor did Mrs. Jennings look at him as she spoke. Rather, she had directed her words toward the threefold screen. David and Ruby moved farther into the living room, until they could see a much younger man seated on a stool in front of a large white cloth draped over the screen. He was a powerfully built man dressed in a charcoal-gray suit and red tie. He was turned three-quarters toward the painter, his face and eyes gazing unfocused into the distance. He didn't leave the stool to shake hands or nod to acknowledge their presence.

"My apologies for not greeting you properly," he said in a voice softer than his features suggested, "but as you can see, it's best if I not move. It disturbs the artist. Please, step around so I can see you without turning my head, Ms. Dark. Or is it Mrs. Dark?"

"Ruby."

They passed behind the painter, and David got his first full view of the portrait. It was an oil, and nearing completion. Jennings's face was nearly finished. The artist was filling in his chin. It was an excellent likeness, but not a photo-perfect likeness. The painter had been selective about his subject's features, capturing the athletic grace of Jennings's broad face, which was framed by a mass of jet-black hair. There was a suggestion of vulnerability in his brown eyes.

"What do you think of the painting?" asked Jennings as they walked into his range of vision. "My wife commissioned it for my thirty-fifth birthday. Anybody can have a photo taken, but a painting is far more permanent, don't you think? It's fascinating to watch Raymond—"

"I find it pretty scary," said Ruby.

Jennings flinched, momentarily ruining the composure he had obviously worked hard to achieve. "Sorry about that, Raymond," he said, glancing out of the corner of his eye at the painter. He reorganized the muscles in his face to recapture his portrait-look. "Why on earth do you find my portrait scary? Raymond's a wonderful artist, and I'm not an ugly man."

"It's not you or Raymond. It's the bluntness of a portrait.

The permanency you spoke of—that's what I find frightening."

"Ah, very interesting. I know exactly what you mean. I've encountered the same feelings. It takes some getting used to, watching yourself emerge on canvas in the hands of someone else. It's like seeing a stranger born. In fact, I would argue that having to pose is a form of deep therapy. It forces you to face yourself in ways you've never done before. I find it a very daring process. Everyone should do it at least once in his life. We might need fewer psychiatrists."

"I don't think most people could handle that," said Ruby. "Most people don't want to look that closely at themselves—or have others look at them that closely."

Raymond laughed. Like his wife, who had left, he had perfect white teeth. "That is a point . . . Ruby. People usually only glance at a photo, but they'll study a painting. They don't 'see' you in real life—even your friends. They turn away or never get below the surface. A painting forces them to know you, perhaps even come to terms with you."

"That's not necessarily a good thing."

"Then you think only the self-assured should have themselves painted?"

"Or those with no hope of ever seeing themselves."

"Have you ever been painted, Ruby?"

"Only face-painted at the county fair."

"You should. You seem a very self-assured and lovely woman. I would highly recommend Raymond, here. Raymond Draper. He's one of the top portraitists in the nation. He came all the way from Virginia to paint me. Very much in demand."

"Personally, I like the mystery of people. Painting seems to take that away."

Jennings laughed again. "Then you don't think a painting can lie?"

"I assume liars can paint." She turned toward the artist. "Though I'm sure you're not a liar, are you, hon?"

"Painfully not, ma'am."

"There you have it, Ruby," said Jennings. "Through Raymond's brush, I will be exposed for all the world to see. But I'm sure you didn't come here to philosophize on art, did you?"

"No. I came to ask you about a man named Earl Brown, sometimes known as 'Bullet Joe' Brown."

"*Bullet Joe*? How quaint. I assume from your line of work you are looking for this man?"

"He skipped on a forty-five-thousand-dollar bond a few days ago."

"Why on earth do you think I would know him?"

"He mentioned your name to a friend just before he skipped."

Jennings furrowed his brow, then caught himself and tried to relax. "How do you know he was talking about *me*? I'm not the only Todd Jennings in Denver."

"You're the only one who owns a large construction company. Bullet Joe worked for you four years ago, repairing equipment."

"Ruby, I employee a hundred and fifty people in Denver alone. That's not counting several hundred more we hire for our projects in other states and overseas. I don't know them all. I try to know as many of them personally as I can, but as you can imagine, I cannot know them all, especially the line-workers. I rely on my managers to hire good people."

"This good person is an ex-con whose rap sheet would paper over your portrait, hon. Maybe *that* Earl Brown sticks in your mind."

"Actually, Ruby, we've hired numerous ex-offenders over the years. It's a company policy."

"Why's that?"

"I believe in giving people second chances. I don't believe in contributing cash to charities. They just waste it. My civic contribution is hiring people others won't. I provide them with a good wage, hard work, and high expectations. We've had excellent results, with a very low recidivism rate. We've been written up in penal and industry publications, but otherwise we've kept a low profile.''

''Bullet Joe was arrested and jailed while he was working for your company.''

''Unfortunately, some backslide. No program is one hundred percent effective. What was he arrested for?''

''Burglary.''

''He didn't steal from us, did he?''

''No.''

''I didn't think so. I would have remembered that. I don't hire ex-convicts for office work, so they're usually not around money that might tempt them. They can always steal a road-grader or a big cat—there's a healthy black market for stolen construction equipment—but that's not easy. Exactly in what context did this Earl Brown mention my name?''

''That's a little unclear. He was incoherent at the time.''

''Incoherent? What does that mean?''

''He was drunk and having nightmares and scared as hell.''

''That's it? A drunken man mentions my name—or the name of a Todd Jennings—and you barge in here thinking I can help you find this man?'' Anger flared in his face.

''Mr. Jennings!'' The painter stepped back from his easel. ''We're losing your pose.'' His voice was insistent, without a hint of obsequiousness.

Jennings nodded apologetically in the painter's direction and promptly readjusted his position on the stool again. His face relaxed but his eyes held their hard edge.

''I find it a little strange,'' said Ruby, ''that he would mention your name under those circumstances, especially if the two of you had never personally met. I don't think he was reviewing his employment history at the time.''

''I really can't help you. I don't know him, I don't know anything about him, and I certainly don't know where he is, though I could have our employment records checked if that would help.''

''Does anyone in your company drive a white Lexus?''

Jennings kept his face relaxed for the painter, but David detected puzzlement in the man's eyes.

"*I* don't drive one, and I'm not aware that any of my close executives do. I don't know, of course, about my line-workers, but I would rather doubt it. Most of them drive pickups or four-wheelers. However, I don't pay a lot of attention to what people drive. I run a construction company, not a car dealership. What does this Lexus have to do with the man you're looking for?"

"He was seen in a Lexus after he skipped. Someone else was driving."

"Are you suggesting that I or someone in my company in some way is *assisting* his avoidance of his legal obligations?"

"I doubt it, though it strikes me that if you've done so much public good for ex-cons, Bullet Joe might want to make contact with you."

"Certainly if Mr. Brown drops by the house or my office, I'll do my civic duty and call the police. We don't want any burglars running loose in our city."

"It's gotten a little stickier than a burglary charge, hon. Since he jumped bail, Bullet Joe is now the prime suspect in a murder case."

"Good heavens! How horrible! Who—who did he murder?"

"I said he was a suspect, not necessarily the killer."

"Yes, of course. Presumed innocent until proven guilty, right?"

"The dead man's name was Sean Powell."

Jennings maintained his pose, but his voice sounded fainter when he spoke. "I don't know him either."

"I didn't suggest that you did."

"Ma'am," came the painter's voice. He stepped away from his easel, his paintbrush and palette lowered at his side. "I need the complete cooperation of my subject. I can't paint when there is so much tension in his body."

"Doesn't look tense to me," said Ruby.

"It's as plain as day on his face. It affects the lines."

"Please, he's right," said Jennings. "I must insist that you leave. I have limited time with Raymond. He's scheduled to leave soon for a portrait in Austin, and my wife wants the painting completed and hung in time for my birthday party. It's obvious that I can't assist you. I simply don't know anything about the man."

"I gave your wife my card. If Brown contacts your company or anyone there, call me."

She stopped directly behind the painting and studied it for a moment, looking at Jennings and then at the portrait and then back at Jennings.

"You're right, hon. Raymond here has permanently exposed you for all the world to see."

12

David was slumped over Ruby's desk, dozing with his face pressed against an open copy of *Gilbert Law Summaries*, when Ruby came into the office through the back door. He blinked his eyes several times and yawned. He fumbled for his watch but couldn't find it.

''What time is it?'' he asked.

'' 'Bout six. Tired?''

He stretched his arms above his head. ''Beat. I've got two hundred pages to read in the next four days.''

''Sounds like you need food.'' She held up two white paper bags.

David looked dubious.

''Don't worry,'' she said, plopping the bags on the desk. ''I didn't bring you anything that has grease, cholesterol, animal fat, red dye number two, caffeine, sodium, pesticides, anything that was deprived of life, or, for that matter, anything with taste. It's from the deli. Vaguely Californian, I think. Tofu and bean sprouts on rye.''

''Thanks,'' he said sarcastically. He retrieved a bottle of mineral water from the small refrigerator in the back room—Ruby had coffee—and they took seats on opposite sides of her desk. She'd brought a greasy-looking grilled Reuben and chips, set out now on waxed paper.

''Any luck at the Veterans' Center?'' he asked his aunt.

''They don't know where Bullet Joe is . . . or if they do,

they aren't telling,'' she said, her mouth full of sandwich. ''But I did come up with a possible lead.''

''What?''

She wiped mustard from her mouth. ''I think we've found the Lexus.''

The Veterans' Center was located in a run-down building on a run-down stretch of Ashbury Street on the south edge of downtown. Ruby thought she remembered the building as once serving as a union headquarters, but she wasn't certain.

The office of the Center's director had a spartan look. The linoleum floor hadn't seen a coat of wax since Ford was President. There was a shortage of filing cabinets, so manila files with bright-green labels were stacked on the floors and chairs. The walls, a light gray, were covered with two dozen pieces of artwork and posters espousing the value of veterans. The artwork, done on 11 x 14 sheets of white paper and thumbtacked to the walls, showcased a mixture of media, quality, and styles ranging from crayons to watercolors, from childlike stick figures and crude, bursting yellow rays, to subtle abstracts and haunting gaunt-eyed figures.

''Art therapy,'' said Samuel Hollingsworth, who'd described himself to Ruby and David as a clinical social worker. He was a black man in rimless glasses. His dark beard was going gray, and he was casually dressed. He appeared to be in his early fifties, but it was difficult to tell, since his shoulders were hunched and he looked as worn down as his surroundings.

Ruby sat on a small, cushioned metal chair while Hollingsworth read her business card. He set the card aside, pursed his lips, and said, ''Sara said you're looking for someone you *think* may be in our support group.''

Sara must be the frizzy-haired young receptionist in the outer office.

''I *know* he is,'' said Ruby. ''His parents said he went to a rap group for Vietnam vets at this center. Earl Brown, a.k.a. Bullet Joe. He skipped sentencing . . . and a forty-five-thousand-dollar bond I posted.''

''Because a man's parents say he's coming here doesn't mean he is. Men lie to their parents—and their wives—about coming to groups like ours.''

''Maybe you saw Bullet Joe on TV the other night.''

''TV? I'm not sure I under—''

''He was the guy sprinting across the field in the middle of the Rockies' game. Hear about it?''

''That was—'' Hollingsworth stopped.

''The other man running after him—the one the guards tackled instead of Bullet Joe—was my associate.''

''I'm sorry to hear that . . . this person . . . failed to appear in court, but I really don't see how I can help you. I'm not at liberty to discuss who uses the services of our center. It's a matter of client confidentiality.''

''Look, hon, it's obvious that you know Bullet Joe. So let's just work from the premise that *you* know that *I* know that *you* know Bullet Joe.''

The therapist shook his head. ''I still can't tell you anything about any of the individuals in our group or anyone we counsel on a one-to-one basis. Not unless they give us written permission to release information.''

''I'll be sure to get that from ole Earl as soon as I catch him.''

''Ms. Dark, I appreciate your situation. I don't wish to see a man who's facing a mandatory life sentence out on the streets any more than you do. But I can't help you.''

''I guess Earl talked pretty openly with the group about his criminal life.''

''Why do you say that?''

''I didn't say anything to you about his facing a mandatory sentence.''

The therapist grimaced but said nothing.

''You can't—or won't—tell me if he's contacted you in the last coupla days?''

Hollingsworth shook his head.

"Or whether he may have contacted anyone in your little rap group?"

"No."

"Or whether he dropped any hints where he might like to go if he wasn't planning on going to prison?"

"The issue is much more complicated than just the professional obligation of client confidentiality, Ms. Dark. If I told you anything about anyone in our group and word got back to them, the walls would go up faster than a pup tent in a rainstorm. I've worked long and hard to get through their distrust and suspicion to establish rapport. I won't jeopardize that. They watch out for each other. It's as if they're . . . joined at the hip."

"The problem we have here, hon, is that Bullet Joe's become more than just a skip." Ruby leaned forward in her chair to underscore her point. "He's now a murder suspect."

Hollingsworth shut his eyes. When he opened them he asked, "A suspect in whose murder?"

"Someone who, I understand, also was in your group. Sean Powell."

Hollingsworth looked shocked. "*Sean*?"

Ruby described the murder and the fact that the police hadn't released the dead man's name yet because they couldn't locate his family.

"Maybe you'd like to reconsider your reluctance to talk about Earl," she said.

He put his hands out in a plea. "I wish I could help, but confidentiality rules—"

"Screw your confidentiality rules! A man's been murdered. I don't want to see Earl—whom I personally don't think killed Powell—or anyone else get hurt."

Hollingsworth rose, his voice hostile. "Ms. Dark, this discussion is pointless."

Ruby stayed seated and raised both hands. "Okay, okay. No more questions about Bullet Joe or Sean Powell. But I would like to ask you about your support group. Nothing that involves confidential information."

The therapist remained standing.

"Please," said Ruby, her hand inviting him to sit down again. "Certainly you can describe your work here in general terms, without names. This place isn't a government secret. It's our tax dollars at work, right?"

Hollingsworth wavered for a moment, then said, "Actually, it's *not* your tax dollars at work here. We're not part of the V. A. hospital system or the government's Outreach program. We're a nonprofit organization. Understand that a lot of vets were alienated by the V.A.'s treatment of injured Vietnam veterans and by its generally hostile attitude toward them—and I don't blame them. The V.A. had become more of a nursing home for World War One and Two vets than a place to handle crippled or mentally wounded men from Vietnam. We had an estimated seven-hundred-thousand vets suffering from post-traumatic stress disorder by the early eighties, and the V.A. hadn't even recognized it as a legitimate mental disorder. A lot of the men also saw the V.A. as part of the military establishment they had come to distrust, so self-funded groups like ours were established. We run support groups, provide individual therapy and job counseling, try to find housing, help with vocational training and college admission—whatever it takes to get these men back into the mainstream of society. Come on, I'll give you the Cook's tour."

He led her out of his office and down a short hall to a doorway. He opened it, revealing a large room with a small stage at one end. A dozen metal folding chairs made a neat circle in the middle of the room. They looked somewhat forlorn in the large space. The walls were covered with paintings and uplifting posters.

"This was a union hall once, wasn't it?" said Ruby.

"Yes. Teamsters, I think."

She stepped into the room. Her footsteps squeaked on the old wooden floor. "You meet with the group of vets in here?"

"Once a week, every Thursday night. We've been meeting here for several years."

''The *same* men?''

''More or less. There's around ten or twelve in the group. It varies because men come and go.''

''You mean like visits to prison?''

Hollingsworth ignored her. ''Typically, we have seven or eight at each meeting. Usually a core group. Several of the men have been with us for a long time. They're extremely close. For some, this group is the only family they have.''

''So when you get together, you just what—talk?''

''That's putting it too simply. This isn't a social club. The men are very open about their lives—particularly the troubles in their lives. They have a more difficult time discussing their successes. That's what we always try to get them to focus on, their successes. We don't do trauma regression—trying to get them to relive the trauma. I don't believe you can integrate horror. We focus instead on trying to reestablish a foundation of trust, hope, a more positive outlook on living that can outweigh the horror.''

''It must be a difficult job for you.''

Hollingsworth shrugged. ''I've lasted longer than most therapists who do these groups.''

''You served in Vietnam?''

''I was a medic from the summer of sixty-four to sixty-five. And yes, I suffer from PTSD myself.'' He stepped into the room. ''Do you know what post-traumatic stress disorder is, Ms. Dark?''

''I don't know much about it. It's a psychological reaction to the stress of combat, right?''

''People associate it mostly with combat-related stress, though in fact civilian war victims experience PTSD as well as people who have been through traumatic accidents, violent crimes, terrorists acts, natural disasters, sexual abuse—any violent event or tragedy in which they feel extreme helplessness or terror. We're even finding PTSD among inner-city teenagers who've witnessed drive-by shootings and gang violence. Contrary to popular belief, it is not a mental illness. You're correct in calling it a psychological reaction. It's a reaction to an extraordinarily traumatic event. Usually, it's a delayed reaction. It may not surface for months, even years. The individual is emotionally stripped of his or her psychological defenses at the moment of trauma. The person feels a loss of control, a fear of imminent death, almost a regression to an infantile state."

"But Vietnam veterans have been especially vulnerable to PTSD, haven't they?"

"That's an issue of much debate. The men who fought in Vietnam generally were younger than soldiers in previous wars, and were thus more susceptible to PTSD. It's also argued that they were betrayed more by their superiors, and they fought in a war where the enemy wasn't always clear-cut. There also was no decompression time for these men. They were in the jungles witnessing grisly deaths one day and walking the streets of America two days later.

"But there also is statistical evidence that these men's rate of PTSD experience was no greater than the rate of veterans returning from World War Two. Of course, the military didn't call it post-traumatic stress disorder back then. Nothing so clinical-sounding. They called it shell shock in World War One and battle fatigue in World War Two and Korea. They generally ignored it except for the most visible cases. We didn't ignore it this time around. So, most of what we've learned about PTSD, we've learned from studying Vietnam vets. But it's hardly unique to them. In fact, there's evidence that PTSD occurred in ancient Greece."

Ruby leaned back on one of the metal chairs. "Tell me about the symptoms. Do they typically include nightmares and flashbacks?"

The therapist sat down across from her. "Nightmares and dissociative episodes are common, yes, but symptoms are as many and as varied as the individuals. There may be paralyzing feelings of shame, drug and alcohol abuse, severe headaches, skin and stomach disorders, outbursts of irrational rage, suicidal ideation, severe depression, a sort of emotional numbness toward the external world, hypervigilance, low self-esteem, inability to have intimate relationships—''

''You said rage. Can PTSD lead to violence?''

Hollingsworth frowned and sighed heavily. ''I know where you're trying to take this, Ms. Dark. Yes, homicidal ideation can be a symptom of PTSD. And it seems to be most prevalent among those who saw the heaviest combat duty. But most of these men are not berserk killers or walking time-bombs like they're so often portrayed in the movies. Most of them struggle more with what we call survivor's guilt. These men, by and large, are victims, not perpetrators of violence. They blame themselves for the deaths of their buddies and for surviving, instead of blaming the V.C. or the damn war.''

''But the war ended twenty years ago,'' said Ruby.

''Not the memories. Understand that PTSD is chronic. Without early and appropriate psychological intervention, it's progressive. Imagine finding the body of your best friend with his hands nailed to a tree and his head stuffed into his stomach. I've talked to a man who saw that. That's not an image that will ever go away. It's hardwired into his brain. In fact, we now know that symptoms of PTSD can lie dormant not only for years, but *decades* before it surfaces. There's much anecdotal evidence that many World War Two vets didn't display PTSD symptoms until after their kids were raised and the men had retired. Then all that comforting structure disappeared and the horrors of the battlefield began to haunt them. Some of them went through severe personality changes late in life. Of course, they didn't understand that all the anger and guilt were tied back to a war they'd fought forty years before. Fortunately, many of the Vietnam vets at least understand their symptoms for what they are. PTSD is common language today. If we can get them in here, we can work on trying to learn how to cope with those images, maybe force them into remission and keep them there, and to get the men to quit blaming themselves.''

Ruby rose and thanked Hollingsworth for his time. She started to leave when something on the stage caught her eye. She walked to the spot where a heavy canvas tarp was draped over something shaped in a four-by-four box. In one spot where the tarp didn't completely cover the object, she could see what appeared to be bamboo poles.

"What's this?" she asked, lifting the tarp partway.

The therapist appeared agitated. "It's a bamboo cage."

Ruby stared at him. "You use it for therapy?"

"No, no," he said. "Some of the men built it for local POW-MIA awareness rallies. We're storing it temporarily for them. A man will sit in it during a rally. It draws photographers. It's supposed to resemble the conditions POWs were held in."

Ruby looked back at the cage. "It must have been horrible. A man couldn't even stretch out in it."

"The truth is, few POWs were ever kept in these cages, except occasionally for punishment. Did you ever see the movie *The Deer Hunter*? I think that burned the image of these cages into the public mind. Along with the Russian-roulette scenes. In so many ways, a horribly misleading movie about the war. I'd just as soon they junk this cage, myself."

They walked together to the street entrance. Ruby turned to ask one more question. "Can you tell me if anyone in your group drives a white Lexus?"

She thought she saw a flicker of recognition in his eyes.

"I don't pay attention to what kinds of cars the men drive. And if I did, I couldn't tell you."

"I know, I know, confidential information. Okay, hon, can you tell me this? Is there anyone in the group who could *afford* a Lexus?"

"Contrary to popular perception, Ms. Dark, most of the men who suffer from PTSD are not criminals or bush vets who sleep in tents in the rain forests of Hawaii or the backwoods of New Hampshire. Most are upstanding citizens and many hold steady, well-paying jobs."

"I take it that's a *yes.*"

* * *

David wadded up the sack that had held his sandwich and tossed it into the wastebasket. "I still think this PTSD stuff is a lot of bullshit, Aunt Ruby."

"I don't think it is, David. People are traumatized by violence. I've seen it firsthand."

"But these guys are whiners using it as an excuse when things don't go right. Like you said to the doctor, the war ended twenty years ago. How long can you use that for a crutch? You move on, you don't talk about the damn thing every Thursday evening for ten years."

"Speaking of Thursday, you got any exams that night?"

"No. Why?"

"I want you to stake out the Vet Center and watch for a white Lexus."

13

Morgan Reed held up two tickets. "Wanna go out with me tonight?"

"Go where, Morgan?" Ruby asked. "Those aren't baseball tickets, I hope."

"I'm not that big a fool." He pushed the tickets farther and farther away from his face until he got the fine print in focus. "They're to see some guy named . . . Zubov."

Ruby brightened. "Alex Zubov? Really? He's playing at the Jazz Alley, right?"

"Yeah. Who is he exactly?"

"Don't you know what you got tickets to?"

"These sorta . . . fell into my hands today. But I knew he had something to do with jazz, so I figured you'd be interested."

"*Very* interested. He's probably the best saxophonist in Europe."

"Then go with me."

"That's sweet of you, Morgan, and I'd love to hear Zubov. But I got a bond to make in a coupla hours."

"The guy won't go anywhere."

"I promised him. I make good on my promises."

"David can do it."

"I'm studying," said David, who'd come down from his garret above the office a few minutes earlier to stretch his legs and clear his foggy brain.

"If you won't go with me, Ruby, I won't tell you the important information I learned today about your dead man," said Reed.

"What information?" Ruby asked.

The detective wiggled the tickets in his fingertips.

Ruby sighed in a rare sigh of defeat and looked beseechingly at David. "Would you cover it, David? It's a twenty-thousand dollar bond. I know the guy. It's kosher and it won't take long. It's just a matter of doing the paperwork. I really would love to see Zubov."

"Sure, go for it." He cursed Reed under his breath.

"Thanks. Okay, Morgan, what's the news? It better be good."

"Actually, it's not good news. Your dead man isn't who he said he was."

"What does that mean?"

"It means his real name isn't Sean Powell."

"Swell. So who is he?"

"Homicide doesn't know."

"Morgan, if you want to take me to Jazz Alley tonight, you're gonna have to cough up a little more information than that."

He shrugged. "I don't have it. Neither does Homicide. All they know is this guy is *not* Sean Powell. They ran the standard victim-ID. Put his prints through our system, nothing. Ran it through CBI, nothing. You said he was a Vietnam vet, so they ran it through the military. The military says they've got no files on a Sean Powell and his prints don't match anyone who ever served."

"I ran a check myself," said Ruby. "His house, credit cards, bank accounts, car, driver's license—it all looked good."

"Homicide came up with the same thing. Local medical, phone, utility records, the works. They even found a passport. All under the name of Sean Powell. Only problem is, his history goes back just eight or nine years. After that, zip. Like the guy appeared in town one day out of the blue and created an elaborate false ID."

Ruby paced the floor. "Not the first time that's happened."

"Oh, by the way," said Reed, "they found the guy's pickup abandoned in the Northglenn Mall parking lot. No sign of his wife or kid."

"Homicide have any ideas about the fake ID.?" asked David.

"One possibility is the guy was part of the Federal Witness Protection Program. They're checking on it. If he was, that will slow down the investigation."

"Does that mean he may have been murdered by a professional instead of Bullet Joe?" asked David.

"Possible."

Ruby shook her head. "Doesn't strike me as your average professional hit. Pretty messy for that."

"More likely the guy was on the run from somewhere," suggested Reed. "Might be a skip himself. My hunch is he'll turn up in the AFIS system. Should be pretty quick."

"What's the AFIS system?" asked David.

"It's the FBI's Automated Fingerprint Identification System. Their computers can run through millions of files overnight. The computer can't make a perfect match, but it can pull up several possibilities for the technician to check by eye. It saves a helluva lot of time. If your man's on file, they'll come up with him."

"It doesn't really make a lot of difference who he is," said Ruby. "If he isn't Sean Powell, it's going to make it more difficult for me to close on his collateral if I need to. We better find Bullet Joe."

Two days later, David sat in his 1972 pea-green Duster a third of a block up the street from the Veterans' Center office. He looked at his watch: 8:11 P.M. The therapist's rap group was in session. He got out of his car and walked toward the Center, staying on the far side of the street. He strolled casually in the warm evening. This stretch of Ashbury was primarily light-industrial, with poor residential neighborhoods mixed in. Most of the cars parked along the street were clunkers. A white Lexus would stick out like a sore thumb. David doubted that the owner would be foolish enough to park such an expensive car around here, unless he wanted to become another auto-theft statistic.

David passed the Center. Through the plate-glass window he could see a desk and scattered chairs in the waiting room, but no people. They were probably doing their thing in the room where Ruby had seen the bamboo cage. He was walking south of the Center when he spotted the Lexus half a block down, across the street but on the same side as the Center. He continued to the next intersection, crossed, and came up the other side. He figured no one in the Center could see him from this angle, but to play it safe, as he neared the rear of the car he stopped, knelt on one knee, and retied his shoelace.

By lifting his head slightly, he could read the license-plate number. He memorized it. Then he noticed the black-and-white bumper sticker. He retied his other shoelace. The bumper sticker resembled the one described by the Hispanic woman at the trailer park. It was a sticker he had seen before: a white silhouette of a man, his head slightly bowed against a black background, a guard tower behind him. A line of barbed wire ran under his chin. Above the image were the words POW MIA, with a black star between them. Below the man's silhouette ran the words, "You Are Not Forgotten."

David walked back to his car and wrote down the license number. Then, as the light in the sky waned, he sat in the car and briefed a case for his civil-procedure class, *Guilford v. Yale University*, about a man who'd sued the university back in the 1930s because he'd hurt himself while taking a piss at night on school property. Even then, thought David as he scribbled notes in the margin, people were blaming others for their own stupidity.

Around 9:20, men started coming out of the Veterans' Center. It was nearly dark, with only smudges of light in the summer sky. Faces were hard to distinguish under the weak streetlamp. David looked through the expensive night-vision binoculars Big Jim Brodie's widow had given them.

Nine men exited in the space of a few minutes. Several stopped outside the entrance to shake each other's hands, then headed off to their respective vehicles. None of them resembled Bullet Joe. Not that Ruby expected him to be there. If she had, she would have turned Reed down and come along, probably with hired muscle. After the chase at the ballpark, she figured Bullet Joe was in deep hiding and not likely to show up where his buddies would question him or where Hollingsworth might try to persuade him to turn himself in.

With the binoculars, David trailed the men who were headed in the direction of the Lexus. One almost reached it, but instead climbed into a Toyota pickup directly in front of it. Another walked by the Lexus and drove off in a rusty Datsun. Only two men were left standing in front of the Center. They talked for a few minutes, shook hands, and walked off in opposite directions. David tracked the man heading south. He was well-built, around six feet, with dark, curly hair. He wore a dark suit, as if he'd come to the meeting straight from his office. All the other men had been casually dressed.

The man walked briskly, but he didn't appear wary. He didn't look around to see if he was being watched. He cut through the open spot directly in front of the Lexus, unlocked the driver's side, and got in.

''Bingo!'' David said under his breath.

The Lexus pulled away and passed David, the driver never looking his way. David waited until the car was well out of sight before he pulled out. Ruby had instructed him not to follow. Just get the license plate. They could track him down with that.

14

The next morning, while David lay on the mattress on the floor of his attic room and cracked a law book, his aunt worked her magic with the computer and the telephone. In less than an hour, she called David downstairs and laid out the life history of the driver of the white Lexus.

The vehicle was owned by a Joseph C. Caffarelli. An abstract of his driver's license provided the following:

Date of birth: 6/19/49
Sex: M
Weight: 185
Height: 6' 1"
Hair: Black
Eyes: Gray

As always, David was amazed and disturbed by the amount of information and ease with which his aunt could obtain it through electronic databases and a few phone calls. Caffarelli had been born in Saginaw, Michigan, graduated from Michigan State with a bachelor's degree in business administration, and served four years in the Marines in Vietnam. His home address put him in an expensive suburb southwest of Denver. He was married (his first), had a daughter age seventeen in an expensive private school, belonged to a local athletic club, was executive vice president of marketing for a satellite TV service, was a registered

Democrat, and had a clean criminal record except for two drunk driving convictions, both in the past four years.

A phone call to Caffarelli's office turned up that he was in, but unavailable to speak to her. Not that Ruby had expected Caffarelli's secretary to patch him through to a "Lillian Holmes of Aspen MicroCom Incorporated." But now she knew where she could find him.

CTX Telecom, Inc., was a square, three-story building that sprawled on treeless land south of the Denver metro area. An array of gleaming white satellite dishes, aimed at different locations in the sky, some of them the size of backyard swimming pools, flanked two sides of the building.

Ruby bypassed visitor parking in front of the building and drove around the side to employee parking. It didn't take long to find the spot reserved for the Executive Vice President of Marketing. A white Lexus sat in the space.

"That's our car," said David, noting the license plate number and the POW-MIA bumper sticker.

They parked in visitor parking and went inside. The huge lobby was silky smooth marble, dotted with soft light-gray leather chairs.

From behind a circular desk large enough to defend a well-armed platoon, the receptionist quickly informed them Mr. Caffarelli was busy and that they would have to make an appointment with his secretary.

"Fine, we'll make an appointment right now," said Ruby. "Tell him we want to talk about Bullet Joe Brown and Sean Powell."

The receptionist blinked. She obviously had never come across anyone in the high-level corporate executive world with a name like Bullet Joe. Maybe a Chuck or Bob or Dick if the exec didn't have serious ambitions for making company president, but not Bullet Joe.

"Go ahead, call up there, honey," said Ruby, giving a little brush with her hand.

Reluctantly, the receptionist did as Ruby commanded.

After a long pause and nod, she hung up with a defeated look. "He can see you now."

"What lucky timing," said Ruby.

Two minutes later, logged in and wearing visitor passes, they were ushered into Joseph Caffarelli's third-floor office.

It was what David would expect of an executive vice-president of marketing of a TV-satellite company: corner location, glass-topped meeting desk, a jungle of large green plants, framed print-ads on the walls, and several muted television sets built into one wall. They cast a flickering blue glow into the room. Directly in front of a gigantic window overlooking the majestic Colorado mountains was a long desk of textured glass trimmed in enameled metal. Behind it sat the curly-haired man David had seen driving off in the Lexus the night before.

Ruby was halfway across the expanse of marble floor before Caffarelli rose and said, "What do you want?"

"I want to know where I can find Bullet Joe." Ruby dropped her business card on the desk and introduced David.

Caffarelli, dressed in a custom-made dark suit, white shirt, and a red-and-blue tie with duck decoys, glanced at the card but didn't touch it. He glanced up with a mixture of wariness and hostility. He looked tired, as if he hadn't slept well the night before—maybe for several days. "Why do you assume I know this . . . Bullet Joe?"

"You mean, beyond the fact you wouldn't have let us up here if you didn't?"

Caffarelli smiled but said nothing.

Ruby went on. "For openers, he attends the same weekly rap group at the Veterans' Center that you do—which, by the way, I learned from independent sources, not from Hollingsworth. He wouldn't tell me anything because of confidentiality rules. More important, someone saw your white Lexus leave with Bullet Joe—from his parents' trailer park, a week ago Sunday—the day before he jumped bail."

Ruby seated herself, uninvited, in a black leather chair directly in front of Caffarelli's desk. David took an adjoining chair. Their chairs faced the Front Range, and David wondered for a moment why Caffarelli hadn't arranged his desk so that *he*, not his visitors, faced the mountains. Then he realized that the power came from letting visitors know that his office commanded a stunning view and that he, the all-powerful executive, could turn his back and let the underlings gape.

Still silent, Caffarelli ambled to a floor-to-ceiling credenza and poured himself a glass of water from a pitcher. Mentally, David inventoried the contents of the wall-unit. It held black ring binders, books, and framed family photos. A cap with ''Da Nang'' on its front was flanked on each side by tiny American flags. A fine leather attaché case lay on its side, unopened, the handle broken. But what struck David as odd were the red and blue Lost-in-Space robot, the metal lunchbox with a picture of Lassie, the set of bongo drums, the Superman model, and the pair of P.F. Flyers canvas sneakers occupying one end of the credenza. A hotshot executive who collected Baby Boomer memorabilia!

Not that he should be surprised. David felt that he and the rest of his generation lived under the boot of cultural imperialism imposed by his aunt's generation. Much of the stuff of their childhood could still be bought in shopping malls, when it should have been relegated to museums. Half the movies released today seemed to be remakes of Baby Boomers' favorite childhood TV shows. Couldn't this damn generation ever grow up?

''All right, I gave Earl a lift to his folks' place,'' admitted Caffarelli, leaning back against the credenza and taking a drink. ''That's not a crime, the last I knew. In fact, he apparently didn't *jump bail*—is that the expression you used?—until the next day, so I wasn't helping a fugitive escape. I knew he was facing sentencing, of course, but—''

''Where did you take him after you left the trailer park?''

''I took him out to Lakewood and dropped him off at . . . Wadsworth and uh, Alameda, I think it was.''

''What's at Wadsworth and Alameda?''

"A street corner. He asked me to drop him off there. That's all I did. I didn't wait around to see where he went."

"You didn't drive him downtown, near Coors Field?"

"No."

"It's where he ended up that night, down in a squatters' camp near the river. That's quite a ways from Lakewood."

"I don't know how he got there. *I* didn't take him."

"Where did you pick him up?"

"Here."

"Here? What was he doing way down here on a Sunday?"

"I don't know. He called my home and they told him I was at work. When I came out, I found him waiting by my car. He said he was in the neighborhood and needed a ride. He didn't say why he was in the neighborhood."

"What were you doing here on a Sunday?"

"I work most weekends. This is a new company in a very competitive business. A lot of us work weekends."

"So, after this long, grueling week, you play the Good Samaritan and drive the man all the way to the north side of town and then all the way out to Lakewood."

"That's right."

"You don't strike me as the kinda guy who would provide gratis taxi service to three-time losers. Why didn't you just put him in a cab?"

Caffarelli flushed with anger. "You don't know me, so don't judge me. Earl's a fellow vet. One of our group. We look out for each other. He was pretty distraught and disoriented when I saw him. I think he'd been drinking heavily. He'd been having a lot of flashbacks lately. I wasn't just going to stick him in a cab and say *adios*."

Caffarelli put down his glass and returned to his desk, where he remained standing. "How did you find me, exactly?"

"We traced your license plate. Public records."

"I don't have to talk to you."

"No, you don't. I could just pass my information on to the fugitive division of the sheriff's department. I'm sure they'd love to talk to you since Earl has a bench warrant out for him."

"I really couldn't tell them more than I—"

"Oh, there's one other little reason they might like to talk to you, hon. Since Bullet Joe jumped bail, he's become a murder suspect."

Caffarelli didn't flinch, but he finally sat down in his high-backed leather chair. His voice was subdued when he said, "Sean's murder?"

"Yes."

Caffarelli nodded solemnly and bowed his head. Now David knew why the executive looked so tired. "That's all we talked about last night in the group. But I hadn't heard Earl was a suspect."

"The cops found his prints at the murder scene."

"I can't imagine he's really involved."

"Did you know that Powell put up the collateral for his bail?"

"No. But I'm not surprised. Sean was that kind of guy. He gave the shirt off his back to other vets. He was a good man. A very good man."

"Your good man was living under an alias. Sean Powell was not his real name."

Caffarelli leaned forward in his chair. "What was it?"

"I don't know. The police don't know. I was hoping you might. He went to a whole lot of trouble to build himself a fake identity. Any ideas why?"

"I don't have the faintest."

A loud pop, like a car backfiring, sounded outside the window. Caffarelli jerked and swiveled around in his chair to look down into the parking lot.

"How long did you know Powell?" Ruby asked.

Caffarelli swiveled back to face them. He seemed unsettled. "What?"

"How long did you know Sean Powell?"

"Two or three years."

"Did you know him before he started in the group?"

"No."

"The day you gave Bullet Joe a ride, he changed clothes at his parents' trailer."

Caffarelli shrugged. "Maybe so. I didn't pay much attention."

"Were his old clothes bloody?"

Now the man stiffened. "Are you implying that I may have helped a murderer get rid of evidence?"

"We know he was at the crime scene the same day you picked him up."

Rising, Caffarelli said, "I think you'd better leave."

15

"Give me Ruby Dark." The voice at the other end of the line was male, bristling with authority, and loud—so loud, David held the receiver away from his ear.

"She's not here right now."

"How soon will she be back?"

"I don't know. Can I take a message?"

"I'll call back."

"I'm her associate. If it has anything to do with the posting of a bond, I'm a licensed—"

"It has nothing to do with a bond, son. But you can tell her I have information about the man she found dead."

"What information? Who are you?"

The man hung up.

Ruby returned an hour later. Mr. Congeniality didn't call back for three. Ruby asked the same questions, got the same answers. Except for one. David saw her rock forward in her chair.

"You know his real name?" she said. "Why can't you just tell me over the phone? . . . No, I won't meet you alone. If you want to talk to me, it'll be in the presence of my associate . . . Yes, you can trust him."

She scribbled on a pad of paper. "Nine-thirty, then."

"He knows Powell's real name?" asked David when she'd hung up.

"That's what he claims. But he won't tell me what it is

over the phone. Claims my line could be bugged. He wants us to meet him.''

''Where?''

''At the movies.''

The movie house was one of those budget places where films were shown after their major run but before they came out on video. It was stuffed into the corner of a small L-shaped shopping center on the east side of town.

Ruby bought tickets to the 9:20 showing of *Lord of Illusions*.

''At least he has a sense of humor,'' said David.

The theater wasn't much larger than a walk-in closet with a screen—hardly bigger than a home-entertainment center. In the semidarkness, David made out a few heads, mostly teenagers, scattered throughout the theater. Nobody looked like the middle-aged bull moose he envisioned the caller.

Following instructions, they took seats on the right side, halfway down. Onscreen, a detective was talking to a dying black man stuck full of knives. Ruby and David waited. People made popcorn and drink runs. More waiting. David had begun to wonder if the caller was going to show, when suddenly someone sat down in the row directly behind them. Ruby and David twisted around to see a large man with short-cropped hair, a square, cleanshaven jaw, and linebacker shoulders and chest. Around his aunt's age, David guessed, give or take five years. It was tough to tell in the dark. The man was dressed in, of all things, a coat and tie.

''Ruby Dark?'' he said.

''This is a rather awkward place to talk,'' Ruby said above the din. Onscreen was a magician strapped to a revolving table. In an illusion gone wrong, the magician was being skewered by falling swords.

''Let's go to my car,'' said the man.

They went out through the exit that emptied into a dimly lit, almost empty parking lot behind the theater. The man carefully scanned the lot before leading them to a well-used canary-yellow Cadillac. He'd backed it into a space at the rear, where he could exit quickly. He unlocked the driver's side, then used the power lock for the passenger doors and motioned David and Ruby into the car. Ruby sat up front, David in the back. The man slid his large frame effortlessly behind the steering wheel. Walking across the lot, David had realized that the man was even bigger than he'd appeared in the theater—at least six-five and a paunchy two hundred fifty pounds.

"Is all this James Bond stuff really necessary?" said Ruby.

"I assure you, it is *extremely* necessary," he said in a bullhorn voice that would have filled the theater.

"What's your name?" she asked. "You look familiar."

"We'll get to my name in a minute. First, I want to tell you who Sean Powell really was."

"Actually, I'm more interested in finding the man suspected of killing Powell—Earl Brown, a.k.a Bullet Joe. You know anything about him?"

The man shook his head. "I can't help you there."

"Can't? Or won't?"

"I don't know this Bullet Joe."

"All right, tell me what you *do* know," said Ruby.

The man twisted sideways to face Ruby, his arm draped along the top edge of the seat. A large fraternity ring dominated his thick right hand. "Powell's real name was Alexander Gage . . . *Captain* Alexander Gage, U.S. Air Force."

"That means nothing to me," said Ruby.

"It wouldn't. He's officially been listed as missing in action since 1970."

Rarely had David seen his aunt lack for words, but this time she was speechless. Finally, she said, "Missing-in-action? As in MIA?"

"That's right."

"As in *Vietnam*?"

"Laos, actually. At least, that's where we think he disappeared."

"We?"

"I have a deep source in the Defense Intelligence Agency—that's the agency responsible for investigating all reports of sightings of live POWs and for recovering the remains of American men who Vietnam has refused to repatriate. Obviously, for security reasons, I can't divulge the source's name. I *can* tell you that when the police department here sent Powell's fingerprints to the FBI and the military for identification, it was quickly established that the prints belonged to Captain Gage."

"Who's still missing," said Ruby, still shocked.

"Officially he was declared dead in 1985, just as the government did with hundreds of MIAs who it decided were no longer worth keeping on the books. In fact, Gage's name is etched in the black granite of the Veterans' Memorial in Washington—my source personally confirmed that. But it was a paper death. Gage is still unaccounted for. His death was never confirmed and his body was never recovered."

"The police told me that the military couldn't match his fingerprints—to a Sean Powell or anyone else on military records," said Ruby.

The man smiled patronizingly. "The Denver police were undoubtedly lied to by our government. It is not about to let this information out to anyone. It will stop at nothing to prevent this information from becoming public. *Nothing*. Which is why I'm playing James Bond, as you put it."

David leaned forward to catch the man's eye. The man had ignored him since he'd climbed into the car. "Let me get this straight. You're claiming that Alexander Gage disappeared during the Vietnam War a quarter of a century ago—presumably captured by the enemy—yet this same man turns up murdered in Denver, Colorado, just a few days ago, after living all this time under the name of Sean Powell?"

"That's correct."

"You're crazy."

The man laughed. "I've been called a helluva lot worse,

son. So have others who passionately believe that our government knowingly and maliciously left American fighting men behind, alive, after the war officially ended in 1973 and after the acknowledged POWs were returned. Hundreds of those men remain alive to this day—they're interned in Communist prison camps across Indochina and in Russia, and our government is covering up the truth.''

''*Hundreds* of men?'' asked an astonished Ruby.

''I've seen the evidence. Did you know that since 1975, over eight hundred Vietnamese refugees have reported first-hand sightings of Americans in captivity? That dozens have been interrogated—in some cases put through polygraph tests—and that many of their reports are considered credible by American intelligence experts? Yet our government has officially discounted the reports, deliberately and actively *sabotaging* private humanitarian efforts to locate and liberate those men.''

The words had flowed easily in his broadcast-baritone voice, almost as if part of a canned speech he had given many times. To whom he'd given this conspiracy speech, David had no idea. What audience would listen to even five minutes of this bullshit?

Ruby said, ''If Powell—or as you claim, this Captain Gage—really *was* captured during the war, how did he escape? When? How did he get out of Laos and back into this country without U.S. military authorities finding out?''

''We don't have those answers at the moment. Obviously, my source is attempting to find out. But don't presume our government didn't know about him, Ruby. He may have been part of a secret prisoner exchange or other sub-rosa deal. However, I think it's more likely that our government didn't know he had escaped and made it here—and that somebody in the government finally found out.''

''And *killed* him?'' said Ruby. The same question had popped into David's mind.

''There are certainly government elements who would take such extreme measures to protect their nefarious secret, yes. From what my source told me, the DIA is in a state of panic right now—they fear that this information could become public. And I suspect the State Department and the White House, presuming they've been informed, are also deeply worried."

"That's insane," interjected David. "I don't believe our own government would cold-bloodedly kill a former MIA just to do what—hide their incompetence?"

"Of course they would, son. This isn't the first time our government has botched the handling of our POWs. There's fresh and very credible documentary evidence that the United States knowingly left behind at least nine hundred confirmed prisoners in Korea in the fifties, and that some of those men are still alive *forty* years after that war."

David shook his head. "If this Gage guy really was a POW, *why* did he sneak back into this country and live under a false name? Why not broadcast his escape to the world? My God, he'd have been a national celebrity. He could have written books and appeared on all the talk shows and had a TV movie made about him! He'd have been rich! The fact that he did none of these things tells me he was no real MIA."

"Unless he had something to hide," said the man.

"Like what?"

"I don't have the answers to that yet. All my source knows is that the dead man you found was definitely an MIA."

David looked furtively out onto the parking lot and at the back of the shopping center's buildings, then behind him at a high fence that separated them from a set of townhouses. Were they under government surveillance at this very moment? No, that was preposterous. This guy was preposterous. This guy was a nutcase. Or he had some devious trick up his sleeve. The smartest thing that he and his aunt could do was to get out of the car and call the men in white coats. Immediately.

But Ruby wasn't moving. She was staring hard at the man and saying nothing. David knew she was studying the man's eyes, trying to read his mind—maybe his soul. That was her gift, the ability to see inside people, to know when they were lying and when they were telling the truth. Not that it took a lot of psychic ability to determine if this paranoid crackpot was lying.

"Now I know who you are," she said.

16

"You're Mad Dog Paul Stratton," said Ruby.

The man grinned like a little kid. "*Colonel* Paul Stratton. Bird colonel. U.S. Marines. Green Beret. Retired."

"I know, I know. I've seen your picture in the papers."

"I see I underestimated you, Ruby. I presumed the only pictures you ever see are the ones tacked to post-office walls."

"There are a lot of people who think your picture belongs there, too."

Stratton shrugged. "People who serve their country often pay a heavy price."

"Many would say it's others who have paid *you* the heavy price."

"You don't believe everything you read and hear in the media, do you, Ruby?"

"Not at all. But now that I've had a chance to listen personally to you, hon, I tend to believe them."

Stratton frowned playfully. "You're skeptical of my claims about Captain Gage?"

" 'Skeptical' is a kind word."

"Good. I wouldn't have it any other way. When my source first told me, I didn't believe him, either. It's a shocking story. But I believe it now. He's an extremely reliable source and he's observing this from the inside. There's panic at the highest levels of our government."

"Excuse me," interjected David. "I have no idea what you two are talking about. I'm not familiar with your name or your face, Mr. Stratton. I—"

"Everyone calls me Colonel."

"Okay, *Colonel*, I still don't know who you are."

Stratton tipped his hand toward Ruby. "You seem to know about me. Why don't you tell him? I'm curious to hear your perspective."

David turned toward his aunt, who kept her eyes on Stratton.

"The colonel here is a much-decorated Vietnam war hero who's become this nation's best-known POW/MIA activist. Works out of Orange County, California, if memory serves me."

"That's correct."

"He's publicly claimed several times that he has evidence proving that American POWs are still being held captive in Indochina. He's personally conducted two or three missions attempting to actually enter Vietnam or Laos to rescue, or at least document the existence of, these alleged POWs. However, he's never actually produced a single, living, breathing POW. And virtually all of his *evidence* has been disproved as either poor intelligence, misleading information, or outright fraud. His missions have been privately funded, and he's been denounced by many people, including his own former military superiors and some MIA families, for cruelly exploiting the issue purely for money and publicity. Frankly, I'm inclined to agree. Is that a pretty fair summary, hon?"

The big man smiled. "Most of what you've said is wrong, but certainly as the image portrayed in the biased media, yes, I'd say you've succinctly captured my public persona."

"I read about con men. I've met a few in my line of work."

"No doubt you have."

I've got studying to do, David muttered to himself. Why are we wasting time with this bombastic ex-military fruitcake? Let's say good-bye, thanks for the laughs, and leave.

"Why are you telling us this farfetched story about Powell, hon?" said Ruby. "Surely you didn't go through all this charade just to hit me up for some kind of contribution to your cause."

"Quite the contrary, Ruby. I want to pay *you*. I want to hire your services."

"My services for what? You gonna need bonding-out soon?"

"I want you to help me prove to the American public that Sean Powell was really Captain Alexander Gage, MIA, and that our corrupt government has buried this secret about him and the many others still in enemy hands. I want to expose the duplicity on this issue and liberate those men still imprisoned on Communist soil. I'm not interested in just bringing back bones. I want live POWs."

For a moment, Ruby said nothing. "Beyond the fact that I don't believe a damn word of your story about Powell, I'm a bail bondsman, not a detective."

"Oh, but you *are* a detective, Ruby. A fine one, according to the newspaper accounts. You really embarrassed the police on that big murder case here. Though I gather you have a penchant for finding bodies. 'Angel of Death'—isn't that what the paper called you?"

"I hope you don't believe everything you read in the papers," said Ruby.

Stratton chuckled at her joke. "No, I checked you out through other sources. The papers didn't exaggerate. You're the legitimate thing."

"I still don't understand why you've come to me. Just because I found Powell's body doesn't mean I'm any closer than a total stranger to proving or disproving that he's this Gage guy. I didn't see or take any evidence at the murder scene that would prove your claim, if that's what you're thinking."

"No, I wasn't thinking that at all. I just believe you're the right person to help me."

"Why don't you go to the police?"

Stratton's hearty laugh filled the car. "I don't trust them, and they don't trust me. No governmental agency does."

"Hire a private investigator. There are plenty in the phone book."

"I don't know them. I think I know you."

"I'll recommend a couple of excellent investigators."

"I want you."

"Why don't you call the newspapers? Hold a press conference. That's your S.O.P., isn't it?"

"Normally, yes. But this isn't a normal situation."

Ruby paused. "You mean that before, you knew your claims were false. Now you think you might have a real one on the line and you're worried that nobody will believe you. Like the boy who cried wolf."

"I've always acted in good faith, Ruby. I've never knowingly made false claims about MIAs. I confess to having been misled by unscrupulous people selling false intelligence. I've been, perhaps, too eager to embrace anyone with claims of information about our missing men. But I have never deliberately misled anyone on this issue—unlike our own government, whose treatment of this issue is one of the ugliest and shabbiest episodes in American history. Unfortunately, to be candid, I have somewhat exhausted the goodwill of the mainstream media. I can't risk squandering this opportunity prematurely on the sketchy information we currently have. Besides, public disclosure of what I know at this juncture would drive our government to an even more defensive posture and perhaps put my source in harm's way. I need to prove beyond a doubt that Sean Powell really was Alexander Gage before I make that publicly known. I need your help because I need an independent, credible source to confirm it."

It was Ruby's turn to laugh. "I'm a bail bondsman, hon. We're viewed as anything but credible."

"You're saying our government would kill your source?" interjected David.

"Absolutely. And if our government didn't kill him, the

Vietnamese would. I'm already on their hit list. They run assassination teams out of Toronto."

"I can't help you," said Ruby. She opened her door and began to get out. Stratton put his hand up to smother the center interior light.

"Don't you care that our government left men behind?" he said. "That there are men *still* alive?"

"I don't believe there are. And if I'm wrong, there's not a helluva lot I can do about it. I run a business. It takes all my time and energy. I'm not going to chase ghosts."

"I said I can pay you."

"I'm not interested in money that's been exploited from MIA families who are too distraught not to see through you." She got out of the car and shut the door.

David scrambled out of the backseat. The open air was exhilarating after the claustrophobic atmosphere the colonel had created inside.

The passenger-side window rolled down. "I'll be in touch, Ruby," said Stratton.

"Don't waste your time, hon. Find a detective in the phone book. He'll be glad to spend your money to humor you."

Ruby was unusually quiet and preoccupied on the drive back to the office. The throb of the Lamborghini's engine was the only sound. She didn't even have the stereo system on.

"You don't believe Rambo's story, do you?" asked David.

Ruby kept her eyes on the freeway. Traffic was light. "No."

Her "no" lacked the conviction she'd shown earlier with Stratton.

"The guy's an arrogant, paranoid nut," said David. "I mean, even assuming there really *was* a Captain Gage and somehow, miraculously, he escaped captivity and managed to get out of Indochina, *why* would he sneak back into this country and live under a false name? That's ludicrous. It doesn't make sense."

"No, it doesn't." Her voice was flat.

Neither spoke for a while. Finally David said, "You know, as crazy as this guy is, Aunt Ruby, we probably should tell Homicide about him."

"Why?"

"Technically, he *did* offer potential evidence in a murder case. We shouldn't withhold that from the police."

"You're taking this lawyer stuff seriously."

David bristled. "Actually, I was thinking of it more as ass-covering. Just in case the cops find out about it another way. You've already got enough problems with them since the Gibson case."

"Maybe later. Not just yet."

"You're not going to take him up on his offer and help him, are you, Aunt Ruby?"

"No."

"Then why don't you want to tell Homicide?"

"I don't want to spook him."

Ruby exited the freeway onto Colfax. Off to their left twirled the bright ferris-wheel lights at Elitch Gardens. Beyond lay Coors Field, dark. The Rockies were out of town. At least I won't be on TV, mused David.

17

David couldn't sleep, a rare occurrence. Most of the time he crashed from sheer exhaustion, usually after reading dozens of pages of fine print in a law book. But tonight the bizarre tale of Colonel Paul "Mad Dog" Stratton kept running through his mind—as did his aunt's curiously low-key reaction to the story. Why didn't she want to report Stratton to the police? Why didn't she dismiss his ludicrous tale in stronger terms? Surely she didn't believe the man.

David pressed the luminous interior light of his digital watch. 12:16 A.M. He considered turning on his lamp and reading more—he hated wasting the time if he was going to lie awake—but the thought of plowing through more obscure law made his brain ache. He rolled off the mattress directly onto the floor and crawled on his hands and knees below the low-peaked ceiling of his garret until he could peer out the tiny window just behind his desk (which consisted of an interior door perched on cinder blocks). Below, streetlights cast a sick yellow glow on an empty street. Beyond rose police headquarters. Nothing much happening out there, either.

He had to pee. At least it was something to do. He started down the narrow flight of stairs to the second floor and realized a light was on in the office. Either his aunt had forgotten to turn it off when she left, or she was still here. He'd left her at her desk after their return from meeting

Stratton and he'd been in his room ever since. He slipped on a pair of ragged shorts and tiptoed downstairs.

David peered around the corner of the office. Ruby sat at her desk staring at something in her hand. "Aunt Ruby, what are you still doing here? It's after midnight."

She jumped at the sound of his voice. Whatever she'd been studying she hastily slipped into the center drawer of her desk. She took off her reading glasses and rubbed her eyes. "Just taking care of details," she said huskily.

David entered the room. Collateral was bagged out on the floor. He checked David with a half-opened eye, saw nothing threatening, and went back to sleep. David couldn't see Alabaster, the coal-black Persian who let only Ruby near her. The cat must be off in one of her hideaways.

"Go home," he said. "Get some sleep. Even the Angel of the Outlaws has to sleep now and then."

"Actually, I was about to go over to J.T.'s. He's been out on an account and they thought he'd be back by now. Want to come along?"

"At this hour? What for?"

Her eyes were glassy, and she looked barely able to stand on her feet, let alone traipse out to J.T. Cale's. Not that exhaustion ever stopped her. "I think he might be able to help us get a better line on Stratton."

"What more is there to know about him? I think we saw all we need to see of that guy."

"He knows more about Powell and Bullet Joe than he's letting on."

"And why would J.T. know anything about Stratton?"

"He was in deep recon and intelligence work in Vietnam. I think he keeps up on what's happening in the POW/MIA movement."

"God, did everybody in your generation fight in Vietnam?"

"If they weren't rich, yes."

"Morgan, too?"

"Yes."

"I've never heard him or J.T. talk about it."

"A lot of men I know who served there don't talk about it. Most of them want to forget." Ruby rose from her desk. "Want to come with me?"

David threw up his hands. "Hell, why not? I'm wide-awake now."

The large, nameless, corrugated steel building—an old repair garage—sat among a string of low industrial buildings in Commerce City, barely across the northeast line of Denver city limits. The surrounding buildings were dark and gloomy, but Cale's was open and brightly lit, with country music blaring into the darkness. In Cale's line of work, the repossession business, he and his employees slept days and worked nights. Nights were the best time to steal cars.

Actually, the building had the look of a chop shop. There were always several cars parked inside the building. Most were fairly new. David could imagine a crew of scruffy guys with blowtorches and bolt cutters slicing up stolen cars for parts, or shipping them down to Mexico. The repo business had never enjoyed a healthy public reputation, and more than a few repo men had been caught running stolen cars. Outwardly, at least, Cale was an honest businessman who worked primarily for banks, auto dealers, and savings-and-loan companies by repossessing cars, trucks, and any other portable items on which people had become loan-delinquent. But David knew that Cale was a man with a freewheeling lifestyle that included gambling trips to nearby Central City and Las Vegas. And a couple of off-handed remarks by his aunt had left David with the impression that Cale occasionally crossed the line.

Cale had just returned from a recovery when they walked into the building. He stood in the middle of the garage, alongside a pale blue Subaru whose doors were flung open, the car's stereo blaring a sad steel guitar. Cale was dressed in his usual working outfit: big black cowboy hat with an expensive silver hatband; black leather vest over a dark western-cut shirt; cowboy boots; and a fancy silver belt buckle large enough to serve as a tea tray on an English estate.

Ruby and David were halfway across the garage when Cale looked up from the 3 x 5 cards in his hands—the "accounts" he was working on. He gave Ruby a hug and a friendly hello to David. "They said you called earlier, Angel. What are you doing over here at this hour? Come to spot a deal on a car?" He swung his arm in the direction of the cars.

"Whattya have that's good?"

"I just brought the Subaru in. Six months old, in great condition. The guy made one payment after he drove it off the lot. Got a ninety-four Lincoln, a ninety-three Jimmy, a Volvo . . . oh, we just repo'ed a Harley from a bikers' bar not far from here. There's a repo that'll raise the hairs on your neck. Doesn't that woman lawyer friend of yours like bikes, Angel? What's her name?"

"Cyndee Valone."

A sly grin came over Cale's face. "I'll get her a great deal from the bank and drive it over to her personally."

His blue eyes sparkled against his full white beard and white hair.

"You're old enough to be her father, J.T.," said Ruby.

"Maybe she doesn't have a father and would like one."

"She has a father and she just bought a new bike. I don't think she'd be interested." Cale looked crestfallen. Ruby put her hand on his shoulder, which was several inches higher than hers and twice as broad. Steering him out of the middle of the garage and away from the sad steel guitar, she said, "I need a favor, hon."

"What else is new, Angel? You always come to me for favors. What is it?"

"You know anything about a Colonel Paul Stratton?"

Cale stopped and turned toward Ruby. The grin on his face had disappeared. "Mad Dog? What rock did you find him under?"

"He crawled out and found me."

"Why? He trying to tap your wallet for one of his con jobs?"

"Actually, he offered to pay me to help him. You read about us finding this Sean Powell stabbed to death?"

"Sure. I recognized his name, too. He's active—excuse me, *was*—in the POW/MIA movement. I'm not personally into the network myself, but I have friends who are, so I keep up on things in an informal way."

"Powell was not his real name," said Ruby. "That much I know for sure. But the police can't seem to I.D. him. Stratton claims he was really an Air Force captain named Alexander Gage who was listed as an MIA in Laos during the war. Nobody knew what happened to him—until we found his body."

"You're shitting me!"

"I'm not. But I'm sure Stratton is."

A young man with long, dirty blond hair and a wimpy goatee appeared and handed Cale a piece of paper. David didn't recognize the man. In this business, they seemed to come and go like the cars. Cale slipped his 3 x 5 cards into a shirt pocket, read the paper, flicked a fingernail against it, and said, "Bring the Cowboy Cadillac around, Mike. We better snatch this sucker while the snatchin's good." The man dashed off, and Cale turned to Ruby. "We got a tip on a guy I been chasin' for two months. He's in a bar in drive-by city. Gotta go now or we'll miss him, and I'm tired of chasin' his ass."

Seconds later, a dark extended-cab Ford pickup with a tow unit bolted to the truck bed pulled up in front of the garage.

"Why don't you and David jump in?" invited Cale. "It'll be cheap thrills. We can talk about Stratton on the way. I wanna hear more about this, Angel."

Ruby didn't hesitate. She piled into the bench seat in the back. David, who was not quite so enthusiastic, followed anyway. The pickup roared off with the blond-haired man behind the wheel.

"I never met this sonofabitch, but I feel like I know him," said Cale as they headed downtown.

"He's a strange one," said Ruby.

"No, no, not Stratton. This guy whose car we're going after. I know where he eats and drinks and works, who he hangs out with, who he screws, but I always seem to miss the bastard. He knows we're on the prowl for him."

"We nearly got him at his mother-in-law's last week," said the driver.

"Missed him by that," Cale said, snapping his fingers. "Let's not let it happen again."

The driver pushed the pickup faster.

Cale opened the glove compartment, took out a fifth of Jack Daniel's, unscrewed the cap, and offered it to David, who shook his head. Cale didn't offer it to Ruby, knowing she would turn him down. He took a shot, screwed the cap back on, and put it away.

"Tell me about your meeting with Stratton," said Cale.

Ruby gave him the *Cliffs Notes* version.

Cale shook his head. "Shit, that's really out in left field, even for Mad Dog."

"So you don't subscribe to his claim that we left men behind in captivity in Vietnam?" said David.

"I didn't say that, David. Frankly, I believe our government left guys behind. But I don't trust these shysters who claim they've got evidence of living POWs after all these years. Stratton especially. Word around the network is his last POW rescue mission was a real fiasco."

"In what way?" asked Ruby.

"I don't know the details. Nobody likes to talk about it. It seems to be sort of the black hole of the movement. Whatever it was, it went wrong, real wrong."

"Where did he get the nickname 'Mad Dog'?" asked David.

"That's a little unclear too," said Cale. "One story is, his Green Beret unit was running a top-secret intelligence operation and assassinated an alleged double-agent against the wishes of his superiors. The investigation was hush-

hush and it was dropped. Stratton had a lot of friends in 'Nam. The other story goes that he got the nickname after ordering a napalm strike on his own unit when they were surrounded by Vietcong. I don't believe either story. I think Stratton made them up. I don't mind if guys don't want to talk about the war, but damned if I want to hear 'em lie about it."

Ruby cut in. "You said something about a POW/MIA network. Stratton alluded to that, too. What exactly is it?"

"It's a loose coalition of POW/MIA organizations, former 'Nam vets, and families of missing men who keep track of any POW/MIA information. There's a lot of infighting among the different factions, so life isn't too smooth in the network. But many of them have connections to people still on active duty, people salted inside the intelligence agencies with access to secret documents—people like this guy who Stratton claims told him about Powell—even former vets who work for law enforcement agencies. They trade information—photos, bones, live sightings, intelligence reports, that sort of stuff. Several of them put out newsletters, like *The Bamboo Informer* and the *POW/MIA Insider*. They use the Internet a lot, too."

"You said Powell was part of this network?"

"He was active locally in the movement. But let me tell you about that later. We're almost there."

The pickup turned onto Welton in Five Points and slowed as Cale scanned the line of cars parked along the street.

"There's our baby," he said almost gleefully, pointing to a red Nissan Sentra on the opposite side of the street. "The guy's supposed to be in that bar." He pointed to a joint named Happy Haven several car lengths away.

"Shit!" said Mike. "Look how the bastard's got it parked. We'll never get it outta there."

The Nissan was wedged between two cars, bumpers touching bumpers. Even if the owner handed them the ignition key, they couldn't budge the car, let alone tow it away with their pickup.

''He got friends to block it for him,'' said Cale.

They drove to the end of the block, turned onto a side street, and parked.

''Now what?'' The driver sounded discouraged. ''Can we move the other cars?''

''Not legally,'' said Cale as he dialed his cell phone. ''Besides, that would take too much time. But not to worry, Mike. You can run from J.T. Cale, but you can't hide your car.''

The repo man turned his attention to the phone.

''Charlie, it's J.T. . . . Yeah, I know it's fucking late for you, but I'm only halfway through my working day . . . Yeah, yeah, but how would you like to make a quick C-note plus standard rental? . . . Yeah, right now . . . I don't care what the hell you're in the middle of, Charlie, tell the broad she can finish when you get back. Offer her half the hundred. That's probably double what you're paying her anyway.'' Cale broke into a big grin. ''It's parked by the Happy Haven on Welton . . . That's the place . . . I don't know how much longer the guy's gonna stay, and I ain't goin' in to ask. Just make it fast . . . a hundred and a half if the guy comes out and shoots at you . . . Fine, two hundred if he puts a hole in your truck . . . No, you don't need to bring anything too big. It's just a Nissan. A red Nissan . . . Great, see you in twenty—fifteen, if you can do it.''

''Who was that?'' asked Cale's driver.

''You'll see.''

18

They waited on the side street for fifteen minutes. Cale sent his driver around the corner to make sure the Nissan was still parked between its bookends, then twisted around in the seat to face Ruby and David.

"There were a coupla things I didn't want to mention in front of Mike. You were asking about Powell and the network. Powell got a name among the activists by claiming that an American businessman had bribed U.S. government officials to get them to lift the trade embargo with Vietnam and to normalize diplomatic relations. Now, a lot of vets and MIA families are strongly opposed to normalization until we get a fair accounting of the missing and a return of the bodies. Most of the activist newsletters picked up Powell's charges, but he never got the national media to bite, and I'm not aware of any official investigations into the charges."

"We've already lifted the trade embargo, and we're close to normalizing relations," said David.

"Maybe the guy was successful," said Cale.

"Who's this businessman?" Ruby asked.

Cale thought for a moment. "Powell didn't publicly release the guy's name, but it was spread informally through the network. Guy lives right here in Denver, I think. Name's . . . Jenkins or Jefferson or . . . Jennings—that's it!"

Ruby leaned forward. "*Todd* Jennings? Runs a construction company?"

"Yeah, that's him. Know him?"

"We've discussed art together."

"Why would Jennings try to bribe U.S. government officials?" David asked Cale.

"Apparently his construction company does a lot of international work, particularly in Asia. Supposedly he's got close ties with officials over there, including in Vietnam. Vietnam's in piss-poor shape. Has been since the war. Roads, railroads, the ports, industry—it all needs repair. If U.S. relations are normalized with Vietnam and Jennings can get a piece of the action, he stands to make hundreds of millions of bucks. Mind you, I'm not saying Powell was right about the bribery charge. I don't know if he really had any hard proof."

"But if he did, Jennings would have a hefty motive for destroying that evidence," speculated Ruby.

"I suppose he would," agreed Cale.

"You know a vet named Bullet Joe Brown?" Ruby asked.

"Nope."

"Joseph Caffarelli?"

Cale shook his head. "Who are they?"

"They went to a rap group over at the Veterans' Center. Powell went there, too."

"I know about the place, but I've never been there."

"It's a bunch of guys still fighting the war," interjected David. "Reminds me of that Japanese soldier I read about who hid in the jungle during World War Two and didn't come out until *thirty* years after the war ended."

"You got a lot to learn about war, son," Cale said. "That's the problem with your generation, you never had your own war. The Persian Gulf shoot-out doesn't count."

"You buy this post-traumatic stress disorder?"

"Don't put down PTSD, David. When I came back from the war, I was pretty fucked up. I didn't want to be around people and they didn't want to be around me. My marriage broke up. I started drinking. I fought with every woman I knew. Fought with every guy I knew. I didn't have any real friends except for other drunks. War isolates you like that. The only people you feel comfortable with are the other guys who went to war with you . . . like Big Jim."

"But you don't dwell on the war, right? I've never heard you talk about it before now. You don't make a big issue out of it. You don't use PTSD as some kind of psychological crutch."

Cale's hard blue eyes softened, as did his voice. "I just run fast enough so the monsters don't catch up with me."

The driver's door suddenly jerked open and Mike leaned in. He asked Cale in a breathless voice, "Is the guy you called from the Front Range Equipment Company?"

"That's Charlie."

"Well, he's here." Mike had a wild look in his eyes.

"Our Nissan still there?"

"Yep."

"Then let's boogie."

Mike piled into the pickup and made a U-turn. When they reached the corner, Cale instructed him to pull up even with the car just ahead of the Nissan. Directly across from them, in the opposite lane, was parked a flatbed truck with a forklift sitting on it. As soon as Mike slowed down near the Nissan, the driver of the flatbed jumped out, dropped two ramps to the street, hopped up onto the bed, and unchained the forklift.

"You're kidding me," said David, realizing what Cale planned to do.

Ruby, also watching out the rear window, laughed. "J.T., you're a genius."

"Gotta be smart to survive in this business," he said as the pickup stopped. Cale leaped out of the door and began readying the towing equipment. He and the flatbed driver—Cale's guy Charlie, David assumed—exchanged waves but no words. David guessed they had pulled this stunt before.

Charlie hopped onto the seat of the forklift, started it, raced down the ramps to the street, made a sharp right turn, and aimed it dead-center of the Nissan, its forks low.

Welton was a major street, and traffic began to stall, forced to accommodate the partially blocked lanes. Drivers slowed to gawk. Mike had his door half-open, his eyes on the entrance to the Happy Haven. Two men who'd come out just as Charlie was driving the forklift off the back of the truck had stopped to watch. When they saw the lift slide its forks under the belly of the Nissan and begin to lift the car straight up—like a bakery chef neatly lifting out a slice of a freshly baked cake—they scurried back into the bar. An alarm in one of the adjacent parked cars went off, filling the air with a sharp "*Whoop! Whoop! Whoop!*"

"Better be quick, J.T.!" yelled Mike, jumping out of the cab to help Cale hook up the front of the Nissan. "I think we're gonna have trouble real soon."

Trouble burst out the door of the Happy Haven about the time the forklift gently set the Nissan down. Trouble was a big white guy carrying a steel baseball bat he'd probably borrowed from the bartender. He looked really pissed as he stumbled toward the Nissan. Several men spilled out of the bar behind him, but they moved more slowly, warily.

"J.T. got a gun?" David asked his aunt.

"No. He carries a billy club, but he doesn't allow any of his people to carry guns."

"He might want to reconsider his policy. You bring your gun?"

"No."

"What the fuck you doing with my car!" bellowed the big man, waving his bat menacingly as he stepped into the vacant spot where his carefully parked Nissan had sat only thirty seconds before. "Get away from my fucking car, you bastards!"

Cale approached the man, his arms raised for him to stop. Mike scrambled to fasten up the tow under the Nissan, while Charlie drove his forklift back up the ramps onto his truck bed.

"Just be calm, Steve," said Cale. "That's your name, right? Steve?" The mention of his name seemed to give the man pause. "Your car's gettin' repossessed. The car's going. A legal repo. Ain't nothing you can do about it. It's done, man."

"The fuck I can't do nothing about it!" The man raised the bat unsteadily.

Traffic had stopped. Drivers were honking their horns or yelling obscenities out the windows. The car alarm was still going "*Whoop! Whoop! Whoop!*" The group of men from the bar had worked their way closer, but none had come to assist the man waving the bat.

"It's all legal, friend," repeated Cale, standing his ground although the man with the bat probably had five inches and forty pounds on the repo man. "Let's not get anybody hurt over it. That'd make things a lot worse than they are. It's only a car. There's lots more cars around."

"That's *my* car," the angry man said, pointing the bat at the Nissan.

"The bank says not any longer, Steve. Bank's given you plenty of notice. They don't want to go to all this trouble, but you've left them no choice."

"Fuck the bank."

"You come up with your back payments, they'll let you have it back, Steve."

"I lost my job, dickhead."

"Hey, I understand, friend. Tough times. Been through 'em myself. But you gotta make your payments. Nothing's free, buddy."

Mike scurried out from under the Nissan and headed for the pickup. Charlie had flipped the ramps onto the truck bed, the loud metallic crash startling everyone on the street, and was driving away in his truck. He hadn't taken the time to chain down the forklift or say so much as a good-bye to Cale.

"She's tied up, J.T.!" yelled Mike, piling into the pickup and raising the front wheels of the Nissan off the ground. "Let's get the hell outta here."

Cale backed away from the man with the bat and worked his way around the Nissan. "Gotta go, Steve. Gotta go. It's a done deal. Ain't nothing you can do about it, friend. No hard feelings, okay? Just doing my job. Ain't nothing personal, Steve. I'm sure you're a great guy. If I had the time, I'd come in and have a drink with you.''

The man stood glaring on one side of the Nissan as Cale sidled along the other side toward the pickup. He was still talking, trying to keep Steve calm. Cale waved good-bye as he hopped into the pickup.

''Get the fuck outta here,'' he said to Mike in a shaky voice.

Mike slammed the stick shift into gear and started to pull away. At that moment, they heard the shatter of glass. David ducked expecting to be sprayed with cab glass. Then came more sounds of breaking glass. When he realized the sounds were farther away, he peered out the rear of the pickup. Big Steve was smashing the bat into his own car—well, what had been his own car—shattering windows and denting steel. He pounded the bat on the rear window with enough force to ring the bell at the state fair. A spider web of broken lines shot across the buckled glass. He smashed it again as the car rolled slowly along on its rear wheels. Another swing took off the radio aerial. Then a side mirror.

''Come on, dammit!'' Cale yelled to Mike, reaching over to honk the horn.

The problem was that so many gawkers had slowed to watch that Mike could only inch the pickup through the other cars while Steve continued to pummel the Nissan, putting huge dents in the doors, smashing headlights and taillights. By then, his bar buddies, feeling braver, had joined him, kicking at the doors, ripping off the hubcaps, throwing rocks at the car. Someone had found a tire wrench and pounded fist-sized dents in the hood and cracks in the windshield. Numbers seem to swell until David estimated that fifteen men were beating the shit out of the Nissan. Spectators cheered from the sidewalk and from their cars.

''Push it! Push it!'' yelled Cale, waving an arm out the window to get cars to back out of their way. ''There! There! Through there!''

Mike weaved the truck between two cars, across the opposite lane of traffic, over a corner of the sidewalk, and onto a vacant side street where he was finally able to accelerate and leave the crowd behind. Half a dozen men gave them the finger as their enraged voices faded into the background. One last rock struck the back of the pickup cab with a dull thud.

"Fuck," said Cale looking at the car from the rear of the cab. It looked as if they were dragging a dead animal, ready for burial at the nearest junkyard. "There goes my fucking fee," said Cale. "The bank's gonna just love this."

"Jesus," said David, his body still shaking. "I've never seen anybody do that to his own car."

"It ain't the first time," said Cale. He took a slug from his whiskey bottle. "I had one fucker set fire to his car while I was inside trying to hot-wire it. Another guy found out I was chasin' him, so he left his car parked on the train tracks one night."

"It's like guys who kill their wives when the wife wants a divorce," said Ruby. "They take the attitude that if they can't have her, nobody's gonna have her."

They drove the rest of the way in silence.

"Told you it was cheap thrills," said Cale as they got out of the truck at the garage and stood inspecting the damage in the glare of garage lights.

"Doesn't exactly look cheap," said David. Up close, the car looked far worse than it had appeared on their ride back.

Cale shrugged. "Cost of doing business."

"We gotta go, J.T.," said Ruby. "Sorry about the car."

"Hey, better the car than us."

"Will you see what more you can find out about Stratton for me?"

"Sure thing."

"Oh, and one other favor. Don't mention anything to anyone about Stratton's claims. And don't pass my name around on this POW network. I don't need more nuts calling me."

19

A light evening breeze blew across the rooftop restaurant in LoDo, and David shivered. But he knew it wasn't the breeze that had chilled him; it was the memory of the night before—images of the man with the bat and his bar buddies beating the Nissan to a pulp. He couldn't shake the feeling that it could easily have been Ruby, Cale, and him instead of the car. Anger was a wild wind that could swiftly change directions and catch anything in its path.

"I can't believe these bastards are still milking the MIA issue after all these years," Morgan Reed snapped loudly. Ruby had just finished telling him about their secret meeting at the movie theater with Colonel "Mad Dog" Stratton. "It's the worst myth of the war, all this MIA crap."

"You don't believe POWs were left behind?" Ruby asked, her voice as loud as Reed's.

David kept his eyes on his salad but peeked to see if anyone in the restaurant was watching them. The few scattered patrons seemed to be minding their own business, and two waiters were laughing at jokes while huddling at the bar.

"No, I don't believe it," said Reed, "and if any POWs *were* left behind, I certainly don't believe they're alive today. Especially hundreds of them. That's preposterous."

"I agree with you, Morgan," chimed in David, who rarely agreed with the detective. "Besides being a fraud, the guy's a raging paranoid, suggesting that our own government may have murdered Powell."

Reed took a long draw on his beer and nodded. "I'm glad to know at least one of you has some common sense."

"Why don't you believe men were left behind, Morgan?" said Ruby. "You served in Vietnam. You know what it was like."

"Damn right I know what it was like. That's why I don't believe it. It's triple-canopied jungle. A jet or helicopter going down in that stuff is like dropping a green marble into a huge bowl of split-pea soup. It's gone. You'll never see it again. Hell, the stuff was so thick, sometimes high-explosive bombs didn't penetrate to the ground. And if you walked through the stuff, you couldn't see five feet in front of you. It's a miracle we rescued as many downed pilots as we did. Guys disappear in war, Ruby. That's why they have tombs of unknown soldiers."

"That doesn't mean some of them didn't survive."

"Yeah, but a lot of those MIA reports were bogus from the get-go. Fellow pilots or the wing commanders would officially report seeing a parachute descend, or claim they didn't actually see the plane go down at all, when in fact they saw the plane blow up. Or the pilot got target fixation and flew right into the ground at several hundred miles an hour. Do you think the wing commander's going to tell the pilot's family that? Or a guy disappears in a firefight. Everybody knows he's dead. Body's lying at the bottom of a rice paddy or blown to bits by artillery. If they list him as dead, his family gets a one-time death benefit. But if they report him as missing, his family continues to collect his paycheck. Guys used to tell their commanders whether they wanted to be listed as MIA or KIA, in case something happened to them. That was unofficial policy in some squadrons and combat units. I don't blame them for doing it. Hell, I did it a few times myself. We were looking out for each other. Unfortunately, that perpetuated the myth that many of these guys survived crashes or firefights and were captured. Then lo and behold, they're never accounted for and we accuse the Vietnamese and our own government of covering up the facts.''

''But many pilots *did* bail out,'' said Ruby. ''Far more of them should have been accounted for.''

''But most of those who managed to eject were injured. Broken legs or arms, burns, bad cuts, internal injuries—the kinds of injuries you sustain ejecting at high speed or parachuting into rough terrain from a wounded duck. If they were captured, they didn't have American medics or quick evac to a hospital where there were top surgeons. Virtually any injury, untreated or poorly treated in a prison-camp situation, could be fatal. It wasn't an accident, Ruby, that the majority of guys released as POWs hadn't suffered serious injuries. It was no accident that not a single POW who returned home was an amputee or had suffered serious burns. Anyone with severe injuries couldn't have survived under those conditions. It's as simple as that.''

''Were you a pilot?'' asked David.

Reed laughed. ''Me? No. I was just a grunt. A sergeant in the First Cav in Binh Dinh province. Went through five greenhorned lieutenants in two tours.''

''Went through them . . . ?''

''Killed.''

David could see his aunt getting up a head of steam. She pushed aside her barely touched plate of nachos. ''Tell me, Morgan, why is it our government gave credence to Vietnamese refugee reports of American defectors fighting alongside enemy troops, yet discounted all similar refugee reports about seeing American POWs? *All* of them!''

''Thousands of people have reported seeing Elvis, too, Aunt Ruby,'' David cut in. ''But you're going to have a hard time convincing me he's still among us.''

''Amen,'' said Reed, his mouth full of Philly cheese steak.

''Tell me, Aunt Ruby. Why would Vietnam have kept back POWs? They were just more mouths to feed.''

''There are several possible explanations. They may have been kept for slave labor, but I don't buy that. There's a strong possibility some were shipped off to Russia for their technical or intelligence expertise. That was done during the Korean War. But the most widely held explanation, and the one I tend to believe, is that Hanoi kept men back as a bargaining chip. Nixon and Kissinger supposedly promised to pay Vietnam four billion dollars in war reparations, and when we reneged on the promise, Vietnam kept the men in retaliation. Maybe they hoped the U.S. would change its mind. And of course, our government had no choice but to secretly go along with the situation. The promise to the American public was that the U.S. had brought *all* the men home."

"But why hold them all this time?" asked David. "If there was a political motive at the time, it must have vanished a long time ago. It must have been obvious to Vietnam after a few years that we weren't going to pay that money."

"I doubt they've held them all this time, David." A sadness clouded Ruby's features. "Frankly, they put themselves in the same position as our government did. They couldn't admit to the world what they'd done."

"So they killed them?" said David.

"Probably. But maybe not. They sold French prisoners back to France fifteen years after that war ended."

David shook his head in disbelief. "I just can't believe anyone would be alive after all these years."

"I'll tell you what happened to those men," said Reed, putting down his sandwich. "It's well documented from North Vietnam's own military records that most of the men we strongly believed had been captured but never returned were either killed on the spot by irate villagers whose homes had been bombed, or they died in the prison system from torture or poor medical care. The Communists were too embarrassed by what had happened to them, so they claimed they didn't know a thing. Granted, it wasn't fair to those guys' families, but that doesn't mean we left them behind alive."

Ruby leaned toward the detective. "Tell me, Morgan,

has the FBI come back with an I.D. on Powell yet?''

''No, not that I've heard.''

''Why's it taking so long? You said the FBI should be able to check fingerprints overnight. A man who creates a false I.D. like Powell did is hiding from something, and it's a fair bet he's got his fingerprints in a police file somewhere.''

''I have a theory about that,'' said David. Neither Ruby nor Reed looked at him with any great expectation, but he plunged ahead anyway. ''Powell may have been a deserter. That would explain why he disappeared and why he created a false I.D.''

''You may be on to something there, David,'' admitted Reed. ''Several guys who deserted during the war were arrested Stateside, years later, on unrelated charges. They're found out when their fingerprints end up in the system. In fact, did you read about the guy—some old master-sergeant with a Hawaiian name—who got off a plane in California in 1970, apparently on his way from 'Nam to a new assignment here, and he just walked away? Didn't even contact his family. Because of some bureaucratic snafu, they didn't expect him at his new assignment, so he just disappeared between the cracks. He was reported as missing and eventually declared dead. His name ended up on the Wall. The military even returned someone's bones from Vietnam and told his family they were his. Nobody ever would have found out except that the guy applied for Social Security.''

Ruby shook her head in dismissal. ''If Powell was a deserter, he would have turned up in the fingerprint system. The Defense Department or the FBI wouldn't have any reason for keeping his desertion a secret. It might be a minor embarrassment at best, but it would explain away one more man listed as MIA.''

''Maybe there's some sort of mixup that we don't know about, Ruby,'' said Reed. ''We're talking bureaucracies here.''

''I don't think so. I know Stratton's story is pretty tough to swallow, but so is this silence about Powell. Our government has a long history of trying to cover up on this issue.''

''Hell, Aunt Ruby,'' said David, ''our government couldn't organize a damn backyard barbecue, let alone cover up the fact that it abandoned dozens—or hundreds—of POWs.''

''I didn't say it was a successful cover-up.''

David walked his aunt back to her loft after Reed left. ''You seem awfully well informed about this subject, Aunt Ruby. You knew a lot about Stratton, too. I'd never heard of him.''

Ruby shrugged. ''Vietnam was my generation's war, and the POW/MIA issue was a big one. Some people think it was the issue that finally turned our country against the war. Naturally, I've followed it over the years.''

''Were you against the war?''

''It's hard to be *for* war, David, unless you're a weapons manufacturer.''

''Were you one of the protesters? Did you go on marches and all that stuff?''

''I made my voice heard.''

''I bet you did. Where? One of the campuses? In the streets?''

Ruby smiled. ''Around.''

Around. Rarely could he get his aunt to talk about her past, about those missing years between age sixteen, when she had run away from home in St. Jo, Missouri, and age forty, when she turned up in Denver. Nobody in his family knew for sure where she'd spent those years, though they did a lot of speculating. Her past was as blank as the past of Sean Powell . . . or Captain Alexander Gage . . . or whatever the hell his name was.

''See you tomorrow, Aunt Ruby,'' David said when they reached her building.

''Good night, David.''

''Oh, Aunt Ruby?'' She stopped. ''What are you going to do about Bullet Joe? Any new leads?''

"No. I'm hoping the cops will pick him up. He'll do something stupid and they'll catch him. He wants to get caught. He always does. Old habits are hard to break."

"Maybe not this time. This time it's murder."

20

Three days later, Mad Dog Stratton called, claiming he had developed new information on Powell. It was 9:38 P.M. David had just returned from Professor Gideon A. Rothschild's contracts class, and he was beat. Rothschild's class always left him beat. It came from steeling himself against the professor's Darwinian approach to teaching law—gnawing the weakest students to death.

"You're not really going to see Stratton, are you, Aunt Ruby?"

"Yes. And I want you to go with me." She reached for a straw hat on her oak hat rack.

David threw up his arms. "Why are you wasting your time with this man? You heard J.T. The guy's a fraud. It's obvious listening to him that he's a fraud. In fact, what I don't understand is why anyone—even MIA families—would give a con man like him money to go crusading off into the jungle for MIAs."

"Families believe him because they're desperate to believe him," said Ruby, her voice suddenly low.

"Believe what? That one of their relatives is miraculously still alive sitting in some Commie prison twenty or thirty years after the war? That's nuts. No, that's not nuts. That's sad."

"Put yourself in their place, David. Imagine that you lost a husband or a son or a brother in the war. Yet there's no body. No one saw him die. Maybe he disappeared under questionable circumstances. Maybe there are even reports that he was seen alive in captivity. If there's no body, there's always hope. A slim hope, granted, but hope. By keeping that hope alive, they won't forget. That's what they're afraid of—forgetting. They're afraid of selling out the memories of their husbands or their sons if they accept that death without a body. It's tough to say good-bye."

David shook his head. "But eventually you have to move on. You can't hang on *forever.*"

Ruby adjusted her hat and looked evenly at David. "Sure you can."

The colonel's directions took them to the Hotel Clayton, one of the more upscale hotels downtown. They were to take the far-right elevator in the lobby, push the buttons to floors 8, 9, 15, 16, and 19, and get off on 16. If anyone got on with them on the way up, they were to pass 16, get off on 19, and walk the emergency stairs back down to 16.

The guy must watch bad television, thought David as they entered the elevator and pushed the appropriate buttons. They rode alone to the ninth floor, but there a man got on. He was Asian—Chinese, Japanese, Vietnamese, David couldn't tell. He was taller than the average Asian—around David's height—thin, and wore American jeans, a plain blue T-shirt, a baseball cap slouched over his forehead, and dark glasses that struck David as rather comical. He couldn't determine the man's age, except he wasn't young.

The man didn't say anything or look at them. He pushed the button to the eleventh floor and stood with his back to them. This can't be a coincidence, thought David. It wasn't. When the elevator doors opened on 11, the Asian pushed the open-door button and stood to one side.

"The colonel is this way," he said in broken English.

Ruby hesitated. "We had different instructions."

"He has changed the plan."

Ruby hesitated a moment longer, then stepped off the

elevator. David followed, not taking his eyes off the Asian. He exited with them, walked ahead silently, and led them to room 1189. He knocked softly and Stratton opened the door.

The colonel was dressed in full regalia tonight: polished black shoes, crisp khaki pants, and a chest full of medals on a tan short-sleeved shirt that did nothing to camouflage his paunch. He looked ready to give a speech. A nickel-plated bracelet gleamed on his thick left wrist. David recognized it as one of the bracelets stamped out by the millions in the 1970s by a POW/MIA organization to raise money and public awareness. Each bracelet was inscribed with the name of an MIA or POW, and the wearer vowed not to remove it until the person was accounted for. Somebody will always find a way to make a buck off tragedy, David thought to himself.

Stratton ushered them into the large suite. Nothing in the room looked as if it had been touched since the maid had cleaned it. Even the paper sanitary wrap around the toilet seat was still in place. It's a wonder Stratton isn't wearing gloves to avoid leaving fingerprints, mused David.

Stratton directed them to the couch. Off to one end, directly in front of the drawn curtains, stood a three-legged easel with a blank flip-pad.

"I'll warn both of you up front not to bother bringing anyone to this room after we finish," said Stratton. "I checked in under an assumed name, paid for the room in cash, and will be gone before you reach the lobby."

"We came alone, hon," Ruby assured him. "No one else knows you're here."

"Good. You've met Xiong Pao Lo." Stratton nodded toward the Asian, who had removed his sunglasses and stood silently.

"Not formally," said Ruby.

"Xiong is Laotian," said Stratton. "From a Hmong mountain tribe in northern Laos. He was a child when the North Vietnamese army and the Pathet Lao drove his family out of their sacred mountains into the south. He's grown up fighting the Communists ever since, sometimes from Thailand and Laos, sometimes from here in the United States. He has been instrumental in aiding my efforts to secure the release of POWs in Southeast Asia.''

Part of the con job, too, thought David. The Laotian had said nothing during this laudatory introduction, but watched them with small, intense eyes.

''What do you know about the war in Laos?'' Stratton directed his question toward Ruby.

''Only that officially we weren't fighting there,'' said Ruby.

''Precisely. It was the CIA's dirty little war—something for them to do while everyone else was busy in Vietnam and Cambodia.''

Stratton stepped to the easel and flipped back a page of the pad to reveal a large map of Southeast Asia. He picked up a plastic pointer from the easel and pointed to a salmon-colored country shaped like a key. ''This is Laos. My Pentagon source has learned that this definitely was where Captain Gage—or as you knew him, Sean Powell—was captured and held by forces of the Pathet Lao and probably the North Vietnamese regular army, since they controlled most of Laos. At the time of his capture, the war in Laos was illegal and secret, though every American journalist and Vietnamese hooker in Saigon knew about it. Since we officially weren't fighting in Laos, no Americans could be officially missing there. Hence, under the Pentagon's double-accounting system, Air Force Captain Alexander Gage was officially serving in South Vietnam at the time of his disappearance.''

''What was he doing in Laos?'' Ruby asked.

''He was in charge of a super-secret listening post known as Eagle's Eye, or officially, Site Fourteen. It sat on a remote mountain top, around Sam Neua. Right here.'' Stratton pointed toward a spot on the handle of the key, barely inside the Laotian border with North Vietnam. ''The radar site provided intelligence information to guide American bombers on runs up around Hanoi and the Red River Delta."

"That's where he was captured?" Ruby asked.

"Yes. He shouldn't have been. Supposedly the site was impregnable—heavily fortified, high limestone cliffs, access only by helicopter or a narrow path, and guarded by Hmong tribesmen under the leadership of General Vang Pao. Have you ever heard of Vang Pao?"

"No," said Ruby.

"I have," interjected David.

Stratton looked at him with surprise.

"He ran a guerrilla war against the Pathet Lao," said David. "Supported by the CIA, I think. He trafficked in heroin, too."

"You've done your schoolwork," said Stratton.

"Not everyone in my generation is ignorant about history."

Stratton went on. "General Pao and his army of about thirty thousand Hmong tribesmen battled the Laotian Communists and North Vietnamese for years. And yes, they ran a *huge* opium operation. They'd been cultivating it for centuries. It was their cash crop. Like corn in Iowa. We're talking about the Golden Triangle, after all. Pao and his guerrillas even set up a network of heroin labs and were exporting high-grade Number Four heroin to our boys in Vietnam. From what we theorize, Captain Gage and his men had to walk through poppy fields to get to Eagle's Eye."

Stratton swept the pointer dramatically down toward Saigon. "And of course it's well known that virtually every prominent official in the Saigon regime was involved in the drug trade."

"The CIA looked the other way, right?" said David.

"They didn't just look away, they actively helped ship the opium to Long Cheng and Vientiane with Air America. But what the hell, the money from the sale of drugs was being used to help finance the war against the Pathet Lao. It was for a good cause. Of course, to this day the CIA denies its involvement, but it's well documented. The important point here, however, is that it was the responsibility of General Pao and his guerrillas to guard Eagle's Eye. Apparently they failed in their mission. Or they were bought off. We don't know. We *do* know, according to Defense Intelligence Agency records, that the Pathet Lao overran the site on June fifth, 1970, capturing perhaps a dozen U.S. airmen. We don't know the exact number. After spending time around Sam Neua, the men were moved south as the Pathet Lao drove the Hmong army toward Vientiane, along with the Hmong women and children, which is what happened to Xiong, here. The last known record of the Americans indicated they were being held in caves down along the border, near Tchepone, not far from the Ho Chi Minh Trail.''

Stratton pointed to an area in the south of Laos, just west of the northern tip of what was then South Vietnam and the Demilitarized Zone.

''Officially, of course, Gage was missing in Vietnam. I suspect that at the time, the Pentagon and State Department hoped that by magic he'd turn up on the POW list when it was released by Hanoi, but he didn't. As far as my source could determine, none of the men captured at Eagle's Eye were on that list. Are you aware that only *seven* military men—of three hundred seventeen listed as missing in Laos—were repatriated, and that all of them were released through North Vietnam?''

''How did the Pentagon know so precisely where these men were moved to?'' questioned David.

''The CIA tracked their movements through village contacts. Laos used to be its fiefdom before the Pathet Lao gained control. In fact, the CIA tracked many missing men in Laos. One CIA cable referred to several dozen Lao prison camps, and the presence of Americans in those camps was confirmed by two or more independent sources. And there were more than just village reports. There was multiple-source intelligence, including Keyhole satellite and SR-71 photographs of some of the camps where Gage and his men were held."

"Does the CIA know what happened to them?" asked Ruby.

"DIA and CIA reports from villagers in the Tchepone region claim that several Americans were killed in those caves and buried sometime around late 1974 or early 1975—well after Operation Homecoming. That, of course, couldn't be confirmed by satellite surveillance."

"Killed how?" Ruby asked.

"We don't know. But presumably it wasn't an accidental U.S. bombing, because none was going on then."

"Yet miraculously, Gage was not one of them to die?" David said.

"My source is positive that the man you found dead was Alexander Gage."

"But no one can actually place Gage in those caves, can they?" said David, convinced that if Stratton was telling the truth about Powell's real identity, desertion was the only rational explanation.

"No, we don't have names of the men who were captured, but it's fair to assume Gage was one of them. Obviously he survived the assault on Eagle's Eye, or none of us would be here discussing this."

"But you still can't prove Powell is Gage," challenged David. "Not unless your Pentagon source comes up with proof, or the U.S. government admits it."

"It won't. But I can if you two help me."

"How?" said Ruby. "You've got the contacts in Washington, not me. I'm just trying to find a skip."

"But you know the people here. You've got those contacts. Somebody in this town knows about Sean Powell's secret past."

"Probably his wife," said Ruby, "but the cops can't find her."

"Speaking of his wife, I have another lead for you to follow," said Stratton. He pulled a folded piece of paper from his pants pocket and handed it to Ruby.

She opened it. "Who's Elizabeth Patterson?"

"Gage's former wife."

"Former wife?"

"The one he was married to *before* he went to 'Nam. The one he had two kids with, none of whom he apparently ever contacted after he returned to the States. The kids are grown now. She remarried after he was declared dead in 1985. She and her husband live on a farm outside of Cedar Rapids, Iowa. That's her phone number on the paper. I want you to call her."

Ruby stared at him. "You can't be serious."

"Get her out here to identify Powell's body as the body of her former husband. I'm sure the cops will allow that as long as we can keep the U.S. government out of it."

"Contact her yourself," said Ruby.

"I have. She refuses to cooperate."

"Gee, I wonder why," David muttered under his breath, just loud enough for the colonel to hear.

"Why would *I* be able to get her out here if you couldn't?" asked Ruby.

"She doesn't trust me, but she might trust you. She once was a big cheese in the POW/MIA movement. I think she can be persuaded to come out to look at the body. Call her independently. Don't mention my name. Tell her you're investigating Powell's death and you have reason to believe that she may be able to conclusively identify the body."

Ruby rose from the couch and shook her head. "I won't do that, Colonel. I'm not going to turn her life upside-down based on your cockamamie story."

Stratton glared at her with almost a wild-animal look in his eyes. "Then get more proof. Do what you need to do to convince yourself that I'm either right or wrong about Sean Powell. This is history in the making, Ruby, do you understand that? If Sean Powell really was an MIA in Laos, then we're going to rewrite the final chapter of the Vietnam War."

"If you're so certain, call the cops here and convince

them to get her out here. I'm sure she'd cooperate at their request."

Stratton scoffed. "They'd be less likely to do it than you are. Besides, I can't take the risk. If I contact them, they might call Washington first, and that would bury Alexander Gage's records forever. I have to keep this under wraps. I don't want Washington getting wind of it."

Ruby shook her head again. "I can't help you. I won't help you."

Stratton said something to the Laotian in French, though David remembered far too little of his high-school French to understand. The Laotian nodded and immediately left the room.

Stratton escorted Ruby and David to the door. "I think you'll change your mind, Ruby." He spoke with the confidence of a cold-calling salesman who had been rejected many times, but who knew that in time and through persistence he would eventually make a sale. "You'll turn up something and you'll realize what we're sitting on, Ruby."

21

J.T. Cale leaned back in the chair, propped his dirty cowboy boots on a corner of Ruby's desk, and told them that Colonel Paul ''Mad Dog'' Stratton, former U.S. Green Beret, former war hero, and big-time POW/MIA hunter, was flat-ass broke.

''My buddies who keep up on this stuff say his fund-raising's dried up, he's on the outs with the activist community, and he's even had to go out and get a real job.''

''Doing what?'' asked Ruby from across her desk.

''He runs a security business. His own shop. Provides protection for executives, movie stars, that sort of thing. Trades on his notoriety, but it's not a thriving business, from what I could gather.''

''We just saw him in a damn nice hotel suite,'' said David.

''He's probably trying to put up a good front,'' said Cale. ''It's tough to sell his kind of con if you look down-and-out.''

''I wouldn't believe the man if he was working out of the Taj Mahal in a thousand-dollar suit,'' said David.

Ruby gave Cale a quick summary of their evening with Stratton and the silent Laotian.

Cale's large brown eyes peered out from below his black cowboy hat. ''You want my opinion, Angel? It sounds like the only thing Stratton is trying to rescue these days is his bank account. If he could get somebody to believe in this fantasy, he'd be back in the dough.''

''Did you get any buzz on his claims about Powell?'' she asked.

Cale shrugged. ''Not a whisper. Either my contacts don't know about it or they're sitting on it. I'm not an insider. Maybe something's there and my sources just aren't telling me. But remember that failed POW mission I mentioned? I learned a few more details about it, and I can see why Stratton's been discredited ever since. He ran the mission three or four years ago. To begin with, there were some financial irregularities. Not unusual for these missions, of course. Most of the time, rescuing POWs seems to be a sure-fire method to part gullible MIA families and supporters from their money. But the irregularities in this case apparently were substantial.''

''How substantial?''

''I heard a hundred twenty grand was unaccounted for.''

''That's a chunk of change,'' said Ruby. ''Who funded the operation?''

''Some desperate MIA families with deep pockets. And a rich woman benefactor. They trained on her estate, in fact, somewhere in Georgia or Alabama or someplace down there.''

''They?''

''A dozen or so 'Nam vets. They were the ones who actually made the mission. Another dozen people or so were involved as support: communications, logistics, that sorta thing. Some were vets, some activists. And a coupla MIA wives, I heard. They had sophisticated radios, night-vision goggles, camouflaged uniforms, weapons, the whole shebang. It was a first-class operation. Interestingly, I was told that some of the vets were guys from around here.''

Ruby leaned forward. ''Who? Any names?''

''No. Just that they were local. Nobody seems to know exactly who was involved in the operation. But I got the feeling—nobody said anything, mind you—that some guys didn't come back from the mission.''

"Back from where?" David asked.

"Somewhere in Laos. That's where most of these excursions go. It's easier to get into a country like Laos than into Vietnam. Stratton claimed to have multiple-source intelligence that half a dozen Americans were being held in a camp not far from the Thai border. They made it into Laos, too, but apparently that's where things went wrong."

"How about the name of the mission? These guys always code-name their missions, don't they?" asked Ruby.

Cale laughed. "Operation *Freedom*. Now there's a man with balls."

Ruby wrote out a check. "Thanks, J.T. You did a good job. I may have to hire you again."

Cale folded the check in half and stuffed it in his shirt pocket. "My pleasure. A nice change of pace from boosting cars."

Cale went down the back stairs of the office, his boots clunking on the metal steps.

"Now what?" asked David. "We seemed to be finding out about everything but Bullet Joe."

"I'm going to have another chat with the therapist over at the Vet Center. In the meantime, I want you to go to the library and dig through the newspaper and magazine index. Go back three to five years and see if you can find any stories about this Operation Freedom. Stratton's a publicity seeker, so I'm sure there must have been stuff written about it."

"Ms. Dark." Samuel Hollingsworth rose unenthusiastically from behind his desk as Ruby entered the therapist's office. He didn't offer a hand. "What is it you want to know that I can't tell you?"

"I want to know about Sean Powell."

"I hate to sound like a broken record, but—"

"I know, I know. The damn confidentiality rules. But Powell's dead. He won't care, I assure you."

"It makes no difference. I can't even discuss a client who is deceased."

"Joseph Caffarelli—who happens to drive a white Lexus, by the way—seemed willing to talk about him."

Hollingsworth frowned. "We encourage the men to maintain strict confidentiality, but I can't be responsible for what they may say or do outside these walls. Besides, I don't understand why you're interested in Sean. You said the person you want to find is Earl Brown."

"That's true. But if I can't find Earl, I may need to go to Powell's estate to collect on the collateral he put up for the bond. The problem with that is, Sean Powell is not his real name. But I've come up with a possible identity. Does the name Alexander Gage mean anything to you?"

"No."

"He was a captain in the Air Force."

Hollingsworth shrugged. "Men who come to these groups don't always use their real name. The name they use is not important. Their confidentiality is."

"Don't you check out the men who seek services? To keep out the riffraff?"

Hollingsworth laughed. "We operate on the budget of a church mouse. We don't have the time or the resources to check out the men who come here. We operate on faith."

"I'd say faith was something Powell may have been a little short of, hon." Ruby pushed aside a stack of files on a chair and took a seat. Hollingsworth remained standing while she filled in highlights of the alleged connection between Gage and Sean Powell. She left out any reference to Stratton and his phantom Pentagon source. Somewhere in the middle of her story, Hollingsworth sat down.

"Now, if Sean Powell *was* this same Alexander Gage," said Ruby, "and Gage really was an MIA, that presents something of a problem, wouldn't you say? How did he escape and get back into this country, and why didn't he contact his family or the government?"

The therapist blinked. "Who told you this story?"

"I can't tell you."

"I'd say whoever it was sold you a big lie."

Ruby chuckled. "That's what my nephew keeps telling me."

"Your nephew sounds like a very clearheaded man."

"I wouldn't say that. He's studying to be a lawyer."

"What on earth makes you think any of this story is even remotely possible?"

"Frankly, I doubt it is. On the other hand, I know that Sean Powell was *not* Sean Powell, and the police are having a difficult time coming up with an ID. There are a lot of things that don't add up. I was hoping you could help me out. You're sure Powell never confided even a part of this story to you or the group?"

Ruby sensed from the stunned expression in the therapist's eyes that Hollingsworth had never heard any of it before. But she needed to ask the question anyway.

"If he did, I certainly couldn't tell you." Hollingsworth rose and said, "I'm very busy and I really can't help you."

Ruby remained seated. "Let me ask you something I think you *can* help me with. For the sake of argument, let's say Powell was held captive in the war and managed to escape. Now, wouldn't he have contacted authorities and his family when he returned? Or wouldn't he have said something to the men in your group?"

Hollingsworth returned to his chair, placed his elbows on the desk, and interlaced his fingers. After some thought, he replied, "Not necessarily."

"Why not? Why would he sneak back into this country, live under a false name, and never tell anyone about his experiences?"

"Let me explain something about PTSD, Ms. Dark. Not all therapists in this area are in agreement, but many feel that central to the etiology of these men's stress disorder is guilt. This guilt is often buried deeply in an individual. There may be no consciousness about it. But if you know even rudimentary psychology, you know that any buried feelings will eventually work their way to the surface. It may take a long time, and they may surface in a different form than the original feeling—rage, depression, alcoholism, restlessness—but it all stems from buried guilt. That's one of the issues we deal with in our sessions.''

''Guilt about what?''

''It can be many things. A soldier may feel—justifiably or not—that he let down a buddy in combat and got him—or even his entire squad—killed. He may have killed innocent civilians during the war. That was common in Vietnam—guys would wipe out a village full of suspected V.C. and then find out that all the victims were fishermen and children. He may feel guilt from having fought in a war that people back home didn't support. Or he suffers from survivor's guilt. That's common among combat veterans. He survived, some of his friends didn't, and he's overwhelmed with guilt about it. He feels he should have died with them.''

''But even taking that into account, surely he would have returned to his family.''

''Many men who returned from Vietnam had little to do with their families. The divorce rate among vets was very high. It can be extremely difficult for these men to have a safe, nonviolent attachment to others. I've known men who've left their wives and families because they were afraid they might explode emotionally one day and harm them. There are men—though not many of them—who came home and immediately lit out for the remote wilds of Hawaii or Vermont. They couldn't face human contact. For their families, these men were virtually MIA—in their own country.''

Ruby nodded. ''One other question. What do you know about a POW rescue mission into Laos? It was run three or four years ago and called Operation Freedom.''

The therapist blanched. ''Nothing. I've heard the name mentioned, but that's all. I don't follow those efforts. I think most of them are misguided.''

''I thought you might have special knowledge about this mission. I've been told that local vets were involved.''

''I don't know anything about it.''

''That bamboo cage you store here. That wouldn't have

been used for training for the mission, would it?''

''I told you, it was used for public protests around town.''

The therapist rose once again. This time, Ruby left his office.

''You really think the cage was used for training?'' asked David after Ruby told him about her visit.

''I don't know. But I sensed he knows more about the mission than he's letting on.'' She put on new music in the office.

David threw up his hands. ''So we're still nowhere. I still think Stratton's story is preposterous, and I don't see why you're so fascinated with whether Powell was once an MIA or POW or a damn deserter. He's dead. It's Bullet Joe who skipped.''

''There's a connection there. Powell may yet lead us to Bullet Joe.''

''What sort of connection?''

''I don't know. I just know something doesn't feel right.''

David rolled his eyes.

''Did you find anything at the library about Operation Freedom?'' Ruby asked.

''Not much. I found one article in a Houston newspaper, along with some photos showing Stratton and some men supposedly training for a mission. But no mention of the mission by name. The article was mostly a lot of fluff about Stratton and other MIA activists.''

''Could you recognize any of the men in the photos?''

''No. Stratton was the only one whose face was recognizable. The rest of them probably didn't want anybody to know they had anything to do with him. If there really was an Operation Freedom, Stratton managed to keep it pretty quiet.''

Ruby turned off the music. ''Come on. Let's go talk with a guy who I'll bet knows something about it.''

22

This time around, Ruby figured that Joseph Caffarelli wouldn't let them up to his office at CTX Telecom, Inc. So they waited outside in the employees' parking lot with the Lamborghini stashed between a pickup and a van. It was early evening before Caffarelli came out. Most of the lower-echelon office staff had gone home, leaving just the evening-shift technical crew and the usual late contingency of executives devoting their lives to the company instead of to their families.

After Caffarelli tossed his briefcase into the backseat and climbed into his Lexus, Ruby whipped her car up behind him, blocking his exit.

Caffarelli bolted from his car and approached them. "Move your car or I'll call security."

Ruby rolled down her window. "You know a man named Alexander Gage? He was a captain in the Air Force."

"No. Now move your car."

"Did Sean Powell ever tell you he'd been a POW in Laos?"

Caffarelli stared at Ruby as if she were insane. "Where in the hell did you get that ridiculous information? Sean was never in Laos and he was never a POW."

"Tell me what you know about Operation Freedom."

Like Hollingsworth, Caffarelli paled, even in the warm

glow of the low sun. J.T. Cale had been right about the local vets and their supposed involvement.

"Let's go someplace to talk about it," Ruby said softly.

The executive hesitated, then nodded meekly.

The Lamborghini wasn't built for three, so they rode in Caffarelli's Lexus to a nearby fern-cluttered restaurant-bar called Centennial Sam's. It wasn't crowded, even for the dinner hour, and they found a booth back in a corner of the bar side. Caffarelli quickly ordered a Cambodian Cluster Bomb.

"What is in a Cambodian Cluster Bomb?" Ruby asked.

"Amaretto, rum, orange juice, pineapple juice, and cranberry juice," explained Caffarelli.

"Make me one, too, but leave out everything except the cranberry juice," Ruby told the waitress, who took a moment to digest the end result of the modified order. Ruby skimmed the menu. "I'll take buffalo wings and fried cheese sticks. I'm starved."

David ordered Oriental chicken salad and a Coors Lite.

As soon as the waitress was out of earshot, Caffarelli leaned forward and said in a hushed voice, "What the hell is this crazy stuff about Sean once being a POW in Laos?"

Ruby told him Stratton's claims. The executive kept shaking his head in disbelief as she talked, after which he said, "You can't seriously believe this man. Every one knows he's a fraud. I know for a fact he's a fraud."

"I don't trust him, either. But the police are drawing a blank on a man who should easily be I.D.'d in military records. Besides, I think you know more about Bullet Joe and why he disappeared than you've told us. I know something went wrong with Operation Freedom, and I think it may figure into Powell's murder."

Caffarelli refused to tell them anything until his drink arrived and he'd downed it, then ordered a second.

"All right, what do you want to know?" he said sullenly.

"You were personally involved in Operation Freedom?"

Caffarelli took a big sigh. "Yes."

"How did you get involved? You knew Stratton?"

"I'd never met him before. I'd heard of him, of course. I wouldn't have had anything to do with him, except Sean persuaded us to go along. He knew Stratton from somewhere."

"Us?"

"Me, Earl, and one other man from our group at the Vet Center. The rest were from around the country."

David leaned forward in surprise. "Bullet Joe was involved in the mission?"

"Yes. I wouldn't have recruited him. The man was a loser. He didn't have any real skills to contribute. But Sean liked him. He'd always help out a down-and-out vet. And in all honesty, I have to say I never saw Earl more excited about anything than when he was working on this mission. It was like he'd gotten back some part of his life he'd lost in 'Nam. Hell, I think all of us did at the time . . . before things went wrong."

The waitress arrived with Caffarelli's second drink and their food.

"Tell us about the mission," said Ruby after the waitress left. "What went wrong? Is it true that some people didn't come back?"

Caffarelli winced at her words. He finished most of his second drink before he slowly began to talk. "Stratton claimed he had good intelligence from a primary collector about a POW camp in Laos, around a place called Borikhane. That's roughly thirty miles across the Mekong River from Thailand. Supposedly five or six Americans were being held there by the Pathet Lao."

"What's a primary collector?" asked David.

"An on-the-ground observer who's a highly reliable source."

"You mean a spy?"

"If you like that term. It doesn't always fit. Stratton wanted to go in with a dozen men and bring the POWs out. He said two camp guards would neutralize the other guards on the condition we'd bring them out with us and pay them a million dollars once we were safely back in Thailand.''

''You believed all this?'' asked David.

''Hell, no. Not a word of it.''

''Then why did you go?''

Caffarelli paused and looked at him with bottomless eyes. ''Because I came back from the war and some of my friends didn't, and maybe, just maybe, as bizarre as it sounded, Stratton was right and some of those guys were still alive.''

David started to reply, then stopped. It was pointless to argue this senselessness with him—or with any of these people, including his own aunt.

''Powell believed Stratton?'' asked Ruby.

''I don't think he trusted him any more than I did, but Sean was *convinced* men were there. Maybe not at the particular site Stratton had pinpointed, but they were *somewhere* over there. I didn't believe it, but somehow . . . Sean talked me into doing it. He could be very persuasive. I've never met anyone quite like him. He'd have made a helluva preacher if he hadn't been such a private man. He was a strange, obsessed person. You could tell he was carrying some terrible burden from the war, something he couldn't shake. I've seen that in other vets, but never quite to the degree it was in Sean. I don't know what it was. He'd never talk about it, either in the group or privately, but you knew it was there, just under the surface. Often guys like that eventually kill themselves. I don't know what kept Sean alive.''

''If he'd been a POW himself, that would explain his passionate belief, wouldn't it?'' said Ruby.

Caffarelli shook his head. ''I don't believe it. I just don't believe it.''

''It would explain a lot,'' said Ruby.

''It explains nothing.''

''Go on about the mission.''

Caffarelli briefed them about the planning of Operation Freedom, though he refused to divulge the name of the rich female benefactor who owned the estate where they'd trained. "When we finished our training, we went over almost immediately."

"When was that?"

"In February, four years ago. We each flew into Bangkok separately. We used false passports and paid for our tickets with cash Stratton had given us. We set up a base operation in a hotel in Bangkok. After a couple of days there, we moved to a forward operating station at Chai Buri, which is just on the other side of the Mekong from Borikhane. We established another radio link there. We were to have direct contact with Chai Buri at all times during the actual incursion. If we found the POWs and got in trouble, Chai Buri would relay our situation to the Bangkok base, which would, in turn, relay word to our communications center in San Diego. From there, word would be sent to contacts inside the Pentagon to alert the military to dispatch helicopters from the Seventh Fleet to rescue us and the POWs."

"This mission involved the U.S. government?" said Ruby, surprised.

"Officially, no. Unofficially, yes."

"Did you talk personally with anyone from the government?" asked David.

"No."

"So you had only Stratton's word on U.S. support?"

"That's true," conceded Caffarelli. "But I have to admit, despite my serious reservations, I was impressed by the scope of the operations. I think we had tacit government backing—at least within a part of the Pentagon."

David found that difficult to believe, but he said nothing.

Caffarelli went on. "It also was in Chai Buri where we hooked up with two Pathet Lao resistance fighters."

"Hmongs?" asked David.

"Yes," Caffarelli replied.

"Was one of them named Xiong Pao Lo?" asked Ruby. "A tall, thin man with the sociability of a log?"

"Yes. Where did you hear about him?"

Ruby told the executive about his presence at the hotel meeting with Stratton.

"I never had much to do with him," said Caffarelli. "He and the other Laotian dealt mostly with Stratton. None of the rest of us spoke French or Laotian."

"They were your guides?" Ruby asked.

"Yes. They took us into Laos about three days after we set up in Chai Buri."

"It must have been terrifying," Ruby said, "going into Laos like that."

Caffarelli nodded. Any pretense of being the all-powerful executive vice-president of marketing of a multi-million-dollar company was gone. He looked drained and weak. "I was more scared then than I ever was in any firefight in 'Nam. We wore camouflage uniforms, but we weren't regular military. I figured if they caught us, they'd shoot us as spies. That, or stick us in the camp with the other POWs."

"*Were* there POWs?" David asked.

Caffarelli hung his head low. "No. Nothing. It took us three days of hard marching to get to the target, and all we found were farmers and rice fields. The fields had probably been there for the last millennium. No POW camp, no evidence of a POW camp there at anytime, no evidence of anyone buried there. The farmers didn't know about any POWs. Just the damn rice fields."

"Are you sure you had the right location?" Ruby asked.

"Yeah, we were right on target. We had excellent equipment for verifying our coordinates, and our guides knew the area. We had the right place. Stratton's intelligence was wrong, that was the problem. There was nothing there. Except trouble."

"What went wrong?" said Ruby.

Caffarelli looked up with sad, dark eyes. The man had aged ten years since they'd stopped him in the parking lot. "What *didn't* go wrong? We'd managed to duck a couple of Pathet Lao patrols on the way in, but on the way back out, they hit us. They were waiting for us. They knew exactly where we were going. It probably would have been over for everybody, but our Laotian point-man tipped things early for them. They took him out, but it gave us enough time to scatter and return fire. Frankly, it's a damn wonder any of us got out of there alive.''

''How *did* you manage to get out?'' asked Ruby.

''It sure as shit wasn't the Seventh Fleet or Stratton. The guy may be a great con man, but his reputation as a Green Beenie is vastly overblown. He couldn't lead a bunch of Cub Scouts to the nearest Seven-Eleven. It was Sean and me who got us out, and Stratton's Laotian buddy. We rounded everybody up, directed return fire, and made hasty retreat for the Thai border. Fortunately, we weren't far from it at the time—any deeper in, and I wouldn't be here talking to you. Sean was calm. I couldn't believe how calm he was. I mean, I'd led men in combat, and I relied on my old instincts, but I was scared as hell. He wasn't. It was like he'd already died once, and this stretch was just a bonus.''

''Did everybody get out?'' asked Ruby. ''I mean, besides the Laotian point-man?''

Caffarelli, blinking tears, looked away and tried to compose himself. When he spoke again, his voice was husky and low, almost inaudible. ''No . . . we lost . . . two others.''

''Two? That means some of the Americans.''

''Yes.''

''Jesus,'' said David.

''Who?''

''One was an ex-Marine named McDaniel. From Seattle, I think. The other . . .'' Caffarelli stopped, then continued in a whisper. David leaned in so he could hear above the blare of the television behind the bar. ''The other guy was a man Sean had recruited from our support group. His name was Lewis Howard.''

''You said they were lost in the firefight. They were killed?''

There was a long pause. ''Yes. And a couple of other guys were wounded, but they could still walk out.''

''What about Bullet Joe?'' said Ruby. ''What did he do?''

''Well, not much, as it turned out. He didn't make the trip. The dumb shit got himself *arrested* just before we were scheduled to leave. Some burglary charge, I guess. Old habits are tough to break. He was sitting in county jail while we were getting our butts chased toward the Mekong.''

''You claimed that the Pathet Lao were waiting for you,'' said Ruby. ''How did they know you were there?''

A curious smile broke across Caffarelli's tired face. ''That's a point of much debate.'' He fell silent and stared into his third drink.

Ruby leaned toward him. ''A debate over what?''

He looked up, eyes unfocused. ''Mad Dog and Sean and some of the other guys thought we were betrayed by someone here—someone who knew about the mission.''

''You don't agree?''

''It's not like we were invisible over there. I'm sure the Laotians had spies in Bangkok, Chai Buri, and along the border. How hard is it to spot a dozen blond, blue-eyed Americans setting up base operations in a small Thai town and sneaking into Laos? They probably spotted us ten minutes after we crossed over. But it's certainly possible somebody betrayed us ahead of time. Stratton's security on that mission was about as tight as a political rumor in Washington. He even had a reporter and a photographer come to our training camp to document things. Of course, it was on the condition that they wouldn't do a story until we were safely out of Laos—and presumably triumphant.''

''I saw the story,'' said David. ''But there was no mention of Operation Freedom. In fact, I couldn't find anything in the newspapers or magazines about it.''

Caffarelli smiled sardonically. ''Stratton managed to keep the whole fiasco hush-hush. I don't know how.''

''Who did Stratton and Powell think betrayed you?''

''Stratton had his usual paranoid theories—the CIA,

DIA, State Department, drug dealers, the local Rotary Club, you name it.''

"And Powell?''

"Initially, Sean was in general agreement with Stratton—about a U.S. government agency or maybe drug dealers. But later on, he dropped all that nonsense and focused on a businessman named Todd Jennings.''

Ruby leaned forward. "The same guy who Powell claimed had bribed American government officials in an attempt to normalize relations with Vietnam?''

Caffarelli nodded. "I don't know where Sean came up with the bribery stuff, but he seemed pretty convinced. That's why he believed Jennings got word to the Pathet Lao about the mission. Privately run missions into Southeast Asia to find POWs don't fit real well with his normalization agenda—especially if we turn up somebody.''

"Do you think Sean had any real evidence about Jennings's bribery or his betrayal of your mission?''

"That's the strange thing about all this,'' said Caffarelli. "The morning of the day Sean was murdered, he called me. He said he'd finally found concrete, reliable information about just that.''

"Did he say exactly what this information was?''

"No. All he said was that he could finally nail the bastard. He didn't want to talk about it over the phone. He wanted me to come to his house, but I couldn't just then. When I called him later that evening, I didn't get an answer. I left a message on his machine, but I never heard from him again. And then I heard . . . about his murder.''

"Do you think Jennings killed Powell—or had him killed—to keep the information from becoming public?'' said Ruby.

Caffarelli wrinkled his face in doubt. "The thought crossed my mind, but Jennings doesn't strike me as the type of person who would commit murder.''

"Why, because he's rich? We're talking about millions of dollars in corporate profits. I've bailed out guys who've killed over change for a cup of coffee.''

23

The two men in suits and Ray•Bans wanted to talk to Ruby Dark, but David told them she was at the city jail.

"When's she going to return?" asked the taller of the two men. He had dark, short-cut hair and the look of someone who'd just eaten a grapefruit.

"I don't know. The bond won't take long, but I'm not sure if she was going somewhere else afterward. Could be hours."

The man folded his sunglasses and slipped them into his jacket pocket. "We'll wait."

David offered to help if they needed someone bailed out, but that didn't seem to be what they wanted. He wasn't sure what they wanted. They didn't volunteer their names, and when he asked, they repeated that they'd wait for Ruby. They had the look of detectives, though their suits fit better than those of most detectives he knew.

The two men made themselves comfortable while David busied himself with his law books. They didn't disturb him; maybe that was what disturbed him more than anything. He glanced up periodically, but neither said a word. They were so quiet. And patient. They just sat as if they had all day. David wished he had that kind of time.

Ruby arrived forty-five minutes later. Neither man had spoken the entire time. But they were on their feet and speaking as soon as Ruby walked in the back door.

"Ruby Dark?" asked the man with the sour face.

"That's me, hon."

"I'm Jonathan Schell and this is Tom Graham"—he pointed to his shorter, ginger-haired partner. "We're with the federal government, and we'd like to ask you a few questions."

Ruby sized them up as she slung her purse off her shoulder and dropped it on her desk. "The federal government's a big place. Maybe you could narrow it down for me."

"We'd prefer not to."

Ruby squared off in front of them. "Look, hon, I like to know who I'm talking to. You could be from the FBI or the Farm Bureau for all I know. Are you from the Farm Bureau? You don't look like guys from the Farm Bureau. Not that I have anything against the Farm Bureau, understand. I just like to know who I'm talking to."

Both men gave her a stupefied look.

"No, I know," she went on, wagging a finger at them. "You're here to check up on that awful spay-neuter clinic right below us. The government must have an agency to investigate cruelty to animals. I'll swear in a court of law they do all kinds of unspeakable acts to those animals. I can hear their screams right through the floor. My cat won't go anywhere near the place. You oughta check 'em out."

"Let's just say we're from an interested government agency," said the man who had identified himself as Jonathan Schell.

"Interested in what?"

"Ms. Dark, we're here on important government business and we really need to ask you—"

"If it's that important, you can show me some picture ID. or get the hell out of my office. I've got better things to do with my time."

Schell turned to his partner. The redheaded man forced a smile and pulled out his wallet. He opened it and held it out to Ruby. David glimpsed something with a picture on it.

Ruby put on her reading glasses and peered closely at the man's photo. Then she glared at Schell, who coughed up his ID. as well.

"What the hell is the Defense Investigative Service?" she said, reading Schell's ID.

"We are a personnel security investigative service for the Defense Department," said Graham.

"And you're investigating what?" Ruby asked.

"A leak," said Schell.

"A leak. That sounds ominous. You don't hear about many leaks in the government."

"A rumor, actually."

"Ahhh, you're with Rumor Control. Now there's a government job with lifetime security."

The ginger-haired man smiled patiently. "Someone within the Defense Department is spreading a false rumor about the man whose body you recently found"—he glanced at David as if debating whether to include him in the body-finding business.

David tried to remain civil. He didn't want to end up on some government blacklist.

"Well, the guy's dead, if that's the rumor," said Ruby.

"The false rumor is that the man—Sean Powell—was once a U.S. Air Force captain declared missing-in-action in Vietnam."

"That's some rumor if it's true," said Ruby.

"It's not true!" snapped Schell. "It's an outrageous lie. But a federal employee may be involved in spreading that rumor, and we're trying to find out who that individual is."

"Well, I can't help you there, hon. I don't know anyone who works for the federal government. Do you, David?"

David shook his head.

"I take that back," said Ruby. "I *do* know someone in the federal government. I bailed him out a few months back on arson charges. He worked for the Bureau of Land Management, I think. A cushy office job. But they caught him setting forest fires."

"Have you heard anyone making any claims about Mr.

Powell?'' asked Schell. ''Not necessarily from a federal employee?''

''I read in the paper every now and then about people who claim that hundreds of American POWs are still being held captive in Vietnam. Even in Korea.''

''We're talking specifically about Mr. Powell,'' said Graham. ''Have you heard anyone claim that he was once an MIA?''

''You mean besides you two?''

The ginger-haired man smiled tightly. ''Yes, someone besides us.''

''You're authorized to investigate rumors that even *non*-government employees spread?''

''If we believe the source of the rumor originated within the Defense Department, yes.''

''Is this a matter of national security?''

''We couldn't tell you if it was.''

''It must be, or why else would you two come all the way out here to little ole Ruby's Bail Bonds if the rumor was nothing but a rumor that didn't involve national security?''

''We're concerned that the rumor might find wider circulation and reach sensitive families.''

''You mean those families who haven't been real happy about how our country has handled this issue?'' Ruby's voice took a harder edge.

''Ms. Dark, we didn't come here to argue politics with you. We simply want to get to the root of this rumor. We could use your cooperation.''

''So you're not really here to investigate the rumor, you're here to squelch it.''

''We're deeply concerned that should it receive widespread circulation, it might needlessly create more false hopes among families of MIAs. They've been subjected to enough misinformation and hoaxes.''

''Yeah, starting with the Gulf of Tonkin.''

Schell bristled. ''I take it you don't intend to cooperate with us?''

"I think that's the first correct perception you've had since you got here. By the way, where did you get my name?" asked Ruby. "Why do you even think I would know something about this rumor?"

"We're not at liberty to divulge that."

Ruby ushered the federal agents toward the door. "Then I'm not at liberty to cooperate with you, hon. Client confidentiality and all that."

"What client confidentiality?" asked Graham.

"Sean Powell was my client."

The sour-faced man spun to face her. "Powell told you something?"

"That he was an MIA? No, he didn't tell me anything like that. I don't ask that question on my bond app, and he didn't volunteer an answer."

"There was nothing for him to volunteer," said Schell. "Any claim that he was an MIA is total fabrication, and we hope, for the sake of MIA families, that you would not spread such a rumor. I would also ask you to honor our request that this conversation go no further than this room."

"Honor is not something I associate with guys like you."

"Stratton," said David as he watched the men drive off in a light-blue sedan with rental plates.

"What about him?" said Ruby.

"He put those guys up to this. They're just a couple of actors he hired to play government agents. We've seen that stunt before, remember?"

"Why would Stratton do that?"

"To convince us there's some truth to his claims about Powell."

"They had pretty convincing ID."

"You know IDs can be easily faked," said David, surprised by her apparent lack of skepticism.

"I'll check on it."

* * *

David was sound asleep in his garret when the phone rang.

"Ruby's Bail Bonds," he answered groggily, in no mood to run over to the jail to bail someone out.

It was Ruby herself on the other end of the line. "You asleep?" she asked. "It's midday!"

"I was taking a nap. I stayed up late last night to catch up on my studies—no thanks to this Bullet Joe business." David struggled to one elbow and tried to clear the fog from his brain. It was bright outside. He looked at his watch. 1:06 P.M.

"Hollingsworth was found dead this morning," his aunt said.

David sat upright. "The therapist at the Vet Center?"

"Yes. His assistant found him when she came to work."

"Murdered?"

"Multiple stab wounds. Remember that bamboo cage in the meeting room I told you about, the one Hollingsworth didn't like having around? That's where she found him. He was locked inside."

"Jesus."

"He wasn't killed there. He was killed in his office and then dragged to the cage. Apparently he was working late last night. That's when the police figure he was murdered."

"Somebody he was meeting with?"

"Not on his calendar if it was."

"How'd you find out about this?"

"Morgan called me. He heard it on the noon news. They didn't give Hollingsworth's name, but they mentioned the Veterans Center. Morgan remembered that I'd talked to someone there, so he called the investigating detective and got the lowdown."

"You think his murder has something to do with Powell, don't you?" said David.

"Damn right! Four men from his group were involved in Operation Freedom. One was killed by the Pathet Lao, one was murdered, and one's disappeared. Now Hollingsworth's dead. I don't think that's a coincidence, David. I'm certain he knew something about that mission, and he may have known something about Powell that somebody didn't want him to tell anyone else."

"Then I'd vote for Bullet Joe, though I don't know why he'd be killing people over a mission he didn't even go on."

"I still don't believe it's him, David."

"Maybe this isn't the same Bullet Joe you knew, Aunt Ruby. Have you considered that? From what your friend down by the river told us, Bullet Joe was going off the deep end. All these Vietnam flashbacks and his drinking and facing life in prison—he could be insane. It's not like the guy was Mr. Stability to begin with."

"You're buying into the crazy-vet cliché."

"This whole thing about Powell is crazy."

"Then you'll really love to hear what I found out about yesterday's two visitors."

From his aunt's way of thinking, the two men *were* government agents. Not that she had proof. She couldn't confirm that a Tom Graham or a Jonathan Schell worked for the Defense Investigative Service. She couldn't even find mention of the Defense Investigative Service. But she was able to confirm that a Tom Graham matching the general description and age of the ginger-haired man lived in Alexandria, Virginia, just outside of Washington, D.C., and that a Jonathan Schell, a match with the sour-faced man, lived in Chevy Chase, on the other side of D.C.

"Okay," conceded David, "for the sake of argument, let's say they really *are* from the Defense Department. It only proves that Stratton probably opened his mouth more than he should have, word got back to Washington, and they want to stuff a boot in it."

"So they dispatched two federal agents all the way out here just to squelch a farfetched rumor from a man who's been discredited by his own people?" said Ruby.

"Only liberals ever claim the government makes any sense."

"Rumor control or not, they must be damn worried about *something*."

"So what are you going to do?" asked David, knowing that his aunt would never let things just be, even if it was none of her business.

"I'm gonna make a phone call I didn't want to make."

24

"Is this Elizabeth Patterson?"

"Yes."

"My name is Ruby Dark. I'm calling from Denver. I hope I haven't caught you at a bad time."

It was shortly after dinnertime in Iowa.

"Are you selling something?" The voice was high and slightly nasal.

Ruby laughed pleasantly. "No, I'm not selling anything. I run a bail-bond office here."

There was a catch in the woman's voice. "Bail bond? Is . . . is there some kind of problem?"

"No, nothing like that. I'm not calling to ask you to bail out somebody you know. But you may be able to help me with a client I have."

"I don't follow you. What client? I don't know anyone in Denver, except an old classmate from high school, and I don't think she'd be one of your clients. She's a schoolteacher."

Ruby said, "A man who put up bond collateral for a client of mine was murdered two weeks ago. It turns out the name he was living under was not his real name. I'm not sure how to put this delicately, Mrs. Patterson, so I'll just say it: There's a possibility that the dead man may have been your former husband."

The line went silent. David, who was listening to the

conversation on another phone in the office, could hear a television in the background. He kept his hand cupped tightly over the mouthpiece.

"You work for Colonel Stratton, don't you?" the woman said acidly.

"No, I don't," said Ruby. "I found the dead man."

The woman paused, perhaps wondering what it was like to find the body of a murder victim. Take my word for it, thought David, it's an experience in life everyone should avoid.

"You saw this . . . person?"

"Yes."

"And you think this . . . man was once my husband Alex?"

"I don't know. That's why I'm calling you. To try to find out."

The woman's voice flared. "Stratton called me several days ago and tried selling me this same scam. I didn't believe it then, and I don't believe it now. He's put you up to this, hasn't he?"

"He contacted me after he read about the murder in the paper. He gave me your name. He wanted me to call you, but I refused."

"You didn't refuse very well."

"I had no intention of ever calling you, Mrs. Patterson. But yesterday, two federal agents showed up in my office to investigate a rumor that the dead man may be your former husband. And a second man was murdered last night in connection with this same case."

"Oh God."

"Look, hon," said Ruby, "I don't trust Stratton any more than you, but I find it mighty strange that two federal agents would fly all the way from Washington just to squelch a rumor. Usually when you try to stop a leak, there's a leak to stop."

"Not necessarily. They have a mind-set to debunk any reports about MIAs. If they had put as much effort into addressing the MIA issue as they've put into stopping rumors, it would have been resolved years ago.''

''Well, I don't think it's coincidental that the police department here is having an unusually difficult time identifying the dead man.''

''Look, uhhh . . .''

''Ruby.''

''Look, Ruby, my husband disappeared on a helicopter flight in South Vietnam in 1970, and he was declared MIA. He didn't return home in 1973, and the government declared him dead in 1985. I've remarried and moved on with my life. It's obvious to me—and I'm sure to anyone who is halfway sane—that the man you found could not possibly have been my husband.''

''Was your husband's body ever returned?''

There was a long pause, followed by a deep sigh. ''No. But neither were the bodies of many men in Vietnam. It seems to be a function of war and politics.''

''So you have only the government's word that he died in Vietnam?''

''I'm not going to award Brownie points to the Defense Department. They handled this issue with the tact of a brain-damaged wrestler. But at the same time, I'm not going to swallow a ludicrous claim by a certified fraud that my husband somehow escaped and returned to the United States and went into hiding.''

''Did your husband disappear under mysterious circumstances? Was there evidence that he may have been captured alive?''

''Many disappearances in war are under mysterious circumstances. The truth is, the government has never been very forthright about what happened to Alex. For many years I sought answers—unsuccessfully. You may know from the good colonel that at one time I was extremely active in the POW/MIA movement. I was a damn pain in the butt to DIA. I traveled overseas, hounded Communist governments, generally made a nuisance of myself to everyone, including my friends. But the fact is, Alex was in intelligence work, so I'm not surprised by the military's reluctance to provide me with details of his disappearance. God only knows what clandestine mission he was on. I don't say that as an excuse, I'm simply stating the facts."

"You said he disappeared in South Vietnam. Did he ever mention working at a remote radar site in Laos?"

"No. Stratton claimed that, too, but I have no evidence to support it."

"Our government *did* run a secret war in Laos."

Mrs. Patterson chuckled. "It was hardly a secret. But Alex would have told me if he was going into Laos."

"You had a close relationship with your husband?"

"That's none of your business, frankly. But if you mean, would he have kept secrets from me, no, he wouldn't have."

"Did you call the Defense Department after Stratton called you?"

"No. I don't want anything to do with them any more than I do with Stratton or you. I told him to go to hell and I hung up on him—and that's what I'm going to do with you."

"Wait! Please! Call the Denver Police Department. They know who I am. They can vouch for me. I'm not trying to run a scam on you."

David suppressed an urge to chuckle. The cops vouching for a bail-bond agent? They'd sooner vouch for rattlesnakes. Except Morgan Reed. He'd vouch for Ruby to anyone who'd listen.

"Then why are you calling?" The woman's voice was close to tears. "What is it you want?"

"Look, the man who I bailed out skipped. In fact, he's the prime suspect in the murder. The problem is, if I don't find the skip and return him to the courts, I have to fork over the full amount of his bond. The dead man was the cosigner on the bond. His house is the collateral. I may have to foreclose on the house, and if I do, the question of his real identity creates a big problem."

David noticed that Ruby had been careful not to mention that Powell was married.

"It sounds like you run a wonderful business, Ruby."

"I'm not asking you to like me or what I do, hon, though it *is* a legitimate part of the judicial system. But I think you can help end this once and for all."

"I can end it by hanging up."

"I want you to come to Denver to identify the body."

Elizabeth Patterson said nothing.

"I'll pay your airfare and pick you up at the airport," Ruby went on. "It'll take an hour at tops at the medical examiner's, and I can have you back on a return flight before dinner."

"No, no," said the woman. "I'm not going to fly out there to look at a *body*."

"You're the one person who can confirm whether the man was your husband."

"This is the sickest scam I've ever heard."

"It's not a scam, Elizabeth. The body is being held by the county medical examiner. It's official police business. If this man really was your husband, you'd recognize him."

"I don't want to see a dead man. How . . . how was this man murdered?"

"He was stabbed."

"Oh, God."

Butchered would have been a better word, thought David.

"Was Alex around six-one, sandy hair, blue eyes, maybe a hundred sixty-five pounds?"

The woman didn't answer.

"I met him," said Ruby. "*Before* his death, when he put up the collateral for the bond. Does that match his description?"

"In general terms, yes, though the weight's less than I remember. Alex was very solidly built."

"This man wasn't in the best of health. Imprisonment may have done that."

"You could have gotten his description from military records . . . or from Stratton."

"Are there any distinguishing marks that wouldn't be on his military records?"

"None that would do you any good unless you slept with the man."

"Then we need your personal identification."

"I refuse to come there."

"What if I could get a picture of him—either an autopsy photo or a picture from his personal belongings?"

"Photo scams are the oldest trick in the business."

"Then talk to the Denver Police Department. Arrange the photo ID with them. They could work it out with the Cedar Rapids cops or the state patrol."

"I've been burned once. I won't be burned again."

"Burned how?" Ruby asked. "Stratton?"

"No. You've never heard my story?"

"I never heard your *name* until Stratton told me."

"Well, I'm a legend among MIA families about how to be taken for a fool."

"What happened?" Ruby asked softly.

"There was a Baptist minister from Phoenix. His name was Charles Roark. He'd been very active in the MIA movement and had served on the Remember the Pueblo Committee. He claimed he'd been contacted by three Vietnamese intermediaries who said they had information about Alex that could prove he'd been captured by the Vietcong and was still alive. I met with Reverend Roark and one of the intermediaries in Toronto in August of 1982. They showed me a grainy picture of a bearded Caucasian man. He was holding up a board that read, 'May 25, 1982.' I was certain, even with his beard, that he was my husband. I *wanted* him to be my husband. If several other wives or parents had looked at that photo, they would have claimed he was theirs, too. The intermediaries wanted sixty thousand dollars as a down payment for providing tangible proof that Alex was alive. After that, they would begin negotiating his release—which would cost around a quarter of a million dollars."

"What tangible proof?"

"I would write two questions. The answers would be something only my husband and I would know. Intimate facts. Nothing that could be discovered from outside sources. Alex would write the answer in his own handwriting, and his fingerprints would be on the note for further proof. I didn't have the money, of course. I had some savings, but I had to borrow the rest against our house and from friends and family."

"What happened?"

"I was ripped off. I went back to Toronto two months later with the money. They gave me the photo, took my money, and that's the last I saw of them."

"What about this Reverend Roark?"

"Oh, he was extremely sympathetic. He said he'd lost contact with his sources after they returned to Vietnam. He suspected they'd been caught and executed. He said he was trying to make further contacts, but I never heard from him again."

"Did you tell the government about this?"

"Only afterward. I didn't trust them before. I was afraid they'd interfere. I gave them the photo, and DIA eventually traced it to a 1947 edition of *Soviet Life* magazine in the National Library in Phnom Penh. It was the picture of a Soviet farmer."

"You believed the government?"

"I saw a copy of the magazine. The picture was identical, except that the board the man held had something written in Russian, I don't know what—maybe about his beet production that year. Obviously these con men had doctored the photo and added the date."

"Then you need to come to Denver in person," said Ruby.

"I need to do nothing of the kind," replied Elizabeth Patterson, hanging up.

"Damn!" said Ruby.

25

Bullet Joe's parents were right where David and Ruby had left them two weeks before, mildewing in front of the television in their trailer. Fortunately, the trailer wasn't as hot this time around. The weather had cooled off, and there was a fan in the room. Much to David's surprise, the couple to whom Ruby had given the money had actually bought the Browns a big floor-fan. Another surprise was that the canary was still alive, though he still looked as lethargic as he had on the day the temperature hit 101 degrees.

Ruby flicked off the television and faced the couple. "Heard from your son?"

"We told you, Angel, we ain't seen him for a spell," answered Mamma Brown.

"You're sure?"

"Yeah, we're sure," said Eddie Brown gruffly.

"You know Earl's in real big trouble, a lot more trouble than when we talked last time."

The old woman looked down at her hands folded in her lap. "Yeah, the cops were here looking for him."

"Remember what I told you about Earl being on the run? That's how people get hurt. With the cops searching for him—on murder charges—he could get hurt. So if you've talked to him or you know where he's hiding, it's real important you tell me."

"We ain't seen him, Angel," said Eddie Brown. "That's the God's truth."

"It's not God I'm worried about. Now I want you to answer me something else—truthfully. Did Earl ever say anything to you about Operation Freedom?"

The old woman seemed genuinely puzzled, but Eddie Brown's face tightened.

"What's Operation Freedom?" asked the woman, squinting as if to squeeze out a memory.

"It was a mission to get American POWs out of Laos," said Ruby. "It happened about four years ago. Your son was involved."

The woman nodded. "Yeah, I remember Earl telling us about that. I don't recall what he called it. Operation Freedom, is that what it was called? Do you remember, Eddie?"

Anger filled the old man's face. "Sure. A fool name for it. Earl said he was goin' over there with a bunch of other guys to bring back these POWs. Fool crazy is what it was."

"He was real proud of what they was going to do, rescue those men and all," Mamma Brown said.

"He was a fool, woman. Ain't none of 'em alive after all them years. Fool crazy."

She looked meekly at Ruby. "He pointed out on the map where they was going, more or less, where they thought them POWs was. He seemed real proud they was gonna do that. He told us it wasn't dangerous, but we knew it was. We tried to talk him out of it, but sometimes he don't listen. You know how stubborn he is. He told us they needed him. I remember him standing right where you are and saying, 'They need me, Pops.' "

"Yeah, they needed him like they needed two left feet," said the old man.

"But Earl didn't actually go on the mission, did he, because he was arrested before they left?" said Ruby.

"Yes." There was disappointment in the old woman's voice.

"Was Earl working for Jennings Construction at the time?"

Both of them thought for a moment before Eddie Brown said, "Yeah, I guess he was. In fact, they arrested Earl while he was at work. Somebody tipped off the cops."

"He was trying to go straight," said Mamma Brown. "He just found it so hard." Her voice faded.

"Damn war is what it was," said her husband.

"Did Earl tell you who fingered him?"

"No, but I figure it was one of his buddies trying to brownnose the cops," said the old man. "'Course, I can't rightly say I was disappointed they threw him in jail. If he'd gone, he coulda ended up dead or a POW himself. I was right, too. Some guys got killed and one of 'em was captured."

Ruby shot a glance at David and then stepped toward them. "*Captured*? One of the men on the mission was captured in Laos? An American?"

"Yep."

"Earl told you that?"

"Yeah. Two Americans got killed and this other fella got captured. I told you the whole thing was fool crazy."

"How did Earl find out? He was in jail here at the time."

"His friend told him," said Mamma Brown. "Sean. After he got back, Sean visited him in jail. He told Earl. And Earl told us. He made us promise not to tell anyone, 'cause Sean had made him promise not to. But I suppose after all these years, it's okay to tell you."

"Yes, it's okay, Mamma Brown. The man who was captured, was he ever released?"

"I don't know," she said. "Earl never said nothing about it again."

"Do you know the man's name?"

They didn't.

Ruby drew a long breath. David heard only the hum of the fan. Finally, she said, "People on that mission think they were ratted on, like Earl was ratted on, that somebody tipped off the Pathet Lao they were coming."

"Earl told us that, too," agreed Mamma Brown.

"Did he say who may have told them?"

"No. But I think Sean knew," said Mamma Brown. "Earl told us Sean had found out. Earl seemed real upset. He was gonna go see Sean at his house."

"The day Powell was murdered?"

Mamma Brown nodded slowly, as if against her will.

"Did Earl see him?"

"He left here, but I don't know if he went to Powell's house."

"How'd he leave? He doesn't have his own car. Did he leave in your car or borrow somebody else's?"

"He didn't leave in our car," said the old woman. "It wasn't working. Eddie drove it that afternoon—" She turned to her husband. "What was it you went for?"

"A pair of pants. Down at the thrift store on Broadway."

"Yeah, the brown pants, right? And that white shirt. You got a shirt. Still don't fit you right. Anyway, when Earl tried to take the car later, it wouldn't work."

"Loose wires, I guess," said the old man.

"So how did Earl leave?"

They didn't know. "He coulda took the bus or hitched a ride from Indiana Street," said Mamma Brown. "He coulda called a friend. He did that, too, when he had to go places."

"He came back later that day, right? Somebody in a Lexus drove him here. A white Lexus you didn't tell me about. Earl came inside for a couple of minutes and then left in the Lexus. You told me you hadn't seen him in a week."

"Maybe we wasn't here," said Eddie. "We git out now and then, you know."

"But your car wasn't working. That's why Earl didn't drive it. The Hispanic couple said they were working on your car when they saw the Lexus. You were here, hon."

"Maybe we was, then," he conceded.

"Did you talk to Earl when he got back?"

Both people shrugged.

"Did he change clothes before he left?"

Neither seemed to have paid any attention. The way they watched television, thought David, their son could have dragged Powell's bloody body through the living room and they wouldn't have noticed.

26

The Yellow Flower was a small, nondescript Vietnamese restaurant on South Federal, sandwiched in between a laundromat and an office shared by an immigration lawyer and an acupuncturist. Inside were a dozen Formica tables and virtually no decor that hinted of anything Asian. Except for the telltale aromas, the place could have sold chicken-fried steak and biscuits and gravy as easily as it served Vietnamese fare.

It was just after lunch hour and the place was quiet. One table was occupied by two customers, Caucasians, and at another table a middle-aged Asian woman was totaling the lunch receipts. David stood near the front door while Ruby bent over to speak to the woman, who rose and disappeared through a beaded curtain into the kitchen. A moment later she returned with a young man behind her.

The man joined Ruby and David at a table in the back, near the kitchen, where—Ruby had explained to David on the way over—Lanh Ngo washed dishes. She'd bailed him out two years earlier—when he was nineteen—after he was arrested as part of a Vietnamese gang terrorizing local Vietnamese businesses and families.

''Some of the gangs would travel around the country and find their victims by ripping out the page of 'Nguyens' in the local phone book,'' said Ruby. ''Vietnamese families were especially vulnerable because they tended to keep all their cash at home. They didn't trust the local banks—or the police, which was why many of the crimes went unreported. Lanh Ngo was a peripheral member of his gang and ended up doing only a year in county. He's stayed clean since then, as far as I know." She'd seen him now and then since his release, whenever she dropped into The Yellow Flower for lunch or dinner.

"Try their *pho*," suggested Ruby. "It's their traditional noodle soup. It's delicious. Or their *cha gio*. That's an eggroll. You'll like it because it's greaseless." The middle-aged woman went off with their order.

The young Vietnamese man was five-five, with a wispy mustache and a right eye that was milky and motionless, dead to the world. Compliments of a baseball bat in a gang fight, Ruby had told David. Although obviously Asian, the man had taken on a western look, his head shaved along the sides and short hair on top, a small gold loop in his left ear. David wondered how acceptable that was among his fellow Vietnamese.

Ruby asked the man about Sean Powell, his missing Vietnamese wife, and their Amerasian son. Lanh Ngo knew nothing of the murder, had never heard of the woman, and didn't know how to find her. He spoke perfect English, without a trace of accent. Born here? wondered David.

"C'mon, hon," said Ruby. "I know the Vietnamese community is tight and news travels fast. If this woman and her son are hiding in town, people know where they are. Give me a lead."

The young man stirred the ice in his soft drink with his straw. "I know someone who might help."

The Foothills Greyhound Park was nowhere near the foothills, and it was a far cry from a park. It sat on the north side of Denver amid cheap motels, industrial sites, truck lots, refineries, and the foul smell of a nearby stockyard. Any view of the foothills was obscured by huge grain-storage silos.

They bought general-admission tickets and found themselves in a long, gray, cheerless hall below the grandstands and glassed-in clubhouse. One side was lined with betting windows, the other side with snack bars and beer stands. Banks of television monitors hung from the ceiling. Through portals David could see metal bleachers near the track, the track itself, and on the far side, the odds-board whose electronic numbers changed constantly as wagers were laid down. The dog track had seen better days and so had its clientele. A new coat of paint might have helped the crumbling facade, but it wouldn't have helped the clientele, made up mostly of old men wearing baseball caps and nursing beers and cigarettes; young, scruffy-looking men between jobs or killing time before their night shifts; and a few single women. Most of them clutched white racing programs or scribbled furtive notes on yellow tip sheets while standing in a sea of hotdog wrappers and plastic beer cups. This definitely was not the horsey set at the Kentucky Derby, mused David.

In response to Ruby's query, a security guard directed them to the paddock at the far end of the oval track. There the dogs were weighed, walked in circles around fake fire hydrants, and given race numbers. The area was fenced off. Signs warned that only authorized personnel could enter and that paddock personnel were not allowed to talk to spectators. Behind the fence a row of handlers in matching dusty-rose pants and white shirts walked a set of dogs onto the track and down toward the starting blocks.

An electronic trumpet sounded the familiar racetrack refrain, and the announcer called over the loudspeakers, "Three minutes to post. Three minutes."

Ruby flashed her ID at an armed security guard leaning against the fence. She told him who she was looking for. He offered a bored glance at the documents and jerked a thumb over his shoulder in the direction of a dirt parking lot behind the paddock area. "Think I saw the gook drive in not long ago. Got a brown pickup." He motioned to an unlocked gate. "Just don't hang around the paddock."

They went through the gate and left the guard still bored and still leaning on the fence. The parking lot abutted a steel-fabrication company whose yard was cluttered with huge metal tubes that David guessed were used for storm drains or culverts. On one side of the parking lot was a long, open-sided shed leaning precariously on support posts. It was filled with sand and equipment for maintaining the track. The rest of the lot was full of ratty-looking pickups with big spare tires stuck on the backs of custom-built kennels hanging over the sides of the truck beds. Dogs barked from behind louvered windows. The license plates were not only from Colorado but from Kansas, Nebraska, Wyoming, and New Mexico.

Strange, observed David. Despite all the warning signs and the armed guard on the clubhouse side, access to the parking lot was a wide-open, unguarded gate that anyone could drive through from the public parking area that fronted the dog track. From there, it was easy access to the paddock area. So much for security.

Toward the far end of the lot they spotted a dark brown pickup and two men standing by the open slats of a louvered kennel door. Inside, a dog was barking furiously, its shadowy figure banging against the sides and ready to burst out the moment someone opened the door. The bigger of the two men sported a silver ponytail that hung out from under a grimy baseball cap. He dangled a muzzle over the door in front of the dog. The shorter man, dark-haired, with tinted wire glasses, jeans, and a Chicago White Sox T-shirt was holding a plastic cup of beer while he spoke softly to the dog. The agitated animal calmed a little. David couldn't catch what the man was saying to the dog, but as he and Ruby drew closer, he realized that the man was speaking in a foreign language.

"Thang Truong?" Ruby asked the smaller man. A press-on pass on his coat said "Paddock." She pronounced the name slowly, trying to repeat it just as she'd heard it from Truong's assistant at *Quoc Han*, the Vietnamese-language newspaper Truong owned and edited. The woman had said they would find him at the dog track, where he was running his greyhound.

He turned toward them. "I'm Thang Truong," he acknowledged.

Ruby introduced herself and David. The Vietnamese man extended his hand. No bow. Just an American handshake with a firm grip. He introduced the ponytailed man next to him as Matt Murray, the dog's trainer. "And this is Leaving Cheyenne," he said, proudly pointing to the dog inside the kennel.

"I understand you own this dog," Ruby said.

"I own part of her," Truong said. He held his thumb and forefinger an inch apart. "Just a small part. I come every Tuesday afternoon and Saturday night to watch her run. She's a great dog." Truong spoke with an accent, but his English was crisp.

"Yeah, don't that beat all," said the trainer. "He don't know nothing about greyhounds but buys a chunk of this pup, and damned if she don't turn out to be an A-grade dog—fastest bitch in the state, maybe the whole country. Hell, I thought the Vietnamese just *ate* dogs."

Truong seemed to take the insult with equanimity.

"I don't follow the dogs," said Ruby.

She doesn't even *like* dogs, David added to himself.

"I'm looking for a Vietnamese woman. I've been told you're the man to talk to, that you know everybody in Denver's Vietnamese community."

Over the loudspeakers came the announcer again: "It's now post-time."

"Who are you looking for?" asked Truong warily.

"I don't know her Vietnamese name. She goes by Susan Powell."

Truong was suddenly as agitated as the caged greyhound. He took a swig of his beer, his eyes refusing to meet theirs. He glanced at the trainer, who was preoccupied with the dog. Truong moved closer to them and said softly, "You're talking about the woman whose husband was murdered?"

''Yes.'' Ruby gave him a limited summary of her involvement with Sean Powell and Bullet Joe Brown, leaving out Stratton and his MIA claim.

''You think she can help you find this 'Bullet Joe'?'' said Truong.

''Doubtful. But she could help me answer some questions about her husband so I can resolve the bond situation.''

''Many people wish to talk to Susan Powell.''

''The police?''

''Among others.''

''Who else?''

''A Laotian man.''

''A tall, thin guy?'' said Ruby. ''Name of Lo?''

He looked surprised. ''Xiong Pao Lo, yes.'' From the tone of his voice, either he didn't like Laotians, or he didn't like this particular Laotian. ''You know him?''

''Not on a close personal basis. How about you?''

Truong appeared offended. ''I know *of* him. He's not a man I would want to know. He's a drug dealer with strong ties to the Golden Triangle.''

Not quite the heroic picture Stratton had painted, thought David. And why was the Laotian looking for Susan Powell if Stratton wanted Ruby to do his legwork? Was it as simple as the two-people-are-better-than-one approach? Or was Stratton up to something else?

''Did Lo say who he was working for or why he was looking for Susan Powell?'' Ruby asked Truong.

''No. He just said it was important.''

''Anyone else asking about her?''

''A private investigator named Terry Hawthorne.''

''Never heard of him. Why's he looking for her?''

The man smiled. ''You want me to tell you all I know, yet you tell me nothing. Like the others who asked.''

The dog in the cage was growing excited again. The trainer leaned over to talk to her, but it didn't seem to help.

''All right, fair enough, hon. I'll tell you what we

know." Ruby motioned that they should step farther away from the trainer.

A squeaking sound caught David's ear, and he glanced toward a corner of the track visible between the pickups. A mechanical rabbit was noisily sliding along an inside rail and gathering speed. It disappeared around the far turn as the track announcer said, "Heeeerrreeee. . . . comes . . . *Sparky*!" Then David heard the crowd yelling as the dogs sprinted out of the starting gate and moments later barreled into view. They were banked like motorcycle racers in a tight turn, legs churning, dirt flying, as they pursued the mechanical rabbit.

"Thang," said the trainer, "can you settle this dog down? I gotta take her for weigh-in, and she's goin' wild."

Truong went to the louvered window and spoke softly again in Vietnamese.

The trainer shook his head. "Damnest thing I ever seen. I don't understand a word he's saying, and sure as shit the dog doesn't, but it works. Course, you want the dog excited to some degree. You want her to know it's race day. I always short her rations in the morning. She knows then. But you can't let her get too worked up. She'll hurt herself, and she gets so fidgety, it's hard to get her to stand on the scales at weigh-in."

"Where did she get the name Leaving Cheyenne?" asked David.

"The man who owns most of the dog, Kevin Scharf, he named her after a book he was reading the day she was born," said Murray.

"She's fast, huh?"

The trainer laughed. "We started running her last year as a pup in schooling races, and she took to it right away. Won her maidens. Goes out front like no dog I've ever seen. Doesn't make no difference what starting box she's in. She's too fast, really."

"How can a race dog be *too* fast?" said David.

"They get hurt. All the dogs that run really hard eventually get hurt. Don't know when to quit. Get a stopper bone behind a front ankle or drop a muscle or break a hock—damn near anything. That's why we usually keep her to three-sixteenths. The way she runs, the longer lengths would kill her. Won twenty straight races at that distance and she's still just a pup. Mr. Scharf wants to take her to Florida, to the Hollywood Classic. That's where the big money is. Looking for some match races, too, but nobody's got the balls yet to take her on."

"I was thinking about wagering a couple of races before we leave," said Ruby. "You got any hot tips? Besides your own dog?"

"Sure. Bet on the rabbit. He always comes in first." The trainer grinned; obviously he had told this joke many times before.

David decided it wasn't appropriate to ask if it was true that thousands of greyhounds were destroyed each year because of racing injuries, or because they were too slow to be successful racers, or if it was true that training meant young greyhounds chasing live rabbits and tearing them to bits—firing a dog's ambition to race by tasting blood.

Truong had quieted Leaving Cheyenne. "You can take her to weigh-in now, Matt," said Truong.

The trainer swung open the cage door, put the muzzle on the dog, and lifted her out of the kennel. She was a sleek, jet-black greyhound. A fine dog, no doubt, but David never had liked greyhounds—they looked too fragile and patrician for his taste. Once the trainer and the dog were out of earshot, Ruby gave the Vietnamese man a quick synopsis of Stratton's claim that Powell was an MIA.

Truong listened as skeptically as everyone else Ruby had told.

"I know it's a bizarre story," conceded Ruby. "But his wife may be able to confirm whether the story is true or not. I need to find her anyway, since as his widow, she presumably inherits his estate, and I may need to discuss the issue of settling up on the collateral. Apparently, others think she may know something, too. Did this private detective tell you why he was looking for her?"

Truong hesitated.

"C'mon, honey, I've played fair with you."

"He didn't tell me why he was looking for her, but he offered me a lot of money if I would help him. I said I couldn't. Then he threatened to kill my dog. But I still told him I didn't know anything about her."

"Was that the truth?"

The Vietnamese smiled enigmatically.

"Had you ever met this Hawthorne guy before?"

Truong hesitated again, then said, "Yes. He works off and on for a man with whom I've had several run-ins. Todd Jennings."

"My, my, that name sure keeps popping up," said Ruby. "What kind of run-ins?"

"He spearheads an organization that has been lobbying to normalize relations with Hanoi. I've written several editorials, in English papers as well as my own, opposing his efforts. We've had verbal debates as well. The Communists are liars, and America shouldn't do anything that can strengthen their regime."

"I heard Jennings was doing more than spearheading, that Powell had accused him of greasing U.S. government palms to move things along and Powell was trying to get that information public."

Truong looked alarmed. "Where did you hear that?"

"From people who don't want relations normalized any more than you do."

The Vietnamese man turned in the direction of the grandstands, deep in thought. "I too heard this about Sean Powell, and I went to talk to him. He didn't know me, but I promised him that if what he said was true about Jennings, I wanted to publish it in my newspaper."

"Did he show you any evidence?"

"No. We met three times, but nothing was resolved. I think he trusted me, but he still was reluctant to give me the evidence. We are a small newspaper, printed in Vietnamese. He wanted the story published in *The New York Times* or *The Washington Post*."

"When was this?"

"A month before he was killed."

Ruby told him about Stratton's foray into Laos. The editor had heard stories about the mission, but Powell had never told him of any evidence that Jennings had betrayed the mission.

"Did you ever meet Susan Powell?"

"No. I knew she was Vietnamese. In fact, I tried to get him to involve her, because I thought that might help things along. But he wouldn't. He seemed protective of her."

"Protective against what?"

"I don't know."

"You do realize, don't you, hon, that she could have the evidence her husband talked about, and that's why people are looking for her?"

"I'll tell you what I told Lo and Hawthorne," Truong said. "I don't know where she is."

"But you could find her, couldn't you? Maybe Powell told her about meeting with you. If he trusted you, *she* may trust you."

"But that doesn't mean she'll trust *you*," asserted Truong. "You're associated with the American judicial system, and many Vietnamese don't trust that system. Many who fled Vietnam don't speak English well. They don't understand the laws here. And they grew up with corrupt secret police in Vietnam. They see criminals released on bail here, so they are afraid to report anything or testify in court. They assume all police or anyone associated with them are corrupt."

"Look, hon," said Ruby. "A man who knew Powell and who may have known something about all this was murdered the other night. I think Susan Powell is in great danger, and we need to find her before the killer does."

God, reflected David, his aunt was starting to sound as fanatic and paranoid as Mad Dog Stratton.

27

David closed the office blinds to the outside darkness, turned on the desk light, and began riffling through the center drawer of his aunt's desk. He'd done this many times before, rummaging for a pen or paper clip or stamps, but he'd never really searched it. It was his aunt's desk, after all, not his. He glanced over at Alabaster, who lay on a chair watching him. Collateral was nowhere to be seen. Probably sprawled out in the back room on the cool linoleum. He was surprised to see the cat; usually she fled unless her mistress was around.

"What are you, her guard cat?" he said.

Copper eyes fixed accusingly on him.

"Yeah, I know, I know, I shouldn't be doing this. It's an invasion of privacy, right?"

Alabaster's eyes never wavered. David felt as if his aunt was staring at him.

He knew he should be upstairs writing a brief, not nosing through his aunt's desk. But her visit earlier in the day with the Vietnamese editor, her continued captivation over Stratton's claims and Operation Freedom, her inability to dismiss the preposterous notion that Sean Powell was an MIA, and her seeming lacking of interest in the missing Bullet Joe had finally pushed him to this. At least that was his rationale. He didn't know what, if anything, he would find.

But he remembered the night he'd come down late from his room and found his aunt sitting here, intently studying something that she hastily shoved away in the drawer the moment he appeared. He'd noticed, too, her wiping away what looked like tears, a rarity for Ruby Dark.

"She's off the deep end on this one," he said to the silent cat as he rummaged through business cards, Nuggets ticket stubs, news clippings, tubes of lipstick, aspirin tins, tortilla chip crumbs, and the usual assortment of office supplies. "Nuttier than you."

Halfway back in the drawer he found what he guessed she'd been looking at—a tattered, wallet-sized photo of a teenaged boy. It was a head-and-shoulder shot, black and white, taken in a portrait studio. The keylight had caught the top of his dark hair, cut in a flattop. He wore horn-rimmed glasses. A high-school yearbook photo, David surmised from the age of the subject and by the posed, doofus expression on the kid's face.

It was an old yearbook photo, he wagered. For one thing, the white border had yellowed slightly, and the flattop and horn-rims were a clue. But the real giveaways were the black sport coat, white shirt, and narrow, dark tie. No self-respecting high-school student today would wear a coat and tie like that for his yearbook photo.

He flipped the photo over. No date or identification on the back. He flipped it back and held the picture out toward the cat.

"Any idea who this is, Alabaster?"

The cat made no comment.

He studied the photo more closely. Behind the horn-rims, David saw that the boy's eyes were vaguely almond-shaped, not unlike Ruby's. And he had her oval face and high cheekbones.

He knew that besides being half-sister to his father, Ruby had a full brother and sister from his grandfather's second marriage. He didn't know much about her siblings—not even their names. David's father and other immediate relatives didn't talk much about that side of the family, who lived on the "other side" of St. Joseph, Missouri. The brother and sister were younger than Ruby, and she'd left them and her alcoholic mother when she was only sixteen, disappearing for the next twenty-four years until surfacing in Denver a decade ago. By then, she'd married a bail bondsman named Al Dark.

"Her brother?" he asked the cat.

No reply. Just those unwavering eyes.

"What's the matter? You're as secretive as your mistress. Cat got your tongue?"

David laid the photo on the top of the cluttered desk and dug deeper into the drawer. Hell, he'd gone this far, may as well dig all the way. He pulled the drawer until it nearly fell out of the desk, then fished through it all the way to the back.

That was where he found it—all the way in the back: a shiny silver bracelet, identical to the one he'd seen on Stratton's wrist. A name and a date were engraved on the outside surface. The name made him gasp.

"Damn, Alabaster. You should have told me about this!"

"Your brother's missing in Vietnam, isn't he, Aunt Ruby?"

Ruby, at the other end of the phone line, said nothing.

"Stuart Piszek," he went on. "A half-uncle to me, if I figure it right." No one in his family had ever mentioned anything about Ruby's brother going to Vietnam or becoming an MIA, but that didn't surprise David.

"How did you find out?" Her voice sounded distant.

"I'm holding his MIA bracelet. It's got his name and date engraved on it. March twenty-eighth, 1971. That's when he turned up missing-in-action, isn't it? I assume the picture of the boy with the flattop and glasses is him."

"Those are my personal belongings, David. You have no right to go through them." Her gravelly voice was as cold as David had ever heard it. He felt uncomfortable, but he wasn't going to back down.

"You had no right *not* to tell me I have a missing uncle," he said sharply. "Why didn't you say something after we talked to Stratton?"

"I didn't think it was germane to finding Bullet Joe."

"No, of course it's not germane. It just explains why you've been chasing after ghosts instead of Bullet Joe, why you put credence into Stratton's claims, why you're more interested in a dead man than a live skip. You could have said something to me. You could have taken me into your confidence. You could have trusted me."

"It wasn't a matter of trust, David."

"Then what the hell was it?"

"It . . . it was just not something I wanted to talk about with anyone. I didn't even want to talk about it with myself."

David was quiet for a moment. Finally, he asked, "Do you think your brother is still alive, Aunt Ruby?"

"I don't want to discuss this."

"I do."

"Good night, David."

She hung up.

Fifteen minutes later, she called back. Her voice was subdued.

"Come over to my loft. I have some things I want to show you."

Ruby was nursing an iced tea when David arrived. He took the one she offered him.

"I want to apologize, Aunt Ruby," he said, feeling the wet chill of the glass in his hand as he stood by the kitchen counter. "I know I had no right to go digging through your desk. But frankly, you've been acting very strange these last few days, ever since Stratton showed up. I saw you looking at something at your desk the other night, so I . . ."

"Come here," she said. Her voice was commanding, but not cold. She led him to the couch. On the coffee table were spread out a manila file folder, official-looking government documents with thick black lines drawn through much of the text, a picture book on the Vietnam War, and a yellowed newspaper clipping tucked inside a glassine envelope. She handed him the clipping first.

It was a brief article from the daily paper in St. Jo. A date was written in black ink, now partly faded, at the top of the clipping: 4/3/71. The clipping announced that Corporal Stuart C. Piszek, age nineteen, U.S. Army, had been killed in action in South Vietnam. No details were given about exactly where it had happened or the circumstances of his death. His surviving family members were mentioned by name, including Ruby.

"The paper got it wrong," said Ruby as he read it. "Or the Defense Department told them wrong. I don't know which. He wasn't killed. At least not officially. DOD listed him as missing-in-action."

David set the clipping down on the table. "What happened?"

"Stuart was a truck driver. He drove those five-tons, I think. He and another soldier were on a road near Quang Ngai—that's below Da Nang seventy or eighty miles. Delivering medical supplies. Just their truck. They never arrived at their destination. The next day, a patrol found the truck all shot up. Obviously they'd been ambushed by the V.C. The soldier with Stuart was dead. They found him a few feet from the truck in a ditch. But they couldn't find Stuart, even after a thorough search in the surrounding jungle. He'd just disappeared. He only had forty-seven days left on his tour. I . . . I didn't find out about his disappearance until quite a while later. I was . . . I wasn't around at the time."

"That must have been very difficult."

"It was like someone ripping open a wound and never letting it heal. The last time Stuart and I spoke, we'd argued."

Just before you left home? David asked silently. Aloud,

he said, "Did the army ever find out what happened to him?"

"That's the sixty-four-thousand-dollar question."

"What do you mean?"

"For several years, Stuart was listed as MIA. North Vietnam never mentioned his name, and he didn't come home during Operation Homecoming. The military told my parents they had no information, and since he hadn't come home with the others, he was presumed dead. In 1979, they officially declared him dead. Your uncle's name is on the Wall in Washington, D.C."

"My uncle," repeated David softly. He had never personally known anyone who'd died in Vietnam, though he knew a student whose father had been killed there when the student was still the size of a baseball in his mother's womb.

"Did your parents protest his status change?"

"No."

David could tell from her expression what she had left unsaid. "But you objected, didn't you?"

"I couldn't understand why one soldier was left dead at the scene and Stuart was gone. That told me he may have been taken captive."

"Or that he escaped into the jungle during the firefight and died there. Even the search could have missed his body."

"Ever the realist, aren't you, David?"

"Morgan said it's like pea soup. You can't see five feet."

"That's what my parents believed," said Ruby, her voice bitter. "To be honest, it would be the likely scenario. My brother was a feisty kid. He wouldn't have just thrown up his hands in surrender. He would have fought, and what you say could easily have happened. Except for this."

She handed him a photocopy of an official U.S. Army document, the one he had seen on the table with words, sentences, sometimes entire paragraphs blacked out. He read through what was left. Stuart Piszek had been seen alive—at least, it was what a source claimed. It wasn't clear who the source was, so much was blacked out. Presumably the army did not want to compromise the source. A "primary collector," wasn't that what Caffarelli called spies? David also couldn't determine how long after his uncle's capture Stuart had been seen in captivity. Days? Weeks? Months? Years? Or where he'd been seen. A Vietcong prison camp? On a road headed north to Hanoi, where they kept most of the prisoners? There were references to his uncle suffering from a leg wound. He was described as "limping."

He held up the document. "Where'd you get this?"

"Someone gave it to me," she said.

Ruby pulled a manila file from an envelope. She opened it and handed him another official document, a memo, also from the army. Nothing was blocked out here. David read it. It wasn't about Stuart Piszek. It was about Ruby. The lengthy memo chronicled her numerous phone calls and letters with the memo's author, as well as her contacts with other military officials, the Defense Intelligence Agency, and even members of other MIA families. The memo's author also had chronicled what he perceived to be Ruby's state of mind. At various points he described her as aggressive, argumentative, persistent beyond comprehension, hysterical, unstable, and obstinate. The memo was addressed to a Major Robert Friedland and signed by a Lieutenant Peter Waldman.

David laughed to himself. Except for "hysterical" and "unstable," they were descriptions he couldn't disagree with. But they also were characteristics he liked about his aunt—as maddening as they could be at times.

"Who's this Waldman?" David asked.

"Stuart's case officer. The one who communicated with the family."

"Why did he write this about *you*?"

"The military was more concerned about the MIA families than about the MIAs. They treated us like you'd treat a dead skunk you find in your backyard. You know what you do when you find a dead skunk, David? You scoop it up with a long rake, hold it as far away as possible from you, and drop it in the trash."

David put the memo back on the table. "Did you ever show any of this to your family? I mean, especially the report suggesting your brother was captured?"

"No."

David was surprised. "Why not?"

"Would you have, under the same circumstances?"

"Don't answer with a question," he said. "That's a lawyer's tactic."

"My family had already buried him."

"What about your sister? Had she buried him, too?"

"I don't know."

"You didn't talk to her?"

"No."

Was there a touch of regret in his aunt's voice?

"What happened with all this?" said David, sweeping his hand over the papers.

"Nothing."

"No subsequent reports about his being alive?"

"Not that I'm aware of."

"Do you really think he could be alive after all these years?"

Ruby looked away for a long time before she faced him again. "I want him to be. More than anything in the world. But I don't believe he is. He probably died from his wounds. Morgan was right about health conditions being poor . . . infections, that sort of thing. Medical treatment was poor even for the Communists, let alone for their prisoners."

"You eventually quit contacting the military?"

"Eventually."

"When did you take off your brother's bracelet?"

"Years ago."

"Why?"

"It was keeping the wounds open."

David looked into his aunt's green eyes, which she held

steady. She had never let him look so deeply into her before.

Finally unable to hold her gaze, he said, "So when Stratton showed up out of the blue and made these wild claims about Powell, it reopened the old wounds about your brother?"

"I don't think they had ever completely healed."

"How old was your brother when you last saw him?

"Twelve."

"What was he like?"

"He was a great kid. He had a great sense of humor. Always pulling practical jokes. And he loved magic. He wanted to be a magician."

David smiled. "I didn't know sisters got along with their brothers."

Ruby shrugged. "Maybe I didn't. Maybe I've forgotten all that. Maybe I just remember he was my brother."

David rose, went to a window, and looked out on the empty alley below. He wasn't sure how to say what he knew was touchy, but finally he turned to her and said, "I know you said you think your brother's dead, but I keep wondering if . . ."

"If what?"

"If you think there's some chance he came back and is living under an assumed identity—like Stratton claims Powell did."

"Sure, the thought crossed my mind. But I don't think that happened."

"It's just that you've been so . . . *obsessed* with all this business about Powell. You don't even seem to be trying to catch Bullet Joe. I was wondering if maybe . . ."

"Maybe what?"

David felt awkward, but he went ahead anyway. "That maybe you've been obsessed about this because you feel you let your brother down in some way because you left home so young. Maybe if you hadn't left, he might not have gone off to Vietnam and he'd still be alive. That kind of thinking."

Ruby's voice turned cool again. "What are you, an amateur psychologist? Like the memo-writer?"

"I just . . . look, you once told me that guilt is a wasted emotion. We can't undo what we've done in the past, so there's no point in feeling guilty about it. Guilt won't change history."

"It *is* a wasted emotion. I'm not trying to atone for what I did when I was young."

"But this Powell business, Stratton's claims, it's—"

Ruby rose from the couch. "If Sean Powell really was an MIA, and he really *did* manage to escape from Laos and slip back into this country, then I'm not trying to recover the past. The past has stepped into the present."

28

The instructions arrived by messenger this time. Mad Dog Stratton's note said he had new information about Alexander Gage and wanted to talk with Ruby as soon as possible. He no longer trusted her telephone line, however, so the written instructions outlined three meeting options, each one with a different time and place, and a different arrangement for avoiding surveillance. They were to choose an option, call the phone number at the bottom of the paper, and leave the letter of their choice—nothing but the letter—with whoever answered the phone. They were then to destroy the note.

"The man's getting more paranoid by the hour," said David.

"*A*, *B*, or *C*?" said Ruby.

David sighed and looked at the choices again. "*C*."

"You would!" she said, disgust in her voice.

David had picked *C* because he found it the simplest of the three options. But simple may not have been best—at least twice en route, he spotted a light blue sedan with rental plates following them. Two men were in the car. David mentioned his suspicions to his aunt, and twice she deviated from Stratton's written instructions to shake any possible tail.

"I still think those alleged government agents are plants

by Stratton to lend credence to his claims,'' he mumbled.

David also had picked option *C* because the meeting place was a Mexican restaurant, a place he thought his aunt would prefer. But as it turned out, El Taco was, according to Ruby, a tourist trap that attracted the novices who didn't know a genuine tamale from a tire wrench. In fact, when they pulled up to the grandiose pink facade with a large water fountain out front, a tourist bus and a large van from a senior citizens' center were emptying their loads.

In the cafeteria line, David chose a salad and Ruby ordered fried chicken, which looked more appetizing than the Mexican dishes, which were smothered in something that resembled Cheez Whiz. They carried their trays through the crowded, multi-story restaurant, past walls with fake plaster peeling off fake brick, colorful sombreros and serapes hanging from the ceilings, and pots of cacti—as if this was supposed to mimic a grubby little café on the high Sonoran desert. In a relatively isolated corner on the second floor, behind a welter of plants and a support post, they found Stratton.

He was alone and dressed in civvies. The Laotian was not with him.

''You're not a fan of Mexican food, Ruby?'' he said, eyeing her chicken as they took seats opposite him.

''I worship Mexican food, but *that*''—she pointed to his plate—''is not Mexican food.''

Stratton laughed, then said, ''Okay, let's get to it. I've found out that—''

''I've found out a few new things, too, hon,'' interrupted Ruby. She launched into what they'd learned about Operation Freedom and the fact that Stratton had known Sean Powell *before* he was murdered. And that he knew Bullet Joe.

Stratton took Ruby's rapid-fire assault without blinking. It was not the first time he had been under fire, David knew, both in war and with his MIA missions. Men like Stratton were impervious to criticism—or reason.

When she'd finished, Stratton swore that he hadn't

known until Powell's death that the man was anyone but a Vietnam veteran with a deep, abiding concern for the POW/MIA issue. He conceded that two Americans had died on the mission into Laos, but he vehemently denied that a third had been captured by the Pathet Lao. "That's a lie spread by people out to bury the truth about what our government did to the brave men who fought in Vietnam." He also dismissed any speculation that Todd Jennings had betrayed Operation Freedom and murdered Powell to keep the fact secret. The mission had been sabotaged, contended Stratton, by the CIA and Drug Enforcement Agency, who were running drug operations in that area.

David looked at him in dismay. "You're saying our own government betrayed your mission?"

"Remember what I told you about General Pao and his CIA-supported heroin operation? That continued after the war, even with the Communists in control. The DEA joined the CIA in running drug operations to fund off-line covert operations. Several private POW missions into Southeast Asia have been sabotaged because they could compromise the drug operations."

Ruby cut in. "It seems rather odd, Colonel, that your mission would have been betrayed because of drug operations, considering the fact that your Laotian buddy is himself a drug dealer with Golden Triangle connections."

"That's bullshit!" flared Stratton, raising heads at nearby tables. "Where the hell did you hear that? Xiong Pao is not involved in drug running and I defy anyone who claims otherwise to prove it!"

"Proof seems to be a short commodity in your world," said David. "Do you have proof that your mission was sabotaged by the CIA?"

"No. But I think Sean may have found the proof. That would explain why he was murdered."

"By DEA or CIA agents? You've *got* to be kidding," said David.

"Did they kill Hollingsworth, too?" asked Ruby.

"I heard about that," Stratton said.

"Did you know him?"

"No."

"Did he have anything to do with Operation Freedom?"

"No."

"People who were connected with the mission are dying or have disappeared, hon. And whether it was the DEA or Todd Jennings or Santa Claus who tipped off the Pathet Lao, I suspect you were ratted out by someone inside who knew about your mission."

"They were handpicked people! None of them would have jeopardized the mission!"

"Somebody let the cat out of the bag, intentionally or unintentionally."

Stratton had no reply.

"Okay, so what's this *new* information you claim to have about Powell?" asked Ruby.

The colonel's face brightened. "My source in the Defense Department says the Defense Intelligence Agency—along with the rest of the military, the State Department, the White House, the FBI, the CIA, *and* a few security groups you've never heard of—have been rooting under every stone they can find for information about Alexander Gage. They've turned up an Air Force intelligence officer who was friends with Gage during the war. This officer now claims that Gage talked to him—*in Saigon*—in March of 1975, four and a half years after Gage disappeared and just a month before PAVN tanks rolled into the city. The officer was shocked when Gage showed up on his doorstep. He knew Eagle's Eye had been overrun and that Gage and the rest of the airmen were presumed dead, since they hadn't been released in 1973. Apparently, Gage wouldn't tell him where he'd been held or how he'd escaped, or the fate of the other men—or how he'd gotten into Saigon. He refused to discuss any of it. Gage only seemed interested in how he could secretly get himself and a Vietnamese woman companion out of Saigon and into the United States."

"A *Vietnamese* woman? Susan Powell?"

"They don't know who she was. But I'm sure they can add like you can, Ruby. I'm sure they've got people looking for her here."

"Yes, a lot of people seem to be looking for her," said Ruby, "including your buddy, Lo."

Stratton smiled. "A good officer sends out more than one patrol if the enemy is near."

"In case one patrol gets ambushed?"

"I thought we were on the same side."

"My problem is, hon, I don't know what your side is."

"I hate to interrupt," said David, "but I want to know how the hell Gage got from a supposed prison camp in southern Laos to Saigon in the middle of a damn war? Bus? Rickshaw? Rescue chopper? What? He didn't say *anything* to this intelligence officer?"

"No. Nobody knows," said Stratton, "or they're not telling."

"What did the intelligence officer do?" asked Ruby.

"Apparently, he told Gage how to get out. Not that it was difficult. Saigon was in complete chaos just before it fell. There were hundreds of refugee flights leaving Tan Son Nhut Airport those last days. When they landed at California air bases, if you were Caucasian or black, you were waived through immigration. It would have been easy for Gage to fly in, walk right off the base, and disappear. That's how a lot of deserters came home. No doubt some of the government's official MIAs were really deserters. When Saigon fell, they got out and sure as hell didn't tell anyone. That, of course, is the official line our government will take when all this shit about Gage hits the fan. They'll brand him a deserter. Except we know different, and I intend to make damn sure that everyone in America comes to know it."

"Why didn't this intelligence officer say something to his superiors back in 1975?" asked Ruby. "Why keep it a secret all these years?"

"He claims Gage swore him to secrecy. Gage told him he was on a government black-box operation that he couldn't discuss. The guy figured Gage had gone over to the CIA. It would have been convenient for Captain Gage to die in the war and then assume a new identity. Not the first time the CIA has killed someone on paper in order to launder a new agent. The officer said he never saw Gage again, and he never said a word to anyone for what he assumed to be reasons of national security."

David guffawed. "This is too damn bizarre."

Stratton ignored David and turned to Ruby. "Find Susan Powell. She's got the answers. Maybe then you'll find out that all this is not as bizarre as you think."

29

David had just returned from a night class and was dumping dog food from a bag into Collateral's huge plastic bowl when Joseph Caffarelli walked into the office. *Stumbled* into the office might have been a better description. The man looked as if he had guzzled a load of Cambodian Cluster Bombs. His clothes were rumpled, his eyes bloodshot, his skin waxy, his hands shaky. From his appearance, he couldn't get a job cleaning his corner office, let alone running the company's marketing operations.

At first he said nothing to David as he surveyed the office with unfocused eyes. The view of police headquarters out the window caught his attention. He stared at it for a long time. Maybe he was comparing its view with the more impressive one from his own office, David speculated. Maybe he was contemplating a visit there. Then again, maybe he was staring at nothing in particular.

The executive finally directed his attention toward David, who still held the bag of dog chow in one hand. "Where's Ruby?" he asked.

"I don't know. I just got back myself."

"I need to . . . I need to talk to her." There was no self-assuredness or cockiness in his voice, only the slurring of words.

"It's pretty late. What's the problem?"

"Earl Brown called me tonight."

David promptly telephoned his aunt at her loft. There was no answer. He tried her pager. She phoned back immediately on her cell phone but she didn't say where she was. He conveyed to her what Caffarelli had just told him.

"Sit on him. I'll be there in twenty minutes."

Twenty minutes? Where was she—at a restaurant? A jazz joint? Morgan Reed's bedroom?

Ruby arrived in exactly eighteen minutes, according to David's watch. By then, Caffarelli was slumped in a chair. He'd said little while they waited for Ruby, and he was dozing when she arrived.

She strode in briskly and tossed a straw hat onto her oak hat rack. Caffarelli barely stirred. She glanced quizzically at David, then walked to Caffarelli and said—loudly enough to wake the dead—"Bullet Joe called you?"

The executive jumped at the sound of her voice. "I hate that name," he mumbled.

"So does his mother. What did he want?"

Caffarelli drew himself up a little in the chair. "He wanted to meet me."

"Where?"

"I don't know. We didn't get that far. I told him I wouldn't meet with him unless I could bring the police. He wouldn't do that."

"Where was he calling from?"

"He didn't tell me."

"A pay phone? A bar? Any noise in the background to give you a clue? Cars? A baseball crowd?"

"A pay phone somewhere, I suppose. It had that kind of echoing sound. Not a clean line like from a home or office. But that's all I could tell."

"He say anything—*anything* to give you a clue where he might have called from?"

Caffarelli bent over and stared at the floor, but he said nothing.

"*Think!*" snapped Ruby.

Still Caffarelli said nothing.

"All right, let's try it from a different angle, hon. Repeat to me exactly what he *did* say."

"He didn't say much. He was drunk."

"You don't look any more sober than he sounded."

"I'm not. But I was when he called."

"Why did he want to talk to you?" said Ruby.

"I don't know. Maybe he just wanted to talk. Drunks do. I know about that. Sometimes they just need to talk. No particular reason other than to hear their own voice. Hear your own voice, you know you're still alive."

"But why call *you*? If he only wanted to hear his own damn voice, he coulda sat in a bar and done that—it's what bartenders are paid for. Bullet Joe has talked to bartenders most of his life. In his situation, that woulda been a lot less risky than calling you."

"Look, I didn't psychoanalyze the man."

"He must really trust you to call and ask you to meet him."

Caffarelli was still hunched over in the chair, still staring at the floor. It was a nice oak parquet floor. David worried that he might throw up on it.

"Why did he trust you, hon?" badgered Ruby.

"He knows me. He's part of our group. You know that. A fellow vet."

Ruby leaned over him until her mouth was near his ear. "But why *you*? I didn't have the impression you two were buddies. He coulda called others in the group if he just wanted to chat. Doesn't he know the other guys?"

Caffarelli sat upright again, his upper body weaving for a moment before he righted himself. But he continued to be at a loss for words.

"Did Bullet Joe want to turn himself in?" pressed Ruby.

"I told him to. He said he couldn't."

"Why not?"

"He wouldn't say."

Ruby stepped away from him. "What other coherent things did he say? Anything about Hollingsworth's murder?"

The mention of the dead therapist seemed to sober Caffarelli. A shiver rippled through his body. ''He knew about it,'' he said, his voice as pale as his skin.

''You discussed it with him?''

''I wouldn't say *discussed.* I asked him if he'd heard about Sam, and he had. That's all he said. We didn't talk about it anymore.''

''Helluva subject not to talk about. How long were you on the phone with him?''

''Just a few minutes. Even drunk, he finally figured out I wasn't going to meet him alone, so he hung up.''

''How long ago did he call?''

Caffarelli looked at his watch. ''Two . . . three hours, maybe. I'm not sure.''

''Did you call the police?''

''No.''

''Why not?''

''What could I tell them? I didn't know anything more than I did before Earl called, other than the fact that he's still around town, which isn't big news.''

''You coulda agreed to meet him. You coulda said yes and arranged it, then called the police. That woulda been the smart thing to do.''

''I guess I was too shocked by his call,'' he said in a low voice. ''I didn't think about that.''

''He's wanted for suspicion of murder, hon. I don't think he did it, but he's still wanted. And he sure as hell is a convicted, habitual criminal looking at life in stir. You shoulda thought about it. You shoulda called the cops.''

Caffarelli looked numb. ''I couldn't do that to him, lie like that and bring the cops. Not to one of our own.''

Ruby was back in his face again, forcing him to look up at her. ''So if you wouldn't turn him in and you wouldn't tell the cops he called, why the hell are you here telling us?''

Caffarelli blinked his bloodshot eyes. ''Fuck if I know.''

''Sit there. I'll make some coffee.''

Ruby put on some mellow jazz, then ground fresh coffee

beans and put them in the coffeemaker. She didn't offer Caffarelli any of her hot Mexican snacks, no chips doused in salsa with names like Buckshot or Snakebite, or pickled *habañeros* or red chile pistachios. That probably was a good thing, David decided, unsure of just what chemical reaction might occur inside a man with so much alcohol in his system.

The coffee brewed, and the air filled with its aroma. When it was ready, Ruby gave Caffarelli a cup and let him nurse it for a few minutes.

She hadn't asked him further questions, but suddenly he began to talk, as if someone had turned on a switch.

"I . . . I picked Earl up not far from Sean's house."

"What?" responded Ruby. "When? Tonight?"

"No, no. The day Sean was murdered. Earl called me from a pay phone, and I picked him up a few blocks from Sean's house. Not at my office like I told you, but in front of a nearby Safeway. I didn't realize how close it was to Sean's house until much later. I never knew exactly where Sean lived. That's when I . . . when I knew I may have helped a killer escape."

"Why do you think Bullet Joe's a killer?"

"What he said that day in my car. He said, 'I've done something horrible.' "

Caffarelli paused to sip his coffee, so Ruby asked, "Did he say what he did that was so horrible?"

"No. I asked, but he wouldn't tell me. He just kept repeating that it was horrible, like he was in a trance. He was very shaky. His hands were trembling, like an old man with a bad case of palsy. I assumed at first it was one of his nightmares. He'd been having flashbacks lately. He talked about them at group. But when I thought about it after I learned about Sean's murder, I realized that he was just plain frightened. Terrified."

"He didn't say anything about Powell being dead?"

"No."

"When did you pick him up?"

"Late in the day, on Sunday. Maybe five-thirty or six."

"At Safeway?"

"Yes."

"Did he have blood on him?"

"On his right hand. I asked him about it, and he said he'd cut himself on a piece of glass."

"Any blood on his clothes?"

"None that I noticed, but I didn't inspect him, either. I checked the car seat after he left and didn't find any."

"You drove from the Safeway, where you picked him up, directly to his parents' trailer?"

"Yes."

"Where he changed clothes and came out carrying a plastic grocery bag?"

Caffarelli nodded and took another sip of his coffee. He cupped it with both hands, as if it were the only thing solid in his life.

"You told us before that you didn't ask what was in the plastic bag. Still stick with that?"

"He said they were old shirts he was giving to a friend. I didn't pry anymore, and I didn't look in the sack."

"You also told us you drove him from the trailer to a street corner in Lakewood and left him there. But that was a lie, too, wasn't it? You drove him down by Coors Field, didn't you?"

"Yes, I dropped him off by some railroad tracks and got the hell out of there. That's the last I saw of him, I swear."

Ruby paced the office for a moment before she turned again to Caffarelli. "Why would Bullet Joe have killed Sean Powell? You said they were friends."

"They were. It just looked so bad . . . later, I mean, when I realized he'd been near Sean's home. Maybe he wasn't in his right mind at the time."

Ahhhh, mused David, the post-traumatic-stress-disorder defense.

"Try this on, hon," said Ruby. "What if Bullet Joe betrayed your mission into Laos, Powell finally found out, and that's why Bullet Joe killed him?"

Caffarelli frowned. "I don't know. Sean never said Earl was involved. Only Jennings."

"But what if Bullet Joe *was* the one who told Jennings?" said Ruby. "Maybe he was worried that Powell would link Jennings to him."

"I don't know. I don't know."

"You don't seem to know much of anything, hon. Tell me if you know this: You told us two Americans were killed during Operation Freedom? But Sean told Bullet Joe that a *third* man was captured by the Pathet Lao. Is that true?"

Caffarelli looked up, startled. "He wasn't sup—" He instantly stopped short and once again fell silent.

Ruby leaned in. "Wasn't supposed to what? Tell anyone that one of your men was captured? Is that the awful secret everyone on the mission has been covering up?"

Caffarelli was sober enough now to comprehend the horror of her question. He mumbled something, but it was too weak for David to hear.

"What did you say?" prodded Ruby.

He spoke louder this time. "Yes, it's true."

"A man was captured?"

"Yes."

"What happened?"

Caffarelli lifted his head. David had never seen so much emotional pain in a man's face. "The initial firefight caught us by surprise, and we were scattered for a while before Sean and I could get us reorganized. That's when they captured him. I saw them take him."

"Who was he?"

"Ray Perry. He'd been a chicken hawk in 'Nam and flew choppers commercially in Pennsylvania."

"You left him behind?" said Ruby.

Caffarelli winced at her words, and his voice continued trembling as he spoke. "It was that, or get us all killed or captured."

"Did they ever release him?" asked David.

"No. I don't know if they kept him as a prisoner or

executed him after we got away. But they never released him. At least not that I know of, and I think I would have heard.''

''Did our government do anything diplomatically?'' asked David.

''I suppose you could call it that. It wasn't much of an effort. They found out about the raid right away. There was a third-country intercept, probably by a Thai intelligence station, of a Lao radio transmission saying they were chasing Caucasians. Our government was pretty pissed off at us, but supposedly they made diplomatic inquiries about Ray. Vietiane denied they had anybody. That was it. I think the U.S. lack of pressure was a way to discourage other private operations.''

''But you told us the mission had government backing,'' said David.

''Unofficially, yes. But only as long as things went well. You can bet if we'd brought out anybody, the U.S. government would have taken credit. But this was one of those *Mission Impossible* deals—if something goes wrong, we'll disavow any knowledge of your actions.''

''I'd have expected the Laotian government to make a fuss about it if they'd actually captured the guy,'' speculated David. ''You know, complain about the raid and hold the guy up as proof.''

''Yeah, if he was alive, you'd think they would have,'' Caffarelli said gloomily.

30

"David!" Ruby yelled up the stairs to his garret.

"What?" he yelled back. He was scribbling notes for a brief he would compose later in the evening on the office computer.

"Come down. I need you to go with me."

David came to the top of the stairs. "I'm studying, Aunt Ruby. What's so urgent?"

"That Vietnamese editor just called. Thang Truong. He's located Susan Powell. She's willing to talk to us. But we need to go right now."

"What's their rush?"

"I don't think they want to give us time to involve the cops. Truong said if he sees any police, the deal's off. He said she's very frightened. We may not get a second chance."

David flicked off his desk light and hurried downstairs.

"Where is she?" he asked on the way out the door.

"I don't know. We're meeting Truong. He'll take us to her."

David scanned the street for a light blue sedan and two federal agents as they pulled out of the parking lot in Ruby's Lamborghini, but he saw no sign of them. He said nothing to his aunt. He didn't want to admit his paranoia, though he noticed that she, too, seemed to check her rearview and side mirrors more often than usual.

A few minutes later, she pulled up on the west side of a Sears store. They parked, then walked through the store and out the other side.

Truong was waiting for them in a white four-door Mazda in the parking lot on the east side of the store. Once they were settled in his car, he drove north, past City Park and into the predominately black neighborhood around Martin Luther King Boulevard. All along the way, Truong slowed down at intersections, then suddenly accelerated through yellow lights so that his was the last car across.

Light was fading when they parked in front of a complex of dilapidated triplexes set back from the street. Several men of Asian background lounged in chairs and smoked cigarettes while they kept tabs on the kids playing in a grassless yard. It was still muddy from rain the night before. The buildings were in disrepair, the rain gutters and downspouts broken, the paint peeling, windows boarded up, doors poorly hung on their hinges. Yet bright flowers grew in boxes or patches of dirt in front of nearly every apartment.

Truong led them to a unit where an old man sat alone outside the front door. He and Truong exchanged barely perceptible nods. Before Truong could knock, the door was opened by an old woman. The threesome hurried inside to find themselves in a semi-dark living room, the shades drawn and only a small lamp for light. David was struck by three contrasting smells: One was the stale, imbedded odor of cigarette smoke; another was a musty, moldy odor he couldn't put his finger on; the third was the far more pleasant aroma of cooking. The kitchen lay straight ahead, where the old woman had gone after closing the front door behind them. Beyond her was the back screen door, and beyond that, a small, fenced-in yard that was all vegetable garden.

"God, where's the water coming from?" said Ruby, looking down at her feet. That was when David realized that the moldy odor was from the soggy carpet under his feet. He pressed his toe hard against the shag, and it leached water.

"There's a leak somewhere," said Truong. "They don't know where. They tell me it's been this way for two months. The owner won't fix it. It's a disgrace. He won't fix anything. Toilets are cracked, the linoleum floors are rotten, the roofs need repair, and the wind blows through cracks in the doors. And you saw the state the yard is in. The owner won't seed it. The only time anyone sees him is when he and his wife come around the first of every month to collect the rents. He never leaves an address or phone number. That's so city inspectors can't find him. He owns several properties like this."

"Why don't the tenants move somewhere else?" said David.

"The rent's cheap. It's all they can afford."

They're probably illegals, afraid that another owner might ask, speculated David.

A middle-aged woman entered the room. She was Asian, but her black hair was cut short and layered in an American style, and she wore an American-style dress. Her small, dark eyes flitted from David and Ruby to the front door and back again. Truong spoke to her in Vietnamese, and she relaxed slightly.

Truong introduced her as Susan Powell. She offered a restrained smile and no handshake. Truong motioned for David and Ruby to take seats, but Ruby remained standing.

"May I see some identification, Susan?" Ruby said.

The woman looked questioningly at Truong.

"This *is* Susan Powell," said Truong, offended.

"I'm sure she is," said Ruby. "But I don't know her. I've never seen her picture. I just wanna make sure she's who she claims she is."

"What . . . what kind of identification?" Her voice was small and faint, her English clear but laced with an accent.

"Preferably something with a photo. A driver's license will do."

The woman disappeared into the bedroom and came back

carrying a black purse, from which she pulled a loose driver's license.

Ruby examined it. "Thank you. I know you only as Susan Powell. What's your Vietnamese name?

"Mai Lon Chu."

David wasn't sure he could pronounce the name, but he liked its melody.

"Which would you rather we call you, Susan or Mai Lon?"

"Susan. I'm Susan, now."

"Okay, Susan it is," said Ruby.

Ruby, Susan Powell, and Truong sat down. The woman put her purse on a small table and dug out a cigarette, which she lit with a ceramic lighter.

"I know this is difficult for you, hon, and I know you're frightened. But it's very important that we ask you some questions. I need to find out more about your husband and about his murder."

The woman nodded for Ruby to go ahead.

"First question: Do you know who killed your husband?"

The woman shook her head adamantly as tears welled in her eyes.

"Where were you when he was murdered?"

"At a friend's house."

"Here?"

"No."

"She hasn't stayed in the same place longer than three days," added Truong. "They're not staying here. It's only a meeting place."

"They" were Susan and her twenty-year-old son, Allen. Sean Powell's son. He and his mother had gone to the friend's house on the day Sean was killed because he had sent them away. Someone was coming to see him—someone he needed to meet alone. He hadn't told his wife or son who or why. They'd returned late in the evening, around nine or nine-thirty.

"Your husband was already dead?" Ruby asked.

A shiver ran through the woman's body, and her eyes seemed to disappear as she managed a small nod.

"Why didn't you report the murder to the police?"

Susan drew hard on her cigarette before answering. "Sean told me never to trust the police . . . or anyone in the government."

"Is it more than that, Susan?"

"What do you mean?"

"Who else are you frightened of? Besides the police?"

No reply. Ruby ran through names: Bullet Joe Brown, Caffarelli, Stratton, Jennings, Hawthorne. Susan had met Bullet Joe once, but she'd never heard of Caffarelli or Stratton. Her eyes hardened at the mention of Todd Jennings and Hawthorne. She'd heard Jennings's name during an angry phone conversation a day or two before Sean's murder. She hadn't caught her husband's words, only Jennings's name. Sean had hung up when she entered the room.

"Who was he talking to?" asked Ruby.

"I don't know. He wouldn't tell me anything. He said it was nothing. But I could tell he was—what's the word?" She said something to Truong in Vietnamese.

"Edgy," said Truong.

"Yes, edgy. He had been edgy the last few days. But he wouldn't explain why."

She knew from Truong and others that Hawthorne was a private investigator looking for her, but she didn't know why.

"I think you do," said Ruby.

The woman averted her eyes.

"I think your husband's murder is linked to his past," continued Ruby, "and I think you know what that past involves. It's from a very long time ago—twenty years ago."

Susan Powell's eyes grew wide.

"Let me put it this way, hon. Did you ever know your husband by any other name—besides Sean Powell?"

The Vietnamese woman whispered to Truong. David

tried reading the woman's face as Truong whispered back, apparently trying to reassure her.

At last, Susan turned to Ruby. "Yes, I knew him by another name. His real name was Alexander Gage."

David heard his aunt sharply suck in her breath. Or was it his own?

Susan said she'd first met Gage in the fall of 1972 in Laos, where he was a prisoner of the Pathet Lao until his escape in early 1975.

"Jesus," David said.

"Did he ever tell the U.S. government about any of this?" asked Ruby.

The woman shook her head.

"Did you know he had a wife and family here in the United States? And that they don't know he came back alive?"

She nodded sadly. "Yes."

Ruby leaned back. "My God, how did he escape? And *why* did he sneak back into this country and never tell a living soul? Why didn't he contact his family? Why did he assume a false name?"

The woman turned to Truong and after their exchange, he said to Ruby, "She wishes to tell you everything she knows about that time, but it is a long, complex story and will be easier for her to speak in Vietnamese. She has asked me to translate."

Ruby hesitated.

"I will interpret faithfully," insisted Truong. "She can stop at points and repeat slowly in English, if you prefer. But please let me interpret the story for her."

"Okay," said Ruby.

31

The early part of Mai Lon Chu's story paralleled—David was loath to use the word "confirmed"—the information Mad Dog Stratton had sketched out for them at the hotel: Captain Alexander Gage was in charge of an Air Force radar site on a remote, heavily defended mountain in northwestern Laos, near Sam Neua, on the edge of the North Vietnamese border. On June 5, 1970, following a dangerous night assault, the Pathet Lao, with the aid of North Vietnamese regulars, overran the site and captured ten Americans—three others were killed in the firefight, along with most of Vang Pao's Hmong tribesmen guarding the site.

However, it wasn't until two and a half years later, in the fall of 1972, that Mai Lon Chu first met Gage and the other Americans. She was a cook with the People's Army of Vietnam, though her duties sometimes extended well beyond what a woman of the revolution should have had to endure at the hands of men fighting for that revolution. But it was wartime, and she had no choice but to submit or be shot.

The unit she was assigned to had been sent into Laos to relieve the PAVN unit that was guarding the Americans jointly with the Pathet Lao. When Mai Lon's unit caught up with the POWs, they had been moved well south from where they'd first been captured and held. The Pathet Lao had driven Vang Pao's Hmongs as far south as Vientiane, and the POWs had moved with the victors. When Mài Lon met them, they were being held in two large limestone caves east of Tchepone in southern Laos, not far from the Ho Chi Minh Trail and the northwest border of South Vietnam. The caves lay under a three-story-high rock overhang that was virtually undetectable by air.

Mai Lon didn't understand why the PAVN was involved in the imprisonment, other than the fact that Hanoi ran much of the show in Laos. It didn't take a lot of manpower or skill to guard the ten Americans, most of whom by that time had lost forty or more pounds and were weak from ailments ranging from dysentery and malaria to malnutrition, pneumonia, and, of course, the random beatings administered by camp guards.

In truth, the physical abuse inflicted at the camp was minor when compared with the brutal interrogations conducted by North Vietnamese intelligence in the days immediately following the capture of the radar site. They focused their cruelest attention on Gage, commander of the site, and left him with a broken arm that never healed properly. What information, if any, they tortured out of him or the other men, Mai Lon didn't know. Gage never spoke of it to her, even years after she joined him in America.

In late spring of 1973, the American prisoners were told of the Paris Peace Accords and that nearly six hundred of their comrades had returned home. But these men would not be joining them, insisted the Pathet Lao commander, a short, chubby man the POWs had nicknamed Little Hitler. He claimed that the American government knew of their existence, but the Nixon administration had already reneged on its agreements with the Lao Patriotic Front for reconstruction aid and was more interested in hurriedly exiting the war than in securing the return of its own military personnel. As long as the American government refused to cooperate, Gage and his fellow Americans would remain prisoners of the Pathet Lao.

Gage accused the Pathet Lao commander of lying and

managed to deliver several blows to Little Hitler's face before the guards beat Gage senseless.

Four months later, a gloating Little Hitler handed Gage a copy of *The New York Times* dated March 30, 1973. It carried the full text of President Nixon's address to the nation, in which he asserted that, "For the first time in twelve years, no American military forces are in Vietnam. All of our American POWs are on their way home."

Mai Lon was surprised that the *Times* could be obtained and delivered so deep into Laos, considering the difficulty of getting sufficient food supplies. But there seemed to be no doubt among the Americans as to its authenticity, and the shock of Nixon's statement was as severe as if food supplies had been completely cut off. The prisoners' health deteriorated over the next several months, the men growing weaker and increasingly despondent. Mai Lon tried to fortify them by sneaking in extra food—heavy, sticky Laotian rice caked into round balls, hot red peppers, and the rare piece of fruit—or deer meat, if one of the guards got lucky with his rifle. She even siphoned off provisions of the camp guards, a bold act that could have resulted in severe beatings—or execution—if she'd been caught. The extra rations, however, seemed to help only the Americans' bodies, not their spirits.

Gage and his second in charge, a hulk of a man named Davidson, were the only two who managed to keep their spirits up. During this period, Mai Lon became friends with Gage and the others. The camp commander had no objection—in fact, he encouraged it, then debriefed Mai Lon after each of her conversations with them. Initially she assumed that he hoped the Americans would divulge information that the PAVN hadn't tortured out of them earlier. Yet it seemed unlikely that any intelligence information they divulged to her—none of which even hinted about the operations they'd conducted atop the mountain—would serve any useful purpose at this point, since the war with America was over. But the lack of intelligence data did not discourage Little Hitler; Mai Lon soon realized that he was seeking personal information to use to control his prisoners—and perhaps to pass on to the Pathet Lao and North Vietnamese hierarchy to help them achieve their political ends.

Alexander Gage understood this. He was an intense, self-assured man, even under the incredible cruelty to which he was being subjected. In their hours together, he and Mai Lon talked and argued about many subjects—philosophy, science, American movies, politics, literature. A university student in Hanoi when she was recruited to fight in the war, she found the discussions with Gage stimulating, especially in the midst of such miserable surroundings. She found Gage surprisingly learned for an American soldier. He spoke decent Vietnamese, and she knew some English, so they managed to communicate reasonably well.

During his captivity, Gage never spoke of his personal life. He knew that Mai Lon was being debriefed by his captors, and he understood the risks of divulging to the enemy any information that could be used against him or the other men. A smart enemy could use a man's family as an effective weapon against him—far more effectively than beatings or torture or threats of death. A man's family could be used against the one thing that kept a prisoner alive: his heart.

It was not until later, after their escape from the Pathet Lao, that Gage told Mai Lon of his family—his wife, Elizabeth, their two children, Terry and Shawn, and his hunting dog, a black lab named Whizzer, who had died of liver disease just before Gage's departure for Vietnam.

As Mai Lon Chu related her story, David noticed that her voice was stronger than when she had spoken in English. The problem with her speaking Vietnamese and Truong's translating was that David found it difficult to assess the tone behind her tale—and whether it was matter-of-fact or full of lies. David tended toward skepticism, as he had from the beginning. For all he and his aunt knew, the woman seated innocently across from them—somber and smoking nervously—was in cahoots with Mad Dog Stratton to spin this web of cotton candy.

The months passed with boredom for Mai Lon and the guards, as well as for the Americans. But a singular event occurred early in 1974, and it would change all their lives forever. One of the prisoners had become so despondent that after the story in *The New York Times* that he refused to eat, drink, or clean himself. His fellow prisoners struggled to keep him from starving, forcing him to eat some of their own scant rations, making him drink, talking to him, imploring him not to abandon hope. For some of the men who had contemplated death, their dying companion provided a kind of reverse psychology. In their effort to sustain him, they sustained themselves.

Mai Lon, too, encouraged him to live. She warned Little Hitler of the man's deterioration, but the commander dismissed her concerns. Perhaps he saw some useful political gain from the man's condition.

The dying prisoner lingered for several months, sometimes rebounding for a brief period and buoying the hopes of the other men, then slipping back into his death wish. Each relapse took him deeper and deeper toward death, until finally he gave up in February of 1974.

His death crushed the hopes of the other men. Those who had regained their will to endure fell into deep despair and worse health. Against this backdrop, Alexander Gage and two other POWs began to plot their escape.

Escape, of course, had always been on their minds. But for a long time they had set aside any serious consideration because they still hoped for rescue or for an end to the war, which would bring their release. *The New York Times* article had shattered both illusions. But now, with escape their only hope, it seemed an impossible goal. They were a handful of unarmed, weakened men held captive by armed guards in a hostile land. What would escape do, except get them killed? And if they *did* escape, where would they go?

But the worsening condition of the men convinced Gage

they had to make the attempt; otherwise, death was a certainty. Better to be killed trying to escape than die like sick dogs in a dank cave, abandoned by our own country.

The arguments flew back and forth for weeks, months, causing deep rifts among the men. As their ranking officer, Gage could order his men to participate in an escape plan. But he knew that such an order could be disobeyed, and he feared that one or more of the weaker, skeptical men might even inform the camp guards if an escape plot was hatched. He knew he would have to persuade them—not order them—to go along.

Mai Lon knew none of this. Gage had told her nothing, and for a time, she wasn't even at the camp. She had left to work with another PAVN unit across the border in northern South Vietnam. However, after four months, without a word of explanation, she was ordered back to the prison camp.

When she returned, she sensed something different in the attitude of Gage and some of the other men. They seemed more upbeat, emotionally and physically stronger. Gage persuaded Mai Lon to continue sneaking extra food and water to them; he explained that they had renewed their hope that America and the Laotian Popular Front and the North Vietnamese would negotiate their release.

She later learned that their *real* hope was for an opening, however remote, by which they could engineer an escape. It came unexpectedly, in mid-January of 1975, when the PAVN unit was pulled out to reinforce North Vietnamese units engaged in a flare-up of fighting along the South Vietnamese border. Mai Lon was left behind with a light contingency of Pathet Lao guards.

Three days later, early on a Sunday morning, the prisoners made their break.

They had timed it perfectly. On that particular morning, the small number of guards were reduced even further, with several men sent to pick up fresh provisions. Even Little Hitler was gone, having left to consult with superiors a day's distance away. The few remaining guards, as bored as their captives, were taken by surprise.

Mai Lon later discovered that one of the POWs, Gage's second in command, Davidson, had been escorted to a nearby stream to bathe. After overpowering the guard, Davidson killed a second guard and released the POWs from their caves. Together, they attacked the remaining Pathet Lao. Their only weapons were the rifles Davidson had taken from the two dead guards. But two weapons were enough. In fifteen minutes, they managed to kill every remaining guard without suffering a single loss themselves.

"All right!" Gage yelled when the last of the guards was dead. "We're out of here!"

The men knew that under the Geneva Convention, a POW who killed or harmed a guard during an escape attempt could face execution. There was no turning back.

During the brief battle, Mai Lon took refuge in thick undergrowth and came out only when Gage called her name and reassured her that she had nothing to fear.

She was suspicious of some of the POWs—even among those she had befriended and helped to keep alive, she was still "the enemy." But she trusted Gage and Davidson. In addition, she realized they needed her alive. She was their ticket out, their guide to freedom—no matter how many miles away freedom lay.

They packed as much food as they could carry and headed off in the only direction she knew, east toward South Vietnam.

The front door to the apartment opened abruptly, startling everyone and interrupting Mai Lon's story. She bolted from her chair. The old man who'd been sitting outside appeared. He spoke to her in Vietnamese.

"What's the problem?" demanded Ruby.

Truong replied. "He says someone spotted a car parked down the street on the other side. There are two men in it. Everyone's afraid they're I.N.S. agents."

"If it was Immigration, they'd be raiding the place, not

sitting on their butts,'' said Ruby. She went to the window and peered through a parted curtain. ''Come here, David.'' He peeked out. ''Can you make them out? I think it's the car behind the Pontiac. I can't be sure in this light.''

It had turned dark. There was only a single streetlight on the block. David spotted the Pontiac and a car parked behind it. He couldn't see much, either. But then another car came down the street, and its headlights caught the suspected car. David thought he could see two men inside, but he wasn't sure. He *was* sure, however, that the car was a light blue sedan.

''It's them,'' he said to his aunt.

''Who's 'them'?'' asked Truong.

''Federal agents from the Defense Department,'' said Ruby.

''You know them?'' said an increasingly agitated Susan Powell.

''We've met.''

''I *told* you to be careful!'' yelled Truong. ''I told you—''

''Hey, we followed your instructions,'' reminded Ruby. ''We were very careful not to be followed. We rode here in your car. Maybe they picked up on *you*, did you think of that? These guys have resources, you know.''

Susan Powell started toward the back of the apartment.

''Hold it!'' yelled Ruby. The woman stopped. ''They may have people out there, too. You wouldn't get ten feet. Besides, they're just watching us right now. Maybe they're not sure what they want to do.''

''What are *we* going to do?'' said Truong. ''My car's out front. We can't get to it without them seeing us.''

''I got an idea,'' said Ruby. She pulled her cell phone out of her purse and punched in a phone number. ''Jimmy, it's Ruby Dark . . . I'm doing okay, but I'm in a bit of a jam at the moment. You got your rig with you? . . . Great. Look, I need a big favor . . .''

Twenty tense minutes later, ''Jimmy'' arrived—rather, Jimmy and his truck arrived. A huge tractor-trailer rig that barely fit between the parked cars as it drove down the street. Which was precisely the point.

The truck, whose side panel advertised "Jimmy's Trucking Service," passed the apartment and headed in the direction where the two agents were parked. The truck slowed, then braked in the middle of the street opposite the apartment. David could hear the driver grinding gears, as if he was having engine or transmission problems. The truck lurched forward again and proceeded down the street, but as it neared the light blue sedan, it slowed again. When the trailer portion was directly opposite the sedan, the truck suddenly stopped, completely blocking the sedan's view of the apartment.

"Now!" yelled Ruby. By prearrangement, the four of them bolted from the house to Truong's car, which was parked facing the opposite direction of the agents' sedan.

As they piled into the Mazda, David could hear the truck driver loudly cursing his rig, jamming gears, and acting as if he had the most cantankerous rig this side of the Mississippi.

"Thanks, Jimmy," Ruby said aloud to the gods as Truong's car rounded the corner and shot off down Martin Luther King Boulevard. The sedan was still blocked from view by the truck.

Two dozen streets away, Truong pulled over and exchanged places with David, who took the wheel so Truong could continue translating. He climbed in back with Susan Powell, who had calmed somewhat since their escape. Ruby sat up front with David.

"Just drive south," Ruby said. "It doesn't make any difference where. Just obey all the traffic laws. The last thing we want is to get stopped for a stupid traffic violation."

Mai Lon resumed her story.

32

The POWs were free for three days.

Despite their renewed spirits and bodies, they were still weak and could not travel fast. Pathet Lao and North Vietnamese units quickly hunted them down. They put up a valiant fight but were badly outnumbered and had a limited number of weapons, with little ammunition. Gage's second-in-command, Davidson, and another POW were killed in the battle; the rest were captured, some of them badly wounded.

Except for Gage and Mai Lon. Somehow in the dense jungle they had eluded capture, though twice Pathet Lao soldiers passed within three feet of them.

They didn't move from their hiding place for another full day, until Gage was confident the soldiers had given up and left the area. That was when he told Mai Lon he was going back to the camp.

She didn't understand at first. Why in the world did he want to go back?

''To rescue them,'' he said.

''That's insane,'' she told him. He couldn't rescue the men all by himself. The camp would be more heavily guarded than ever. They needed to take the opposite direction. She could guide him into South Vietnam, into friendly territory—if they weren't caught or killed on the way. If they made it, Gage could tell the Americans where the camp was located, and armed military personnel could rescue the men.

Gage argued that by then, his men would have been moved. "I can't leave them behind," he said. "I was in charge. I talked them into escape, and now they'll be brutalized for the attempt. I won't abandon them."

In the end, Mai Lon couldn't persuade him to go with her. He was determined to return to the camp. He didn't know how to get there, of course. He didn't know the territory as she did. Finally, out of frustration and fear, she agreed to return with him. She knew if they were caught, the Pathet Lao would rape her, then torture her to death as a deserter. But she went anyway.

The Americans had been returned to the same two caves, and as Mai Lon had predicted, they were heavily guarded. She and Gage observed the camp for two days, mostly from a high bluff that provided a clear view of the caves below, yet was well hidden and not far from a source of water. The camp guards made no serious effort to scour the area around the camp; undoubtedly they assumed that Gage and Mai Lon were long gone.

There was a great deal of activity at the camp. Troops came and went. With the binoculars Gage had taken during their escape, he and Mai Lon could observe Little Hitler in heated discussions with his superiors. Then, toward the end of the second day, the camp commander and a dozen guards approached the cave entrances.

Truong suddenly stopped translating. David glanced in the rearview mirror of the car. An expression of shock covered Truong's face as Mai Lon continued. Then she, too, went silent.

"What is it?" asked Ruby.

Truong said nothing.

"Truong?" repeated Ruby.

He turned to Mai Lon and addressed her slowly in Vietnamese. She nodded, and Truong resumed translating.

* * *

The Pathet Lao commander and his guards had lobbed grenades into the two caves and fired their automatic weapons. It continued for several minutes, the sounds of the explosions and gunfire and the cries of the dying echoing off the limestone bluffs.

Mai Lon struggled to prevent Gage from shooting at the guards. He could do nothing to stop the slaughter; to try would expose them both to certain death. It was more important to escape, she argued, to reach friendly territory and tell their story, to expose the horror committed by the Pathet Lao and PAVN so the world would know they had kept American POWs imprisoned after the cease-fire—and might still be holding more men captive.

Finally dusk settled over the land, and Mai Lon was able to persuade Gage to leave with her and begin their long journey to freedom.

It seemed impossible. Seventy-five miles to freedom. Beyond the challenge of avoiding countless enemy units and crossing the heavily traveled Ho Chi Minh Trail, they faced booby traps, mountainous terrain, dense jungle, bamboo-viper snakes, poor water, leeches, B-52 strikes that shook the ground with earthquake-force—all this in addition to Gage's poor health.

For a few days after the executions, they moved slowly. They soon exhausted their rice balls, so they began to scavenge food supplies: frogs, eaten raw; wild berries; and, once, a four-foot-long iguana they slaughtered with a machete and whose snow-white meat sustained them for days. Another time they stumbled across an empty village where they scrounged fresh fruit.

Beyond the fact that Gage was underweight and weak, his physical condition was worsened by his emotional state. The slaughter of his men had turned his initial rage to a dull, numbing shock. It was all Mai Lon could do to prod him forward, one step at a time. More than once she feared he would collapse and die on the trail. Some days they didn't travel at all, resting instead until Gage summoned the will to go on.

Mai Lon had traversed the territory enough to know which routes held the least danger. She led Gage almost due east, across the succession of ridgelines flanking the heavily guarded Ho Chi Minh Trail into South Vietnam; she was heading for Hue, which she hoped was still under control of South Vietnamese troops. It was an arduous, perilous journey, weeks long and often requiring them to travel at night and sleep by day. That they managed to avoid North Vietnamese and Vietcong units seemed a miracle. More than once they nearly stumbled upon an enemy camp or patrol.

In early March 1975 they made it into friendly territory—what little was left of it. They joined thousands of Vietnamese refugees and South Vietnamese troops, many with their families, retreating into Hue ahead of advancing PAVN and VC forces.

By then, Gage was dressed in black pajamas stripped off a dead VC. As the only American, he was often questioned by South Vietnamese troops. He told them that he was a member of the U.S. Agency for International Development, that he'd been working in the highlands east of Hue before being compelled to flee. He introduced Mai Lon as his wife.

They had barely reached Hue when they were forced south, along with waves of refugees, onto Highway One to escape the shelling of the city. Once they reached Da Nang, they were able to board a World Airways jetliner loaded with refugees. They probably wouldn't have made it, except for the fact that Gage was an American.

In Saigon, Gage contacted an American intelligence officer he knew. Mai Lon wasn't at their meeting.

Gage didn't tell her what was said, but soon after they were forced to separate. She had no exit papers, and despite his protestations that she was his wife, she was not allowed on any of the refugee flights headed for Camp Pendleton and other California bases. Everyone knew the city would fall soon. Reluctantly, Gage agreed to leave without Mai Lon. But he made her promise to flee Vietnam as soon as it was possible and make her way to America. He would contact her once she arrived.

How? she asked. Where would he be? Could he give her the address of his family?

He didn't know. He wasn't sure even then whether he would return to his family, or—if he did go home—whether he could stay and face them. But he would write Mai Lon a letter once a month and send it, care of general delivery, to Los Angeles. If she did reach California, she was to go to the central post office in Los Angeles. The letters would be addressed to Mai Lon Chu; they would tell her where he was, and how she could contact him.

She didn't believe him. She didn't understand why he was so unsure about returning to his own wife and children, but she was certain that once he was home, once he touched foot on American soil, Laos and his captivity and their miraculous escape together would quickly become a distant memory. How could he resist returning to the family she knew he loved? His own flesh and blood?

She was wrong. She survived the fall of Saigon by joining the general population of refugees who had flooded down from the north months earlier. For a long time she feared she would be questioned by the Communists and they would discover that she had deserted the North Vietnamese army and had helped an American POW to escape. But she eventually realized that she was inconsequential to the new regime, that they were more interested in rounding up former South Vietnamese troops and government officials and the professional class for reeducation than they were in finding Mai Lon Chu, who had disappeared in the jungles of southern Laos.

In 1979, she fled on a Vietnamese fishing boat, survived a raid by Thai pirates that left many dead, and ended up in a Malaysian refugee camp. She might have remained there for years, as many did, but her education and ability to speak passable English caught the attention of camp authorities, and she was able to come to America in 1980. To her surprise, she found a letter addressed to Mai Lon Chu, general delivery, Los Angeles, California. It was the most recent of many letters Gage had mailed, she would later learn, but the previous letters had been discarded by the post office after no one claimed them. The letter carried a Sacramento post-office-box number and was signed *Sean Bell.* There was no mention of Captain Alexander Gage or Laos, but she knew from the personal references that only one man could have written the letter. She wrote back to him immediately from the post office.

They were reunited one week later. She still couldn't believe it was Gage—even when she saw his face. After all this time, he had kept his promise.

But Mai Lon Chu was not alone when Gage came to meet her. She had with her someone he knew nothing about—a young boy named Nguyen Huu. The child, conceived during their weeks in the jungle and born after Gage's escape from Saigon, was now nearly five years old. Mai Lon had kept him hidden from the conquering North Vietnamese; being Amerasian was not something one advertised after the fall of Saigon.

Gage embraced his son as warmly as he had embraced Mai Lon. They lived in Sacramento for a while, where he worked at odd jobs, then they moved to Phoenix, and finally, in 1987, they settled in Denver. Each time they moved, Gage created a new name and history for himself and his new family. After only a few years in Denver, he was eager to move again, but Mai Lon refused, arguing that their son was growing too old to be moved from city to city and being given a false identity each time. She wanted to establish roots for him, and she liked Denver. Finally, although reluctant, Gage agreed.

Mai Lon Chu was silent once more.

"What's the matter?" asked Ruby.

"There is nothing more to say," said the Vietnamese woman, speaking directly to Ruby in English for the first time since she'd begun her story. "We came to Denver nine years ago. You know the rest."

Mai Lon—now Susan Powell—wiped away the tears in her eyes, but she did not cry.

33

Ruby took a tissue from her purse and handed it to Susan Powell.

David's eyes were on the road, but his mind was on the Vietnamese woman's story—the most incredible story he had ever heard. What were the odds that anyone could have made the escape she claimed? A Las Vegas bookmaker wouldn't have bet on them. This wasn't *Rambo* or a fantasy movie. These were *real* people. Life just didn't happen the way Susan Powell had described it.

Yet if she had fabricated the story, presumably with the aid of Stratton, she had fabricated a helluva good one. She would have to be a born storyteller or have meticulously rehearsed a script to tell a tale as detailed and convincingly as this one.

Still, when all was said and done, the truthfulness—or deceitfulness—of her story made no difference. Either way, she couldn't prove it. The only other witness was dead. What evidence could she possibly offer to substantiate their amazing escape? It wasn't as though there were credit-card receipts and phone records and reputable eyewitnesses that could be tracked down—the kind of trail one followed to catch a skip. If her story was true, there might be long-buried documents in Pathet Lao or North Vietnamese archives—documents confirming the imprisonment of a band of Americans captured at Eagle's Eye in June of 1970. Records might show that one of these Americans was a Captain Alexander Gage, U.S. Air Force; that he disappeared following a prison break in early 1975; and that the recaptured POWs were executed six days later. Records might even prove the existence of a woman named Mai Lon Chu who served in PAVN units. But neither David nor Ruby nor American authorities would ever see those files . . . *if* they existed . . . *if* this story was true.

Ruby spoke slowly to Susan Powell. "Did your husband *ever* tell anyone what happened in Laos? About his captivity and your escape?"

"Not that I know of. We never talked about Laos, even between ourselves. He said it was in the past and he never wanted to talk about it again. Our son still believes his father was an American soldier who served in South Vietnam and came home like most American soldiers. He knows nothing of Laos."

Ruby was baffled. "Why didn't he tell anyone? Why didn't he go home to his own family? Why didn't he tell someone in the American government who the hell he was? There must have been other Americans alive when he escaped. Surely he didn't believe that he and the others were the only ones held back by the Pathet Lao. Or by the North Vietnamese, for that matter. He was living proof of it . . . if what you're telling us is the truth."

Susan Powell spoke defiantly. "It *is* the truth."

Ruby's voice suddenly grew high-pitched and angry. "Then he could have saved lives! How could he have kept that a secret? *Why*?"

"I am not, as you say here, a—" The woman paused for the word, then spoke rapidly in Vietnamese to Truong.

"Psychiatrist," he said.

"Yes, a psychiatrist. I do not know why. Sean refused to discuss it. I asked many times. I asked why he didn't go back to his family. He wouldn't say. He got angry at me when I asked."

"Then why didn't you tell the authorities?"

The woman shook her head. "I could not do that to my

husband. They were his wishes. And if I had gone to the authorities, who would have believed me?''

Ruby's voice calmed. ''Susan, do you think anyone—*anyone*—could have found out—*before* your husband was murdered—that he had been an MIA?''

''I do not know.''

Suddenly Truong directed David to pull into a convenience store's parking lot.

''I don't want to ride around any longer,'' said the editor. ''I have to get her back to where she is staying. I must leave you here. You'll have to find your own way back. We can't risk taking you to your car. I'm sorry.''

Ruby nodded. ''I understand. I appreciate what you've done tonight, Truong. And you, too, Susan. I know it was very difficult.''

Ruby and David climbed out of the car, and Truong and Susan Powell moved up front. Before Ruby closed the passenger door, however, she leaned in and said, ''You need to go to the police, Susan. If for nothing else, for the safety of your son. If you're in danger, so is he.''

The woman said nothing.

''I found a small gold picture frame in your living room,'' said Ruby. ''What picture was in that frame?''

The Vietnamese woman appeared puzzled by the question. ''It was a picture of Sean and me. Our son took it two or three years ago in the mountains. Why?''

''Because the frame was empty. My guess is the killer removed that picture—which means the killer knows what you look like.'' Ruby turned to Truong. ''Hide her well, hon. Until we can find her husband's killer, her life is in grave danger. If she's telling the truth, she holds the key to a story many people don't want told.''

''What do you think?'' Ruby asked David after they'd taken a cab from the convenience store back to Sears and retrieved her car.

''You mean, do I believe her story? I wanted to ask you that question. You're the expert on tall tales.''

"It's a pretty tall tale."

"Paul Bunyon-tall," said David. His skepticism had risen like bile in his throat. "Breaking out of the camp isn't so difficult to accept, but making it as far as they did—safely, through all that enemy territory—is pretty tough to swallow. No American POWs ever escaped to freedom during the war, right?"

"That's not quite true. A navy pilot did, in the sixties. A guy named Dieter Dengler. In fact, if I remember correctly, he went down in Laos not far from where Susan claims her husband was held. I read his book. He and two other Americans and some Thais overpowered their guards. They split up. One American traveling with Dengler was killed and the other disappeared. Dengler hoofed it for twenty-three days in the jungle before he was picked up by an American helicopter. Turned out that all he did was go around in circles. They picked him up only five miles from the camp. But he had managed to elude the Pathet Lao all that time."

"But Powell was gone a lot longer and traveled a helluva lot farther, according to her."

"But he had a guide. She knew the territory. Dengler didn't."

David sank back into the plushness of the Lamborghini and crossed his arms. "I still find it impossible to believe he wouldn't have told *someone*, that he wouldn't have contacted the government or his family sometime during all those years. Why keep it a secret?"

"Maybe he made a pact with the government," said Ruby without conviction. "You know, a trading of spies or something. Or maybe he really *was* mixed up in some drug operation."

"Or he was simply a deserter," offered David. "Maybe she told us that story as a way to rewrite the harsh truth."

"Maybe. But I keep remembering what Hollingsworth said about the trauma of PTSD. Gage could have been so *traumatized* by the massacre of his men that he never forgave himself. As their leader, he felt responsible. He was the one who persuaded them to escape, and they all were killed—except for him. He believed he should have died with them.''

''They would have rotted to death if they hadn't tried,'' said David.

''Sure. That's easy for us to say in hindsight. But he survived and they didn't, and that can be a terrible burden. So you simply deny it ever happened.'' David could hear his aunt's voice grow distant. He wondered if she was talking about herself as much as she was about Gage. ''You seal it off from the rest of your life. It's the only way to protect yourself from the pain. Maybe that's why he couldn't face his family. He would have had to tell them the truth, and he just couldn't do it. Hollingsworth said a lot of men who came back from Vietnam left their wives and their families. They couldn't face people. They were virtually MIA in their own country.''

''Then why did he attend the veteran's group?'' asked David. ''And why was he active in the POW/MIA movement? Or for that matter, why'd he go on the mission with Stratton? That doesn't sound like denial.''

''But that didn't come until much later, years after he'd returned. It's hard to keep the pain buried forever. And it may have been his way of atonement. He knew the Communists had kept POWs back, that probably there were others besides the men he was with.''

Like your brother? David said to himself, unable to voice what his aunt must be thinking: if Mai Lon Chu's story *was* true, and if Gage *had* spoken out immediately after his escape, maybe her brother would be alive and home today.

''He couldn't bring himself to reveal his own truth, but he could work toward other POW releases,'' Ruby went on. ''Gage obviously didn't trust the American government to get men out. How could he, after seeing that *New York Times* article with Nixon declaring that all POWs were free? They'd been betrayed by their own leaders. After he got home and saw how the government was handling the POW issue, he wasn't going to expose himself to the Defense Department. And of course, the longer he remained silent, the more difficult it became for him to go public. Everyone would have asked the same question you just did. He would have been condemned for his years of silence—or branded a deserter. He must have felt he'd betrayed the MIAs twice. That's why he hooked up with Stratton and went on the mission. If there was any chance of freeing men, it would be a private effort. He may even have had a suicidal drive at that point."

"That is still a helluva lot of speculation," said David. "That woman can't prove a thing about her story. And neither can we."

Ruby pulled the Lamborghini into the parking lot behind the office. "There's still one hope."

"What's that?"

"Do what Stratton wants us to do. Prove that Sean Powell really was Alexander Gage."

"And how are you going to do that?"

"I'm going to tell the story to Elizabeth Patterson and try to convince her to come to Denver to ID the body."

34

The low evening sun gave the Denver International Airport a polished golden sheen visible from miles away. David had never been to the new airport, but it struck him, as he approached in the van-shuttle, that the jagged, tentlike roofline rising on the Colorado plains—designed to evoke the solidity of the Rocky Mountains—instead conveyed the impermanence of the nomadic Indian encampments that once occupied the land.

Inside the main terminal, he hurried across the shiny granite floors, through security, and out to Concourse B on the underground train which *whooshed* past hundreds of propellers fastened to the tunnel walls. They were called an action work of art, but their small, rotating blades made his eyes whirl. He arrived at Gate B-34 four minutes before the early-evening United flight from Cedar Rapids, Iowa, was due.

''David, what are you doing here?'' said Ruby as she came out through the gate. She had driven to the airport the afternoon before and flown directly to Cedar Rapids late in the day. Her plan was to speak in person on Saturday with Gage's former wife. Ruby hadn't given advance warning; that might scare her off.

''I've got news that couldn't wait,'' said David.

Ruby cocked her head under her broad-brimmed black hat. ''What news?''

"Let's talk on the way," he said, eyeing the crowd of deplaning passengers and greeters around them. "You have luggage to pick up?"

"Everything's in here," she said, patting the dark blue carry-on bag hanging over her shoulder.

They headed toward the train, ignoring the moving walkway that sliced down the center of the concourse. At Ruby's brisk pace, they outwalked most of the people on the walkway.

"Todd Jennings is dead," David said.

Ruby glanced sharply at him. "Murdered?"

David nodded. "Multiple stab wounds to the chest."

"Where'd they find him?"

"A bicyclist found his body early this morning. Jennings was in his car at a small park up on Lookout Mountain, just a few minutes from his house. Right next to Buffalo Bill's grave."

"*One* of his graves," said Ruby. "From all the places that claim to have his body, parts of Buffalo Bill must be buried all over the West. How'd you find out? Was it on the news?"

"No. A Jefferson County detective called the office this afternoon. Mrs. Jennings told him her husband had been very upset ever since two people from Ruby's Bail Bonds visited him. The detective was, naturally, a little curious as to why we were talking to such a rich and prominent man like Todd Jennings."

"What did you tell him?"

"Nothing. I said he'd have to speak with you, but that you were out of town on business and wouldn't be back for several days."

Ruby laughed. "For someone studying to be a prosecuting attorney, you really shouldn't be lying to the cops."

"I thought you might not want to deal with him right away. Besides, I didn't like the tone in his voice. I don't think he likes bail bondsmen."

They rode the underground train back to the main terminal, this time passing an art display of lights and steel cutouts.

"You coulda called me on the car phone instead of coming all the way out here," said Ruby, hanging on to one of the perpendicular handrails in the quiet train.

"I knew we needed to do something. I wanted to be along—just in case you needed my help."

What that help might be, David had no idea. All he knew was that he'd been "wired" ever since the detective's call. The killing had to stop.

"That's kind of you, David."

"So what *are* we going to do?" he asked as they rode the escalator up from the train to the main terminal.

"We gotta reach Susan Powell again," said Ruby. "She's in real danger."

"From who? Jennings is dead."

"I don't know. Not for sure, anyway. I just know we need to find her before it's too late."

"What about the Patterson woman? Did you have any luck with her? Did she agree to come out to ID the body?"

"I'll tell you about it in the car."

35

"Aunt Ruby?" said David as she drove her Buick along the four-lane boulevard across the darkening prairie toward Denver. Knowing that car thieves targeted airport parking lots, she had left the Buick overnight, instead of the Lamborghini.

"Aunt Ruby," David repeated more loudly. She'd been distant since they left the terminal.

"What?"

"You said you'd tell me about the Patterson woman. Did you see her?"

"Yes."

"What did she say? Is she going to come out to ID the body?"

His aunt began her story.

Ruby was lost.

She'd driven northwest out of Cedar Rapids early Saturday morning in a rented Olds Cutlass Supreme; she was on some godforsaken, narrow country road heading toward a tiny spot on the map called Shellsburg. It would have been difficult enough to find the farm on a clear day—a farm whose only address was a rural route-number—but it was chilly and gray and so foggy, it would be tough finding Coors Field, even if it were standing half a block in front of her.

It was when she nearly plowed into the back of a huge, slow-moving green tractor that she decided to ask for directions.

"I'm looking for the Patterson farm," she said over the hood of the car, after apologizing to the tractor driver.

He tipped back his John Deere cap, showing off his farmer's tan along the top of his forehead. "Which one?"

"There's more than one Patterson farm?"

"There's two of 'em, ma'am. Brothers. Michael and Jerry. Three miles apart."

"I don't know the man's name. Whichever one is married to Elizabeth."

"Oh. Her."

"Why do you say that?"

"She's an odd one. Kind of a recluse. Never see her at the church socials or potlucks or the county fair. She came from one of the big cities back east—Baltimore or Boston, one of them."

"So which Patterson farm does she live on?"

"She belongs to Jerry. His place is on down this road about three miles, then you take a right turn onto the Old Henderson Road, gravel road, right by Tucker's place. Can't miss Tucker's place. He hasn't taken a brush to his barn since Benson was ag secretary. Go on down the Henderson Road for another half mile. Jerry's place is on the right. It's set back a ways from the road, behind a grove of trees. Can't miss it, though. Jerry collects a lot of antique farm equipment. Yard's full of it."

Ruby drove the three miles slowly in the fog. The gravel road by Tucker's place wasn't officially marked—Henderson was probably someone come and gone, the road owing its name from local lore—but she couldn't miss the long gray strips of peeling paint on Tucker's barn. She turned onto the gravel road and watched her odometer. At the half-mile mark, a silo loomed up out of the fog, followed by pieces of old farm equipment scattered in the front yard, just as the tractor driver had described. It was neat though, more like a museum than a junkyard. She could barely make out the faint outlines of a house behind a grove of trees, but the name Patterson, painted on the mailbox by the road, confirmed that she had the right place.

She pulled into the driveway and drove up to the house, a well-kept white, two-story place with a large, lazy front porch. The only thing missing was a barking dog. All farms had barking dogs that came up and sniffed your crotch.

Ruby heard nothing—not even her own footsteps—as she walked up to the porch. The fog had stilled everything, even sounds.

She knocked on the screen door. The inside door was open, and she could see into a small living room. She knocked again, louder. When no one answered, she went around the side of the house. In the back she found a large, flourishing garden and the hazy shape of a slender woman on her knees, weeding around caged tomato plants. Ruby crossed the yard, her footsteps still muted.

"Mrs. Patterson?" she said as she drew toward the edge of the garden.

The woman jerked her head up, obviously caught off-guard. "Yes?" Her voice was tinged with suspicion.

"I'm Ruby Dark."

"Yes?" The name didn't seem to mean anything to her.

"From Denver. We talked on the phone. I'm the bail bondswoman."

Elizabeth Patterson sat back on her heels, holding a spade in a mud-caked glove. There was a long pause. "You shouldn't have come."

"Is your husband around?" Ruby asked as she settled into a roll-arm sofa in the living room. The room was anything but country: a spare, elegant look, with plain white fabrics, a light blue carpet, little decoration on the walls, no pictures or mementos on the tables. An oak secretary stood in the corner, but it lacked the usual clutter one would expect. A few farming magazines lay neatly on a butler's table next to a green potted plant, but Ruby didn't see any books. The place looked lived-in but not loved.

"No, my husband's over at his brother's farm repairing a combine," said the woman as she sat in a bow-back armchair near the secretary. She didn't look as though she was going to sit long.

It was Ruby's first good look at her. She put the woman in her mid-forties, attractive in a low-key way, with long, straight, prematurely gray hair and no makeup. She must have married Alexander Gage young. Ruby was struck by the smoothness of the woman's pale skin—it wasn't the weathered skin of a farmer's wife. Maybe it was the softness of the light, but Ruby suspected it was due more to the reclusive nature the tractor driver had described.

"And your children?"

"We don't have any children. It's Jerry's second marriage, too. Neither of us wanted to bring more kids into the world."

A white-and-brown cat wandered into the living room and rubbed its well-fed body against the woman's leg. She picked it up and plopped it into her lap. Ruby relaxed a little. The cat might keep the woman put.

"What's its name?" Ruby asked.

"Muffin."

"I like cats," said Ruby.

"Why are you here?"

"I came to tell you a story."

"You could have written a letter. The postal service still delivers, even out here. It's a lot cheaper than flying. Or you could have sent it e-mail. We have all the modern conveniences in Iowa."

"I prefer to tell stories in person."

Ruby related all that Susan Powell had told about Alexander Gage and his years of imprisonment, the death of his men and his amazing escape. She didn't withhold details about Susan, about her coming to America with their Amerasian son, about marriage to Gage.

Elizabeth Patterson didn't move while Ruby spoke—even when the cat grew bored and leaped to the floor. She did not interrupt, did not ask questions. Not until Ruby had finished the story did she move, and then she rose abruptly.

"My apologies for not being a good host. Can I get you some coffee?"

"That'd be great," said Ruby.

"It's not decaf."

"I like it leaded. Black."

Elizabeth returned a few minutes later with two cups of coffee on a tray, along with a plate of store-bought cookies. The coffee was rich and strong, and the warmth felt good. Ruby didn't realize it could be so chilly in Iowa in July. For a few minutes they sipped their coffee in silence. Then the woman asked, "Why did you tell me all this? What do you want from me?"

"I want you to come to Denver to confirm—or deny—that this man was your husband."

"I'm not going to fly all the way to Denver to look at a dead body just because some ex-Vietnamese hooker spins a wild story and claims he's my missing husband."

"I've met a lot of hookers in my line of work, hon, and—"

"I bet you have," interrupted Ruby's hostess.

"She wasn't a hooker."

"You know Vietnamese hookers?"

"I know *people*."

"You're good," she said. "This is a well-done scam. But I don't believe you."

"It's not a scam. I don't want your money, I don't want to sell you evidence. I just want you to identify this man."

"Okay, maybe you aren't lying. If that's the case, then you've been duped like I was duped once."

"The man I described sounded like your husband, didn't he? I could see it in your eyes. Susan Powell knew your name, your children's names, things about you that Gage had told her."

Elizabeth smiled cynically. "I was once very active in the POW/MIA movement. A lot was written about me. Not always nice things, but enough personal stuff that anybody with a library card and reading glasses could have dug up that information.''

''Could they have found out about Whizzer? Mai Lon Chu told me your husband once had a hunting dog named Whizzer. A black lab.''

Elizabeth paused. Ruby had held that little piece of information in reserve, for just this inevitable moment of doubt. ''They wrote a lot of personal things about me,'' said the woman. ''That's what the stories were about when they weren't about my politics—how I lived in limbo while our government dawdled. They took photos of us at home. Interviewed the kids. The dog could have been—''

''The dog died before your husband went to Vietnam,'' said Ruby. ''Liver disease, I think. He couldn't have been in any newspaper pictures, and I doubt he got mentioned in the interviews.''

For a moment the woman said nothing. ''They may have talked to people we know, some of Alex's buddies. I wouldn't hang the veracity of your story on a dead dog.''

''I wouldn't either. That's why I want you to come to Denver.''

The woman looked at Ruby with steady, slate-colored eyes. ''For argument's sake, let's say this man really *was* Alex. Let's even swallow for a moment his unlikely escape. If he really was my husband and he made it to American soil, why didn't he tell the American military? Why didn't he tell the Defense Intelligence Agency back here? Why did he live all these years under assumed names, married to another woman, moving from town to town like a criminal on the run? Why didn't he come home to me?''

The strength and calm had left the woman's face. Ruby could see fear in her eyes now, fear that Ruby would have a plausible answer, one that would tear apart the woman's compromised world.

''I've been wrestling with that myself,'' said Ruby. ''His silence toward the government is pretty easy to explain. He felt deeply betrayed by Nixon's words. I have no answer for why he didn't return to you. Not a definitive one. But I have a theory."

"I bet you do."

Ruby told her what she had hypothesized to David, that Alexander Gage was so traumatized by the massacre of his men, so filled with a sense of betrayal and shame and guilt, that he could no longer face his old world. He could not face telling people about the death of his men. Even his own family. *Especially* his own family.

"Did you ever hear of an MIA rescue mission called Operation Freedom?" Ruby asked.

Elizabeth tipped her head slightly. "Yes."

"What do you know about it?"

"Not much. I wasn't active in the movement by then, though friends kept me informed even when I asked them not to. It was one of Colonel Stratton's scams, that much I know. Operational money disappeared, which is nothing new. There were even rumors that men died on the mission, but I never heard strong evidence of what really happened."

Ruby gave her a condensed version of what she had pieced together. "Sean Powell went on that mission, though he was fortunate to come back."

The woman shook her head vehemently. "I can't believe that someone who escaped from Laos would return there under such circumstances, risk being killed . . . or captured again. I don't think anyone in his right mind would have risked that."

Ruby told her how Powell had become active in the POW/MIA movement, most likely as a way of atoning for his years of silence. "If there was any hope of rescuing POWs—and his own soul in the process—it was through private missions like Stratton's. The government certainly wasn't going to do it." Ruby paused, then added, "Of course, we'll never know . . . unless you come to Denver. If that man *is* Alexander Gage, you can do for him what he was unable to do for himself."

The woman bolted forward, spilling coffee from the cup

in her hand. She glared at Ruby. "That's not fair! You can't put that burden on me. I won't let you! Get the Defense Department or the FBI to confirm his fingerprints."

"They haven't, and I don't think they will," said Ruby. "They're trying to bury this real deep."

"Then track down the intelligence officer who supposedly saw Alex in Saigon."

"I don't know who he is, and I doubt the government will let him talk. You know that."

"You need to go." The woman set down her coffee cup and moved toward the front door. Ruby rose and followed, pausing in the doorway.

"The cops don't know who this dead man is. I can persuade the D.A. to get a subpoena for you to come out and identify the body."

"I'll deny it's him."

"Even if it's him?"

"*Especially* if it's him."

"Why? I don't understand."

"Whoever that man is, he's dead. If he isn't Alex, I've learned nothing, and all I've done is stir up a lot of old, painful memories. If it *is* Alex, how do I explain that to my children? They were one and four when he went off to Vietnam. They think their dad was a war hero. How do I tell them he returned twenty years ago but couldn't screw up the courage to contact his own family? That he even married someone else and fathered another child? How do I explain to them? How do I explain to myself? How do I explain to the nation?"

"The nation? Why the nation?"

"What do you think would happen if I said yes, the dead man was my missing husband? The DIA couldn't bury it this time. I wouldn't let them bury it. Maybe this Vietnamese woman wouldn't let them bury it. But I'd be hounded by every TV network and newspaper and sleazy talk-show host. My children would have microphones jammed in their faces and asked questions for which they have no answers . . . for which *I* have no answers."

"Don't you think the nation should know?"

The woman laughed and stepped out onto the porch. Ruby followed. The fog seemed to almost crush their voices. "The nation doesn't give a damn! It would make the headlines for a few days and then everybody would go about doing their business. But it would destroy my life and my children's lives."

She turned toward Ruby. "You told me you had financial concerns about this business. Why do you care whether the *nation* finds out who he was?"

Ruby looked steadily at her. "Because my brother was an MIA."

The woman closed her eyes. "Now why did I think you would tell me that, Ruby?"

"It's the truth." Ruby dug into her purse and handed Elizabeth her brother's POW/MIA bracelet.

The woman read the inscription. "The last name is different."

"Dark is my married name. Or was. My husband's dead. Stuart Piszek was my brother." She described the circumstances of his disappearance and the government intelligence reports that suggested he'd been captured.

Elizabeth handed the bracelet back to her. Her face was sympathetic but unmoved. She'd obviously heard hundreds of stories like Ruby's. "Do you believe he's alive?"

"No," said Ruby slowly. "No, I don't. But I want to know if he was left behind. I want to know if *any* of them were left behind."

Elizabeth laughed sardonically. "Take my word, Ruby. Men were left behind. Of that I have no doubt. Maybe Alex was one of them. Maybe your brother was one of them. I don't know. Our government knows. The Communists know. Men get left behind in war. So do their families. Nothing you or I can do will change that, short of stopping war itself, and I'm not an optimist on *that* prospect. Learning whether your brother or my husband were left behind alive won't bring them back. They're dead. I accepted Alex's death a long time ago. I sense you haven't accepted your brother's death. It's time to accept it and move on. At some point you have to quit looking over your shoulder. I know a father who talks to his son's green beret every night. Those are the people you have to worry about, those who won't forget about the war."

They stepped off the porch together and walked into the yard amid the antique machinery and painted wooden birds hanging on nylon strings from tree branches.

"Why did you drop out?" asked Ruby. She looked around the yard. The ring of trees seemed to close in on them. But beyond the trees, toward the road, the morning fog was lifting. "This place . . . is as far away as you could get, Elizabeth. It's like you've isolated yourself in a convent."

The woman reached up and pushed one of the birds, setting it into motion. She watched it swing back and forth for a moment. "I got tired of the infighting, the wives against parents, sisters against brothers, those who wanted to stop the presumptive findings of death and those who wanted to get on with their lives. I got tired of the spotlight, the press attention. I also came to realize how the government had used us to prolong the war."

"How?" asked Ruby.

"Think about it. Toward the end of the war we were fighting to bring our POWs home, not fighting for South Vietnam's freedom. The nation quit talking about body counts and GIs in body bags and napalmed villages and started focusing on the image of POWs in bamboo cages. Our government hijacked—manufactured, actually—the POW issue. They used the POW and MIA families. We killed more men trying to get our POWs out than we saved. And frankly, why does our nation get to ride such a high horse on the issue? You think *we* had an accounting problem? We killed ten of theirs to every one of ours. We pitched Commies out of helicopter doors into the South China Sea, atomized them with B-52s, incinerated them with napalm, and left them at the bottom of rice paddies. Do you think we took down name, rank, and serial numbers before we did that? What kind of accounting do you think we could give *them*? We lost the damn war. That's why it's such an issue for this country. We're not used to losing."

She moved away from the bird and walked slowly in the direction of Ruby's rented car. "I might have stayed involved despite all the crap. Much of politics I didn't sort out until years later. But what really pushed me out was a woman I knew, somebody very active in the movement, who finally got her husband's remains back. Hanoi could have returned the remains years before. They knew he was dead, but they didn't tell her. She lived her life all those years on the hope that he might be alive. A year after she buried him, she killed herself. I wasn't going to let that happen to me."

Ruby blocked her path. They stood facing each other only two feet apart. It was the closest Ruby had been to her. She could see deep into the woman's eyes. There was calm, a sense of peace. Yet there was no sense of future. She had come to terms with her past, but at what cost? "Aren't you even *curious* about whether he's your husband?"

"No. I loved Alex. My children loved him. Whatever happened to him in Laos—*if* something happened to him over there—I don't want to know about it. I want to keep him as I remember him, not as someone else tells me."

"If it is Alex, don't you think he deserves a proper burial? Shouldn't he come home?"

"I think his Vietnamese wife and son might have something to say about that. I've already buried him. I made my peace with Alex's death a long time ago. He died in Vietnam. His children believe he died in Vietnam. I don't want him to die twice."

36

Ruby told David about Elizabeth Patterson between phone calls en route from DIA to downtown Denver. Her first call was to Thang Truong at his *Quoc Han* newspaper office, but it was already well into the evening, and nobody answered. She tried his home listing, but no one answered there, either.

Information turned up a listing for Terry Hawthorne Investigations, but there was no answer at his office number. Next, Ruby called Morgan Reed.

''Just sitting around watching the ballgame,'' came the detective's voice over the speakerphone. ''Rocks are up two runs in the third against the Giants.''

''I'm thrilled. You know a P.I. named Terry Hawthorne?''

Reed let out a loud chuckle. ''Sure. Half the guys on the force know Hawthorne. He's a wannabe cop. Couldn't pass the psych screen or the physical. Harmless, really. Went into P.I. work. Guess any dope can get licensed in this state. Actually, I hear he's pretty good at finding people.''

''Where does he hang out?''

''Harvey's Lounge.''

''Where else?'' said Ruby.

David knew that Harvey's was a favorite hangout for off-duty cops and low-end defense attorneys.

"Why do you want to find Hawthorne?" David asked as they headed for South Broadway.

"He was trying to find Susan Powell for Jennings. Maybe he did—though I hope to hell he didn't."

Harvey's Lounge was a standard-issue blue-collar bar: smoky, noisy, crowded, a jukebox blaring country-western tunes, two pool tables, a pinball machine, and every light in the place a beer sign. David wasn't sure why it was so popular with cops. Maybe one of their own owned it.

He and Ruby stood inside the doorway for a moment to let their eyes adjust to the semidarkness. She asked two men if Hawthorne was around. The first didn't know him, but the second pointed him out. He was sitting at a horseshoe-shaped bar, an empty stool on each side of him, despite the crowd. The guy must carry the plague, thought David.

Hawthorne was a short, dumpy-looking man in his thirties, with thinning hair and black-rimmed glasses. Not the kind of guy to kill dogs, as Thang Truong claimed he'd threatened. He was eating a dry-looking stuffed cabbage, nursing a light-colored beer, and smoking a cigarette. He kept glancing around, as if he wanted to talk to someone—anyone—but nobody seemed to catch his eye, not even the bartender. Except Ruby. That lit up his face. She came up to his right side.

"You Terry Hawthorne?" she asked.

"That's me."

"I'm Ruby Dark. This is my associate, David Piszek."

The man cranked his head back over his left shoulder as David took the stool beside him. He looked at David, then back at Ruby.

"Hey, I know you," he said, pointing a stubby finger at her. "The bail-bonds lady. They call you Angel, don't they?"

"My friends do. I hear you're pretty good at finding people."

That brought a smile to the man's face. "Yeah, I'm pretty good. You need a skip found?"

"No. I'm looking for a woman. Her name is Susan Powell. Know where she is?"

The light in Hawthorne's face went out. "Never heard of her." He took a drag on his cigarette, balanced it on the edge of a plastic ashtray, and returned to his stuffed cabbage.

"You've been trying to locate her for Todd Jennings. Any luck?"

"I told you, I don't know who she is. And I don't know or work for anyone named Todd Jennings."

Ruby leaned on the edge of the bar and came close to him so no one else would hear. "Your employer is dead, hon."

That gave Hawthorne pause. He tried to mask his reaction by grabbing a hard roll and tearing it in half. "Sorry to hear that."

"You should be. He was stabbed sometime last night or early this morning. In the chest. In his car. That means he was sitting with somebody he trusted. I don't think it would take much to link him to you. A man like that keeps precise records, canceled checks, logged phone calls. His wife probably even knows your name. You also talked to a Vietnamese guy who could testify that you were looking for Susan Powell on behalf of Jennings. I think Homicide would be interested in all that."

The private detective took a long draw at his beer. "Okay, fine. So I did a little work for him. I didn't kill him."

"Why was Jennings looking for her?"

"I don't know. He didn't say. He just wanted me to find her. That's what I'm good at, finding people."

"Did you?"

"No." He put enough butter on the roll to plaster the side of a building and stuffed the entire half in his mouth.

"Why am I having a tough time believing you?"

He chewed a few more bites and then said, with his mouth half full, "I wouldn't know. I told you, I don't know where she is."

"The problem I've got here, hon, is that Susan Powell is in a great deal of danger, and I need to find her before she gets hurt. So I really need to be convinced that you don't know where she is, and the only way I know that is to hook you up with Homicide. See that man over there?" Ruby nodded toward a corner booth with four men seated in it. "The guy with the black hair that looks like something Elvis wore on his bad days? That's Detective Mulleavey. You know Detective Mulleavey?"

"Yeah," he mumbled. It didn't sound as if he and Detective Mulleavey were the best of friends.

"Detective Mulleavey works homicide. I know him pretty well. A real ball-buster. He owes me a coupla favors. He'd probably enjoying hearing—even in his off hours—all about your connection to Jennings and about Jennings's connection to a very dead Sean Powell. Turns out Jennings had a lot of reasons to kill Sean Powell. Maybe you killed Powell for him and then you killed Jennings 'cause he didn't pay you for the job—some scenario like that."

Hawthorne scowled at Ruby. "That's bullshit."

"Probably. But by the time Homicide sorts it out, you'll have lost at least two or three days of work. And the Jefferson County sheriff's department would probably enjoy talking to you, too, about Jennings. Hell, there'd go another coupla days. You could end up losing maybe a whole week's worth of work, honey. Maybe more, if things go really bad. 'Course, with your employer dead, maybe that doesn't matter. Maybe you don't have anything else going on right now and you wouldn't mind spending time chatting with Detective Mulleavey and his friends."

Hawthorne stared morosely at his half-eaten meal. "The Buckaroo," he said half under his breath. "Room one-thirty-four."

"On East Colfax?"

"Yeah."

"How old's the address?"

"A day. She just moved there. She was tough to find.

The bitch kept moving. But I found her." He lifted his head at this, a matter of professional pride.

"Her boy with her?"

"I didn't see him."

"You give Jennings the address?"

"Yes."

"When?"

"Yesterday."

Ruby turned and headed for Detective Mulleavey. She spoke for a few moments, at one point nodding toward Hawthorne.

"Fuck, she said she wasn't gonna talk to Mulleavey," the P.I. muttered to David.

When Ruby returned, she dropped a twenty dollar bill in the middle of Hawthorne's stuffed cabbage. "Take a long time finishing your meal, hon. Order a second one if you're still hungry. Have a coupla more beers. I wanna know where I can find you in case this address turns out to be a bum steer. Don't call anyone, and don't leave. Mulleavey over there is going to babysit you until I call him. I didn't tell him why. It's just a favor to me."

Ruby hurried toward the door. David didn't catch up with her until they were outside the lounge. His aunt was striding fast down the sidewalk to her car.

"You don't think Hawthorne had anything to do with the killings?" he asked as he came even with her, dodging a drunk begging for change.

"Naw. He doesn't seem the knife-type. Doesn't even seem the gun-type. Besides, Powell's and Hollingsworth's deaths were too messy for contract hits. Somebody killed them in anger."

"What do you mean?"

"Something Elizabeth Patterson said to me—that it's the people who won't let go of the war you have to worry about. I figured she was talking about me. And she was. But now I realize she was also talking about the killer."

"And you think he's after Susan Powell now?"

"Yes. And I'm worried he got her address from Jennings—just before killing him."

37

Ruby stopped at her loft after they left Harvey's Lounge. She told David to drive around the block while she went "to get something." She came out carrying only her purse, but David knew what was inside it: her gun.

The Buckaroo Motel was the kind of place where hookers took their johns and drifters took their bottles. A ten-foot-high neon cowboy, the neon burned out on one leg, rode the roof directly above the office. Room 134 was on the bottom floor, at the far end of the motel from the street side and butted next to a fence. It was safe from the prying eyes of the manager, but not from the prying eyes of a killer.

Lights were on inside the room, and a window was cranked open slightly for air. They could hear television competing with the laboring air conditioner. Ruby sent David along the fence and around the back of the motel. A small, frosted window at the rear looked into what was probably the bathroom. The curtain was drawn, but that window, too, was open for air. It wasn't big enough for a good-sized man to climb through, but a small Vietnamese woman could slip out with the help of sweat and soap.

David pressed himself against the wall. He could hear Ruby knocking on the door. No one answered. A second knock. Still no reply from inside.

"Susan," Ruby called through the open window.

David thought he heard movement inside and he braced himself.

The volume on the TV was lowered.

"Who is it?" asked a man's voice. Not the annoyed, hard voice of an old drifter who wanted to be left alone. Tense. Young. A faint trace of accent, not quite Americanized. A five-year-old Vietnamese boy grown to twenty in a foreign land.

"My name is Ruby Dark. Is Susan Powell here?"

"I don't know who you are."

"Are you her son? Allen?"

"Who are you?"

"I spoke to your mother the day before yesterday. I was with a man named Thang Truong. I'm a bail bondsman. Maybe she mentioned me to you. She told me how she came to America when you were only five years old. Nguyen Huu was your name then, wasn't it?"

There was silence.

"Please, Allen, open the door. I need to talk to your mother. She's in danger."

"What danger?" Genuine alarm in his voice.

"A man was found dead this morning. I think the man who killed him was the same man who murdered your father. He may be after your mother, and I think he knows you're staying here."

"Oh, man! Oh, shit!"

"Where is she, Allen? Trust me!"

"She's not here."

David could envision the young man standing in the middle of the room, unsure whether to trust this woman he didn't know, yet afraid to do nothing.

"Where is she, hon?"

"She went out with Mister Truong," he finally said.

"Truong? Where did they go?"

"The dog track. He said he owns a dog."

"Why was he taking her *there*?"

"She called him. She said she was sure we were being watched. He came over and stayed for a while to calm her down. Then he persuaded her to go with him, just to get out of here. He asked me along but I didn't feel like it."

"Was she being watched, hon?"

"I didn't see anyone. He and I even checked the area."

"You didn't notice anybody suspicious?"

"Everybody around here looks suspicious."

"What about a blue sedan?"

"No. Truong was looking for that. The federal agents, right? No sign of their blue car."

As if they'd be stupid enough to keep driving the same car, thought David. "When was this?"

A slight pause. "Five-thirty or six, I guess. Must have been around then because the news was on."

"All right, son. I'm leaving. Keep your door locked. Call the cops if anything seems suspicious to you. And if your mother shows up or contacts you, call me immediately."

Ruby made him write down her pager number and repeat it back to her.

David waited briefly after she left, listening for anyone else in the room and to hear if the boy made a phone call. But almost as soon as Ruby was gone, the volume of the TV rose again, and all David heard was an MTV video.

His aunt was sitting impatiently in the Buick, the engine already running.

"Damn fool!" she said, after David had shut the door and she whipped the car out into the street.

"Truong?"

"What the hell was he thinking, taking her to the dog track?"

"He probably doesn't know Jennings was killed. I don't think it's been on the news."

"It was still stupid," she said. "He knows people are looking for her."

"What if Truong isn't worried about them?"

"What do you mean?"

"What if Truong's the killer?"

Ruby glanced at David, considered the idea for a moment, and then dismissed it. ''Why would he have killed Powell and Jennings?''

''I don't know. What do we know about him? He's got ties to Vietnam. He knew Powell, and he admitted having run-ins with Jennings.''

''Which is why Jennings wouldn't have let him get that close to him in some lonely mountain park. And why kill Hollingsworth?''

''I don't have answers, Aunt Ruby. I just find it troublesome that he left with her.''

''So do I, but I think it was more out of stupidity than with the intent to murder. Hell, maybe the man's hot for her. Besides, he could easily have killed her earlier, instead of letting her talk to us.''

''If it's not Truong, then who, Aunt Ruby? Do you have any ideas?''

''Hunches.''

David shook his head in exasperation. ''Hunches about what?''

''Anger, David. Somebody with an extraordinary, all-consuming hatred toward the Vietnam War.''

''Oh, that really narrows it down! Hell, everybody we've talked to harbors some sort of animosity toward the war. Including you!''

38

The security guard by the paddock fence at the Foothills Greyhound Park was different from the guard they had spoken to on their first visit. He was burly, with a crew cut and a demeanor that appeared far less lackadaisical than that of the first guard.

"Is Thang Truong here?" Ruby asked, arriving breathlessly at the fence with David in tow. They had run through the lower level of the grandstands.

"Who?"

"Thang Truong. A Vietnamese man with round glasses. He's part owner of Leaving Cheyenne, and I think the dog is running tonight."

"Oh, yeah, him. Yeah, I saw him around here tonight."

"With a woman? A Vietnamese woman?"

"A good-looking broad, if I don't say, for an Asian."

"Do you know where they are? Are they back in the lot?" Ruby pointed toward the area where the dog owners parked their kennels. The lot was poorly lit by weak lights sitting on poles, and it was hard to see anything but the murky shapes of vehicles.

The guard shrugged. "Could be up in the clubhouse. Could be in the can. I don't keep track of him, lady. I don't even know if his dog's run yet."

David glanced at the odds-board across the track. It was being prepared for the eleventh race. He spotted a program sticking out of a trash receptacle and retrieved it. He flipped to the inside, scanning the pages one by one. Finally he saw Leaving Cheyenne's name. "He ran the eighth race."

"He'd probably be back by his truck then, wouldn't he?" Ruby said to the guard as she started to open the paddock gate.

The guard blocked the gate. "Dunno. Can't let you back there anyway. Off-limits. See?" He pointed to the sign warning that only authorized personnel were allowed in the paddock area.

"I need to find them right away," said Ruby. "The woman's life is in danger."

"From what? Got a rabid dog back there?" The guard didn't look impressed.

"A killer."

"I can't just let you waltz back there, lady. You got a legitimate need, you get a pass from security. Office is on the mezzanine-level on the far side."

"This is a matter of life and death!"

"Yeah, well so's keeping my fucking job. I lose this one, my old lady'll shoot me."

"Look, you little twerp, you don't let us through, I'll shoot—"

"Aunt Ruby!" David grabbed her arm and pulled her away.

"Hey, lady, you don't threaten me!" The guard's face flushed, and he started toward her through the gate.

"Sorry, she's had a few too many beers," David said, waving off the angry guard as he steered his aunt, who was fighting his grip, toward the grandstand. When they were a few feet away, he whispered, "Come on, I know how we can get through."

He glanced back at the guard, who had stepped several feet through the gate but then stopped, as if hesitant to desert his post. David kept pushing his aunt ahead. She relented and let him guide her back into the lower grandstands. Only when they were beyond sight of the guard did David release Ruby's arm.

"This way," he said. They went out the nearest exit and hurried along the edge of the spectators' parking lot until they reached the entrance to the lot where the dog owners parked their vehicles. As David had noticed on their first visit, the gate was wide open, and there was no security guard posted—only a metal sign that read, "Beware of Dog."

They slipped through the gate and headed down a short road to the lot, keeping to the shadows as much as possible in case the security guard had alerted others. They heard dogs barking as they drew closer to the uneven rows of pickups and cars, but they didn't see people. The air was heavy with the stench of nearby stockyards.

As they passed the first pickup, a dog inside the kennel lunged against the louvered window. His furious barking made David jump away, his heart in his throat.

"Jesus!"

They moved on. The pickup carrying Leaving Cheyenne was dark brown, David remembered, but it was tough to find dark brown in the weak light. They kept to the back row, Ruby a few feet ahead of David. Each time she passed the rear of a vehicle, she'd peer between it and the next truck. David would mimic her as he reached the next row. Sometimes he could spot the dog track between vehicles in the next row; other times he caught only the back end of a pickup or a car in the next row.

Ruby repeated the pattern several times, until they were two-thirds of the way toward the end of the lot, near the open maintenance shed that backed the yard of the neighboring steel fabrication company.

Suddenly Ruby made a sharp left and disappeared between two pickups. David bolted after her, and rounding the pickup, he found her kneeling by a man's body. He was lying facedown in the parking lot, his head next to the front tire of the truck. A few feet beyond him lay a greyhound on its side. The man was motionless, but the dog was twitching. Its legs jerked, and low, guttural moans escaped its throat.

"My God!" said David, approaching his aunt. She felt the man's neck for a pulse. David spotted a pair of glasses on the ground and a white shirt, its back stained with something large and dark. Then he remembered who he'd seen wearing a Chicago White Sox T-shirt.

"Truong?" he said.

"Yeah."

"Is he dead?"

"Yes."

"Jesus."

David stepped past Ruby, toward the dog. It was still twitching and moaning, a pained sound that made David sick to his stomach. He leaned over the dog. Leaving Cheyenne was jet-black, so David couldn't see clearly, but he was able to make out ragged, dark stains spilling onto the ground. Why the hell had the killer stabbed the dog? Had the dog attacked the killer, or was the killer worried that the dog's barking would attract attention—as if barking dogs would raise an eyebrow around here.

David rose, suddenly aware that he and Ruby were trapped between two pickups in a poorly defensible spot. "We need to get outta here, Aunt Ruby, it isn't safe!"

They moved back out into the open parking lot. David scanned all directions but saw nothing. He couldn't make out much except for the lights of the racetrack. In the opposite direction, another light beamed off the roof of the shed, but it left the shed's open interior in total darkness.

"Where the hell is Susan Powell?" he asked, his whole body shaking.

"I don't know."

"Did *she* kill Truong?" He didn't believe it, but he asked anyway.

"No."

"Then the killer's looking for her . . . or he's already got her," said David, eyes on the blackness of the shed.

Ruby turned her head slowly, taking in once again the parking lot and the steel company's lot next door.

"Maybe she headed back toward the track," speculated David.

"Guards'd be here by now if that was the case."

"Not if she ran into the same guard we did."

From where they stood, they were less than seventy-five yards from the paddock security guard. The track announcer gave the results of the previous race.

"Maybe she made it out the way we just came in," said David.

"Maybe, but my guess is she's hiding around here," said Ruby, still peering into the surrounding shadows. After a long pause, she added, "I hope."

She turned abruptly to David and pointed toward the paddock. "Go get that asshole security guard and have him call the police and the rest of track security. Get 'em over here right away!"

"What are you going to do?" said David, knowing the answer.

"I'm gonna try to find Susan Powell before the killer does."

David stepped toward her. "Aunt Ruby, don't—"

"*Go*, goddammit! Don't argue with me!" Her hand came up out of her purse. She was holding her gun. "I've got protection."

David started to object again, but she said, "Go! Get help as quickly as possible!"

David hesitated only a moment more, then turned and raced toward the paddock. It took less than fifteen seconds, even weaving between vehicles and dashing through a row of handlers leading dogs to the track, to reach the security guard.

The guard's face flared the instant he saw David. "Hey, I told you people to—"

David cut him off. "Truong's been murdered, and his dog's dying! They're back there in the lot."

The guard looked as dubious as he had before. "What are you, as drunk as your old lady?"

"This is no fucking joke! Truong's dead, and the woman

who was with him is missing, and there's a fucking killer out there with a goddamn knife! Now get security down here and call the cops—now!''

This time the guard took David seriously. He reached for his walkie-talkie but kept his eyes on David, who turned to head back toward the parking lot.

''Hey, where the hell you goin'?'' demanded the guard.

''To find my aunt.''

39

Ruby was gone.

David called after her. The darkness seemed to hold back his voice. After no reply, he paced a few steps in one direction and called again. Silence. He went in the other direction and called again, louder this time, fearful of what his voice might summon in the darkness.

He sidled across the front of the maintenance shed, hanging back far enough so if a killer with a big knife was lurking inside and lunged at him, the weak rays of the overhead light might catch his sorry ass before he reached David. He licked his dry lips and tried to swallow. What the hell would he do if he saw the killer lunging at him? His only weapons were his fists and his feet, and he was no Karate Kid.

He crept across the front of the shed, staring into darkness. As his eyes grew more accustomed to the poor light, he could make out piles of sand and maintenance equipment and a tractor with a loader on the front, though there were still enough pools of blackness to hide a bevy of armed killers. But he reached the end of the shed without being attacked.

Just then, he heard a noise behind the shed, in the yard of the steel fabrication company. Something had clanged hard against metal, creating an echoing sound. David dashed back along the front of the shed until he reached the fence separating the dog track from the fabrication company. He stared into the black yard, hoping to catch sight of the familiar shape of his aunt with her broad-brimmed hat, but he could make out only the lumpy outlines of the huge metal pipes.

''Aunt Ruby!'' He yelled loudly this time. No answer. Not that it surprised him. If the killer was out there and his aunt was there too, either he'd already gotten to her, or she was keeping quiet so he wouldn't know where she was.

''Susan!'' he yelled, but again no reply.

Suddenly footsteps fell behind him—someone charging toward him, breathing heavily. David whirled—body crouched, arms out, fists curled to protect himself.

It was the security guard, whose gun was drawn and pointed at David. At the last moment the man realized who he was aiming at.

''Oh, it's you,'' he said, lowering his gun arm slightly.

''Fuck!'' David said under his breath, his heart in his throat.

''I called the cops, and more security's on its way,'' said the guard. ''Where's the dead guy?''

The guard may have been an asshole, but he had done his job and he was no shrinking violet.

''He's back there by the truck.'' David pointed toward the pickup he thought was the right one, though he couldn't see Truong's body from here.

''See anyone?'' the guard asked, motioning his head toward the blackness of the steel firm.

''No. But I heard something.''

The guard started for the truck.

David turned back toward the yard and moved along the fence, trying to glimpse movement or hear sound. He kicked something and looked down. A handbag lay on the ground. He picked it up and held it to the light spilling over from the racetrack. He couldn't make out the color, but he knew it wasn't his aunt's purse. He didn't need to look inside it to know it was Susan Powell's. It felt full, and there was no dirt on it. It hadn't been lying here long.

He dropped the bag to the ground and began looking for a place to jump the fence. It was low chain-link, nothing high-topped with barbed wire. Sections were obscured by weeds and vines. He found a spot where the weeds weren't heavy, grabbed the fence, and leaped over so his feet cleared the top in one smooth swing. He landed in soft dirt with little sound, except for the brief rattle of the chain-link and the slight crunch of weeds. He crouched and listened, not yet trusting his eyes. He could hear the noises of the racetrack behind him but nothing else.

After a few moments he began advancing into the yard. His first priority was to locate a weapon—anything—and he found it a few steps in; a thick metal pipe about a foot long. He picked it up and tested its heft. It would be worthless against someone with a gun, but against a knife he stood a sporting chance of defending himself.

He inched forward again, trying to breath quietly, but his lungs sounded like two giant wheezing leather bellows.

Fifty feet into the steelyard, he passed the first large pipe. As he had done with the shed, David passed far enough away from its mouth so if someone hidden inside charged, he had at least a moment's warning. There was little moon, but the racetrack lights cast a faint glow on the rippled side of the metal pipe. Still, the mouth of the pipe yawned like a black cave until David was even with it and could see straight out the back, perhaps thirty feet away. Only then could he see that no one was hiding inside.

He moved on, deeper into the yard, where more pipes lay. Not all were huge. Some were big enough only for kids or small dogs. But most were enormous, six or eight feet in diameter, certainly wide enough to hide a knife-wielding man. In some places, the pipes were stacked, always in odd numbers—two on the ground and a third resting on top, or three with two on top, stacked like cheerleaders in a pyramid at a football game. Steel cable was lashed over the stack to anchor the pipes in place. They were a nightmare to check, because David couldn't see into all of them simultaneously. He feared that as he searched a lower pipe, the killer would leap from an upper pipe, or vice versa. In some cases, pipes had been laid perpendicular at the far end of the one he was inspecting, cutting off any dim backlighting. By now David had moved far into the yard and was moving between *rows* of pipes. It was impossible to simultaneously check pipes on each side.

Twice he froze at the sounds of something scraping against metal—once as if made by a person moving inside a pipe, and once as if someone had banged an object against the metal. But it was difficult to pinpoint the direction of the sound or its distance. Each time he heard the sound David strained to catch a follow-up noise, something to help him nail down the location. But nothing came. The perpetrator—a small animal, for all he knew—was careful not to make additional noise.

At another point, David froze at the crack of a man's voice—until he realized it was the security guard he had left with Truong's body. But David wasn't about to reply and betray his position. Moments later the guard yelled again, this time from another location.

David quickly moved forward. He was nearing the end of one section of the storage yard and approaching a massive corrugated-steel building when the attack came.

Throughout his journey across the yard, he had tried to scan all directions at once, hoping to spot signs of his aunt or Susan Powell—or the killer. He'd been terrified to take his eyes from the mouths of the pipes, fearful that if his focus strayed for a split second, the demon would come after him.

The demon *did* come after him—not from the gaping interior of a drainpipe but from *between* two pipes, in the gap below where the pipes touched shoulder-to-shoulder like Siamese twins—and where the killer had crouched, waiting in the soft and silent ground. David had *heard* his attacker before seeing him.

David wasn't sure what saved him in the initial assault. The killer moved with terrifying speed. But David's nerves, like those of a cornered animal, were raw and alert. Maybe his youthfulness allowed him to whirl in the direction of the assault and lash out with the steel pipe at the same time he jumped aside. He felt the pipe hit flesh, heard the man grunt, but he knew the blow wasn't hard enough or deep enough to do serious damage.

David couldn't see the knife, but he felt its presence as it passed him in the darkness.

He was slightly off-balance from dodging out of the knife's path, but he regained his footing and turned to face the killer.

The man had stumbled past him, carried by the force of the lunge that had failed to strike home. It took longer to stop his forward motion, right himself, and renew his attack. But renew it he did—with paralyzing ferocity.

David still couldn't see the knife, but he could tell it was in the man's right hand, pointed toward his heart. Again he sidestepped the killer's path. Now he swung indiscriminately with the pipe, striking a solid blow to the man's left shoulder. It brought a cry of pain but failed to knock free the knife.

The killer stumbled past him several feet. He turned to renew his attack, but didn't do so immediately. Instead, he stood bent over, exhausted and breathing heavily. David braced for another assault, his heart still racing at record Olympic-speed.

The two men stood only ten feet apart, yet David still couldn't make out his attacker's face, which was shadowed completely by a baseball cap. He was large, that much David could determine—but beyond that, the man could be anyone . . . Bullet Joe, Stratton, Caffarelli—or he could be a total stranger, a hired assassin carrying out the machinations of someone else.

David poked the steel pipe toward the man several times, then feigned a step forward, trying to draw an unbalanced reaction from the killer. He wanted to get a shot at the man's head—even his kneecap—to bring him down. But he had to strike accurately; a mistake could be fatal.

Neither man had spoken to the other. Shouldn't a future

prosecuting attorney be good with words in a situation like this? wondered David. Maybe the killer, tired and aware that he was facing a younger, stronger adversary, was ready to pack it in. But would a man who had murdered four men and a dog—and possibly two women—simply give it up?

No. The killer renewed his attack, charging as before but yelling this time—as if he was expending the last of his energy in a final assault. David went for the man's head, steering clear of his knife-hand. As the man closed the distance, David swung.

He would have knocked the man cold if the pipe hadn't first caught the killer's shoulder. By the time the pipe hit the man's skull, it was a glancing blow without much punch. It staggered the killer but didn't bring him down.

At the same moment the pipe hit, David felt the shock of something sharp and hot ripping through the flesh of his left bicep. He screamed in pain, dropped the pipe, and grabbed at his arm. He propelled himself away, frightened beyond fear, wounded and defenseless. He tried moving his feet but stumbled—not over anything in the yard, just over his own damn feet. He tried keeping his balance, but he failed, falling to one knee, his arms extended to brace his fall. Pain shot through his left arm as his hands hit the ground and his body crumbled, rolling him over onto his back.

The killer, sensing victory, came at him immediately. But he was slow, still groggy from the blow to his skull. David raised both legs to kick off killer—at the precise moment he heard the wondrously alive sound of his aunt's voice.

''Eddie!''

The man stopped dead in his tracks.

''Put down the knife, Eddie!''

Eddie? Bullet Joe's father? The *killer*? But he was too old, wasn't he? No, recalled David; Eddie was strong and fast, even at his age; that was apparent the first time they'd met him in his trailer. Eddie could have done it, with surprise. Who among the victims would have suspected the old man?

But *why*?

"Put down the goddamn knife, Eddie! Drop it!" shouted Ruby.

Eddie hesitated but didn't drop it.

"Drop it or I'll shoot, damn it!"

Instead, Eddie moved toward David. Maybe he still intended to kill him. Or maybe he just figured it was better to take the goddamn bullet.

He did. Two of them. Soft thuds, like someone punching a pillow. David wasn't sure; he'd never heard someone being shot before. And there was the louder explosion of Ruby's gun firing twice in rapid succession, the sounds reverberating among the pipes.

Eddie let out a grunt and fell to his knees at David's feet. The knife dropped to the ground. Eddie moaned, listing to one side like a capsizing ship. He tried weakly to right himself, then keeled over.

"You okay?" asked Ruby, moving quickly to his side to help him up.

"No." David was clutching his arm and sucking in his breath in gulps. "The bastard stabbed me!"

"Let's see." She pulled his hand away and examined the wound. "It doesn't look that deep. You'll live."

"How can you tell? You can't see a damn thing out here."

"I could see well enough to shoot Eddie."

David glanced at the body.

"I couldn't find him until you two started fighting," she said.

"I couldn't, either." David looked up at his aunt. "Thanks, Aunt Ruby. You saved my life."

He thought he detected a smile in the darkness. "Yeah, but now the world's gonna be stuck with another lawyer," she said.

"Gee, thanks."

"It's okay, hon. The trade-off is I get to keep my favorite nephew."

40

The police didn't find Susan Powell's body. They brought in men and searchlights and dogs and examined through and under every pipe in the yard, and still they couldn't find her. A patrol unit went to the Buckaroo Motel, but the room was cleaned out. The motel manager had not seen Susan or her son leave.

When Ruby learned the boy was gone, she knew that Susan Powell had escaped Eddie's knife. They wouldn't find her again, she told David. Susan Powell distrusted the police and the federal government too much to come forward. For all the woman knew in the dark, her attacker was a government agent or an assassin sent by Jennings. Susan and her son would almost certainly leave Denver, if they hadn't already, perhaps to disappear in Little Saigon in Orange County, or along the shrimping shores of Louisiana, or in some other Vietnamese stronghold in the United States. Or perhaps they would flee the country altogether.

And with her would go the only living testimony, if her story was to be believed, to the truth about Sean Powell and the American government's betrayal of its POWs.

''Do you think Ruby really believes the woman's story?'' asked Morgan Reed.

''I don't know,'' said David. ''I don't know *what* she's thinking right now.''

He and the detective were leaning against the railing where Lawrence Street passed over Cherry Creek. Below them, Ruby was walking alone on the concrete bike path that ran along the creek. She seemed oblivious to passing cyclists, joggers, and skateboarders. David had never seen her like this. His aunt was not the contemplative type. She was always doing something, going somewhere, talking to someone. In many ways she was a loner, yet he rarely saw her alone. But she had never killed anyone before—at least not that he was aware of.

"I killed a pimp once," Reed said to David. "He drew a gun on me. He was as worthless a man as I've ever met, and I still think about it."

"You must know other cops who've shot people," David said, surprised that Reed hadn't killed more perps in his long career. "What do you do when someone you know is going through that?"

"Cops are sent to shrinks," said Reed. "It's required. I went to see one for a while."

"Did it help?"

Reed shrugged. "Some. I guess talking about it's good. But therapy won't make it go away. I can guarantee you that. Nothing will make it go away. Mostly you just hope that over time, you can stick it in a corner of your mind where it won't get in the way of the rest of your life."

"She won't go see a shrink," said David.

"Then you'll have to get her to talk to you."

His aunt had talked that night at the racetrack, when the police were taking statements and trying to find Susan Powell. Ruby had seemed as talkative and snappy as ever. But David didn't see her for the next two days. He called her loft and got her answering machine. She didn't return his paging. The third day, she came into the office but was noticeably morose—no explanation of where she'd been, speaking only when necessary, her voice distant. David knew then that she was in trouble.

The sun was high overhead, and David felt tired in the heat. Maybe he could use a shrink himself. Seeing a man die, a man who seconds before had attempted to kill him, could certainly be classified as a traumatic event. Maybe he, too, was at risk for post-traumatic stress disorder.

"Do *you* believe Susan Powell's story?" Reed asked, his eyes still focused below, on Ruby.

David didn't respond with his usual "no." He still found the story farfetched. How could anyone think otherwise? Yet he was less certain than he'd been before. The problem was, with Mai Lon Chu gone and Elizabeth Patterson refusing to cooperate, they would never know.

"I'm not too certain what to believe right now," he said. "You guys hear from Stratton?"

"Oh, yeah. He's called us several times. Aunt Ruby won't talk to him. The last time he called, he told me he was leaving town to try to find Susan Powell. He's convinced she's his ticket. But I don't think he'll find her. And if he does, she won't help him."

They didn't say anything for a while; they just watched the people on the bike path. David noticed several women in dresses and tennis shoes, probably office employees on their lunch hour.

"I still don't exactly understand why Eddie Brown killed all those people," Reed finally said. "Or when Ruby realized it was him."

"All I know is that I was lying on the ground with this man coming at me with a knife, and she called out Eddie's name just before she shot him—and I know damn well she couldn't have made out his face. The bastard was six feet from me and *I* couldn't see his face."

"But why Eddie Brown? If Sean Powell really was this MIA, as Stratton claims, what difference would that have made to Bullet Joe's father?"

"It didn't make any difference. Eddie didn't kill him because he was an MIA. I doubt Eddie knew that Powell was—or may have been—an MIA. Aunt Ruby thinks Eddie Brown was the man who tipped off the police four years ago about the burglary Bullet Joe had committed. He did that to keep his son from going on Stratton's mission into Laos. He thought the mission was crazy. He was worried—like any parent would be—that his son could end up dead or missing. But he not only wanted his son out of the mission, he wanted to sabotage the mission. So he must have told Todd Jennings about it. He would have known about Jennings, since his son was working for him at the time. He probably knew Jennings had connections in Southeast Asia and that the guy was trying to get diplomatic relations established. Maybe he figured the guy might be interested in Stratton's mission. Bullet Joe had told his folks just enough details about it, so all Eddie had to do was pass that on to Jennings, who in turn passed the information on to the Pathet Lao."

"But why did Eddie want to sabotage the mission? He'd already gotten his son out of it."

"Eddie blamed the Vietnam War for all his son's problems: his troubles with the law, his alcoholism, his inability to hold jobs, everything. I heard that from Eddie, myself. He had a lot of anger. By sabotaging the mission, he was striking back. And that would have been the end of it, except four years later, Bullet Joe tells his folks that Powell has evidence about who betrayed the mission. Ruby suspects that the evidence, whatever it was, involved Jennings. But Eddie was undoubtedly worried that *he* somehow would be linked to the betrayal—and especially to tipping off the cops about his son. So in a panic, he drives to Powell's house, maybe with the intention of killing him, maybe just trying to scare him or learn what information he had. It's speculation. You brought up the fact that the killer used one of Powell's own kitchen knives as the weapon, so I'd wager it wasn't premeditated. Whatever his intentions, things obviously got out of hand. After he kills Powell, he goes back to his trailer and disables the car so his son can't drive it to Powell's house. But Bullet Joe gets there anyway and finds Powell's body . . . *and* evidence that his father was the killer."

Reed looked puzzled. "Evidence? What evidence?"

"A Saint Christopher's medal. That's *my* theory, anyway. The first time Aunt Ruby and I went to their trailer, Eddie's wife gave him a bad time about his losing his St. Christopher's medal. I can't imagine things would stay lost very long in a dinky place like that. But you could easily lose a medal around your neck in a fight.''

''And his son finds it?''

''Right. He recognizes it as his dad's. That's why he skipped bail. Aunt Ruby was bothered from the beginning about his jumping bail, because he wasn't a guy afraid of doing time. Even the Big Bitch. And since he was going to jail for life anyway, he decides to run and incriminate himself in order to steer any investigation away from his dad.''

''And slaps his handprint in blood to leave a big, fat clue,'' said the detective.

''Sure. Joe calls Caffarelli and hitches a ride to his parents' trailer. Aunt Ruby figures the clothes he brought out of the trailer in the plastic grocery sack were probably his dad's bloody clothes.''

''And Eddie killed Jennings because he was the one man who could testify to Eddie's betrayal?'' said Reed.

''Right. It might not have been as big a worry for Eddie, except Aunt Ruby asked him and his wife about the mission, and Jennings Construction came up in the conversation. So he probably got worried at that point that we would link them. It would have been easy for him to arrange a meeting with Jennings. Jennings was probably as worried about public exposure as Eddie was. Comrades in fear. That's why Jennings was hunting for Powell's wife. He thought she might have that missing evidence.''

Reed stood up from the railing. ''Maybe somebody will catch up one of these days with Bullet Joe to see if Ruby's theory's right.''

''She's convinced he'll turn up someplace not far away, like Grand Junction or Craig. There's no real reason to run now, with his father dead. He'll probably want to be around for his mother, even if he's only as close as the state pen.''

"What you say makes sense," admitted Reed. "But why did Eddie kill that therapist?"

"I originally thought Hollingsworth was killed because he knew something about Stratton's mission—especially about that guy who was captured. But Aunt Ruby figures Eddie went off the deep end after killing Powell and started attacking anyone who had anything to do with the Vietnam War. Eddie was a Korean War vet himself, so maybe he was experiencing his own PTSD. Hollingsworth told Aunt Ruby there's evidence that some men from World War Two didn't experience PTSD symptoms until decades later, when everything in their life suddenly came unglued. Maybe that happened to Eddie. He blamed those therapy sessions for prolonging his son's mental problems, and of course that was the group where Bullet Joe was recruited for the Laos mission. The therapist just made a handy target for Eddie's rage."

"And Eddie wanted to kill Susan Powell because she was Vietnamese?" said Reed.

"That, and the fact that Eddie didn't know whether she had evidence that might link him and Jennings. Of course, Thang Truong had the misfortune of being in the wrong place at the wrong time, and being Vietnamese on top of it."

"Amazing the old man could do all that," said Reed.

"Yeah, well, *that* old man moved like a sonofabitch! I'd be dead if it wasn't for Aunt Ruby."

Reed looked at the heart of the city not far away and shook his head. "I still don't understand why Ruby got so involved in this MIA business in the first place. She didn't need to find out all this stuff. She just needed to catch Bullet Joe. And why was she so quick to swallow all this bullshit from Stratton, all this crap about Powell being an MIA and guys left behind in Laos. . . ."

David contemplated telling Morgan about Ruby's missing brother—his missing uncle—but thought better of it. It was her story.

He shrugged. "You know Aunt Ruby," he said. "You never quite know what she's going to do."

Curiously, she had talked with David about her brother the night at the racetrack while the cops searched for Susan Powell. It was the only other time he'd heard her speak about him, except for the day she'd shown him the government documents and talked about how her brother had become an MIA.

It wasn't a long story, and it probably wouldn't have meant much to anyone but Ruby. It was something about her brother trying to catch fireflies on a hot summer's night in St. Jo. David didn't remember the details. He was still shaking from his near-fatal encounter with Eddie Brown.

The memory was obviously important to his aunt. He remembered her laughing during parts of the story, an incongruous sound at such a time and place. David would have to ask her to repeat it later, when he was calm and could really listen.

Of course, whether Stuart Piszek had, in fact, been captured by the Vietcong and held after Operation Homecoming—held until he died of disease or was executed for expediency—they would never know. Yet David wondered whether the whole business with Bullet Joe and Powell and Stratton and Mai Lon Chu, however ambiguous it had turned out, had in some way been therapeutic for his aunt. No doubt, years before, her mind had buried the horror of her brother's disappearance and possible capture. She'd probably discussed it with no one. Then along came Stratton, unwittingly resurrecting her long-suppressed feelings of guilt—a word she would never use—for having left home when her brother was still young. Her brief but impassioned story that night at the dog track later struck David as a sign that Ruby had finally accepted her brother's fate. However Stuart Piszek had disappeared and died, he still lived within her. Maybe now, Ruby could replace the pain with closure, and relegate it to a corner of her heart where it would never again interfere with her life.